LIGHT OF LIGHTS

Lata Pimplaskar

ATHENA PRESS
LONDON

LIGHT OF LIGHTS
Copyright © Lata Pimplaskar 2003

ISBN 1 931456 58 5

First Published 2003 by
ATHENA PRESS
Queen's House, 2 Holly Road
Twickenham TW1 4EG
United Kingdom

Printed for Athena Press

LIGHT OF LIGHTS

Weapons do not cut It, Fire does not burn It
Neither does water wet It, nor does the wind dry It.

Bhagvad Gita II, 23

Acknowledgments

Sharad, for being the spirit of this book, love.

Jane Marston, for meeting on the Internet, then becoming a caring, encouraging even as a faceless friend!

Kiran Desai, for your unconditional support.

Janet Falk and Florence Kapoor, for your enthusiastic review of the book.

Jane Cleary, for checking out the facts.

My book-club members, Kiran and Kirti, Atul, Farhat, Kirit, and Urmila for being the readers that a new writer hopes to have.

Carlene Bauer for your critique.

Uma, for always being there.

Mike, for your valuable corrections.

Ravi and Jessika, for your love.

My editor, Bryan Aubrey, for your guidance.

&

Not enough can be said about the teachings and blessings that I have received from my Guru and through him, from the entire lineage of Vedanta teachers.

THANK YOU!

Part One

Chapter One

A poster of a cowboy advertising Marlboro cigarettes hung right above the food-cart where a woman was arranging and re-arranging packets of Cadbury's chocolates and sprinkling fresh green chilies on a heap of samosas. Next to her sat a man in a red turban, stirring Nescafé in a blackened aluminum pot on a kerosene stove that warmed shapely bottles of Coca-Cola on a bed of melting ice. Hawkers roamed. Many *chaiwalas* rushed about, selling their tea, shouting, "*Chai…i ga…ra…m, chai.*" A boy selling soft drinks sang in his nasal tone, "*Kokha… Kolha*", tapping on a bottle of Coke with a rusty bottle opener.

It was Victoria Train Terminal, definitely Bombay. It was ten o'clock in the morning and the train going to Kulur, a town south of Bombay, was already delayed by four hours. Tony checked his wristwatch again, making sure that it was set to the local time, even though he had done it the night before. He surveyed the other passengers but none of them seemed to be terribly concerned about the delay. It's futile to worry about time or anything for that matter, he thought, observing the relaxed attitude of his co-passengers.

A marriage party sat on the platform where a young girl wearing an ankle-length red dress – apparently the bride – played hopscotch. Minutes later, a train stopped on the opposite platform and a funeral party poured out of one of the compartments, wailing at their loss. A group of orange-clothed monks, leaving on a pilgrimage, forgot their vows of peace and hollered at each other as they rushed for empty seats.

Tony's train finally arrived, and late that afternoon it pulled into the station in Kulur. The loud whistling of the train caused a little stir among the sleeping goats on the platform. A few coolies stood up, wrapping their heads in the bandannas they had been using as pillows while taking a nap. One of the coolies raced alongside the slowing train and climbed into the second class compartment where Tony was sitting. Quickly, he took possession of Tony's luggage. With a broad smile spreading across his face, he signaled Tony to move towards the door.

The platforms were filled with welcoming friends and families. Inside the train people pushed and tugged at each other, though the exit was already jammed. Tony politely stood aside for everyone to step down but the coolie did not have time for such courtesies. He dropped Tony's luggage on the platform and it landed with a thud three feet below on the ground. Pushing the crowd aside, the coolie pulled Tony out of the train.

"Where...?" the coolie asked, using hand gestures.

Tony signed back, "I am to wait for my host to find me."

Leaving Tony's luggage to one side, the coolie took off in search of another customer. Tony looked around, wondering how he would find the person from the mission house in this crowd.

While waiting he was visited by a few half-naked children who begged. Pushing them aside, an old man with a shaven head and an orange cloth wrapped around his body approached him. The old man was holding a couple of torn books tightly under his arms. "You a *mi-shi-nari*?" he asked casually.

Tony nodded, skeptically. At the Catholic missionary training program in New York, he had been told that any missionary's good intentions would be questioned. He was to be always on his guard. But the old man looked harmless and when he asked, "So, you buy poor people, for you?" Tony was taken aback.

"What? Buy for me? No..." Tony grumbled.

The old man bent forward, now angrily pushing his thumb into Tony's face. "*Han han*. You buy and convert," he said, loudly.

Tony stepped backward, looking at the old man's glistening balding head right under his nose. He mumbled, "I am here to help the poor and care for the sick."

The old man only understood the words "poor" and "sick". "*Han, han*. You help then, convert. Feed then slaughter, isn't it?" he asked, shaking his head. "*Bolo*? You convert. So..." He pointed a finger at Tony and then, pointing it upward, he asked, "So you can go to your heaven, correct?"

Tony frowned. What does he know about heaven? And what does he mean by "my heaven"? Yet Tony only mumbled, "My heaven? Sir, do you understand the Christian faith?" He stared questioningly at the old man.

The man kept nodding, and Tony wondered if he had understood a word he had said. But before Tony could repeat his question, another man in a white shirt and brown trousers came to his rescue. Tony was relieved to see a cross on a black thread around the man's neck. He knew it was Joseph from the missionary. Joseph pushed the old man and the begging children away.

Without introducing himself he instructed Tony, "Sahib, don't. Do not give any money to the begging children. It's for your own good. Giving these children will only become a nuisance. The more you give them the more they will bother you." Tony looked blankly at Joseph, who continued, "I am giving you what's practical here. Poverty is a way of life here. If you don't get used to it, it will make you poor."

How could he talk like that? Hasn't he learnt anything about being a Christian? Sympathy for these unfortunate souls had brought him to India, yet Joseph, a Christian man, was telling him to ignore it.

"*Ae*! Mad chap, go. Go away," Joseph hollered at the old man. As the latter straggled off, Tony stood staring at Joseph and the retreating stranger.

Joseph gathered Tony's luggage, placed it on the coolie's head, and rushed them both out of the railway station. Throwing the luggage on top of a bus, he gestured Tony to get on, and gave some instructions to the bus driver. Then, without any explanation to Tony, he vanished into the crowd. Tony had no idea where he was going. When he asked, the bus driver didn't understand what he said and only shrugged his shoulders, signaling him to take a seat.

The ride through the narrow streets of Kulur was bumpy. When Tony looked out of the bus window, he saw bullock carts, rickshaws, horse carts, bicyclists, pedestrians, scooters, hawkers with pushcarts – the entire jumbled assortment of people were moving through their daily life.

The side streets were crammed with street venders. Along the road were rows of shops, medical clinics and Nasta-Houses where people were eating. Above the shops were the homes of people, where they made love behind torn curtains, laid dead bodies at the door steps, and encouraged their children to study English, Sanskrit, algebra, medicine and engineering, all in eighteen-by-sixteen-foot cubicles.

The bus crept along, stopping every couple of blocks. All the bus stands, too small for the crowds, were packed. By the time it reached the outskirts of the city, the bus was almost empty. After a few turns it stopped and the driver's assistant jumped down from his seat. A few people were waiting at the foot of the hill, anxious to meet the white American who was going to reopen the mission house. They rushed to him and, before he could rise from his seat, threw a garland around his neck. Bowing at his feet in the familiar Hindu ceremonious way, they helped him alight as if he was a symbol of their devotion. A few mumbled, "Welcome. *Namaste!*"

After the bus had pulled away, a man crossed the street and shouted at some men who were sitting by the river chit-chatting. A few ran to greet Tony.

He tried to shake their hands, yet they kept touching his feet. When he stepped back to discourage these gestures, they seemed baffled and he felt embarrassed. Most of them wore a cross around their neck, suggesting to him that they were Christians. Then, why this Indian homage? he thought. Is the manner in which people greet each other a matter of religion or culture? And can the culture be taken out of religion or religion out of culture?

Are they really Christian?

Are they?

They all walked with him to a bungalow atop a piece of hilly land near the riverbank. Coconut trees surrounded the red-roofed houses on the slopes of the hills and a winding street enwrapped the hills like a coiled snake. On a pillar of the entrance gate was a sign: Catholic Mission House. Underneath, in Indian script, was written, *Seva Sadan* – the house of service. The gate was open. Beyond, the garden was overgrown with weeds. A small broken cement walk led to the steps of the verandah. Tony climbed a few steps and as he turned, he saw a spectacular view of the magnificent river. The riverbank undulated, providing natural recesses for the mud huts. Along the bank were magnificent giant *pepul* trees. Underneath them, a few men were resting. Children played on the bank, and by the water's edge women were beating clothes with wooden bats. On the far bank was a tall, narrow Hindu temple.

Tony instantly fell in love with the landscape around Seva Sadan. He felt that it promised inner leisure; it would relax him, even when he was in the midst of unfamiliar people.

On the right, next to the verandah, was a small door that led into an office. The front door next to the office, the main entrance, was adorned with marigold garlands. Inside the house, a long front room was partitioned with shelves, for a dispensary. There were no chairs, but there was a bench, and a dhurrie with faded colors was spread on the floor. In the center of the far wall, an oil lamp burned in front of a shrine to Jesus Christ.

Tony's eyes took in all the strange things and came to rest on the lit lamp. Thank God they follow some Christian traditions, he thought.

The next morning, even before the morning light filtered through the trees, the air in parts of Kulur was filled with sounds. The milkmen's cans thumped on the wheels of bicycles and farmers sang tunes to the soft clanking of the bullock cart bells, carrying fresh produce to the markets. The Namaz readings from nearby mosques could be heard clearly only until the hymns of Hindu worshippers, along with Hindu temple bells, began to compete. Minutes later, from a corner teashop, a loudspeaker shrieked with Hindi popular songs. After all this, a rooster awakened, serving as an alarm clock to anyone who was still managing to stay asleep.

Awakened, Tony switched off his alarm clock. Hearing the sounds of morning activities, he felt alive. He rushed to the window. Mist was floating above the river water. Small boats scurried around to fetch the morning worshippers. Fishermen were collecting their catches of fish from the net and throwing them in baskets to sell. Women carried water-filled earthen vessels over their heads and were hurrying home like ants in a squiggly line.

Tony felt excited about his new life. Perhaps, he thought, he would be happy living as a missionary in India.

As instructed by the people he had met the day before, he collected water in two brass buckets and, after a bath, he searched the kitchen in vain for a coffee pot. He tried to turn on the gas stove but found the supply cylinder empty. But shortly a knock came at the kitchen door. He opened it to a boy of twelve or thirteen, who handed him a kettle of coffee and a plateful of toast. Tony offered him money but the boy shook his head, saying that he was a neighbor.

As the morning hours passed, Tony began to feel at a loss. Then a bicyclist appeared at the door and gave him a note from the minister from Church:

Dear Tony,

I have been waiting for your arrival but, now, I have to be away on urgent business. I am very sorry for the inconvenience this may have caused you. The medical supplies have been delivered to the mission house. I am sure you are anxious to get to work like a true missionary and there is lots of work to do. A few people have volunteered to come and help you to set up. You will need to employ a person as your assistant, so you can learn to communicate with the local people.

Looking forward to meeting you. Till then,
Yours truly,

Father Paul

After reading the letter Tony walked around the place. It was still too early for anyone to be there to help him. He assessed the things he would have to do before he could open the clinic.

The house had been used both as a residence and a medical clinic by a doctor missionary from Portugal. After the doctor's death, his wife had used it to help the local poor. Later, she had donated it for the missionary work, but lacking a trained doctor or a lay missionary, the place had been shut. Tony was told they would now have a visiting doctor for a few hours a week. Until then, he was to run the clinic and send critical patients to the hospital in the city.

A few Christian men came by to help him but he couldn't

communicate with them, and one by one they drifted away. By noon half a dozen people had come for medical help, but he was unable to communicate with them either. He realized the urgency of finding someone to translate the people's needs to him, and his instructions to them. But he would have to wait until the minister returned before he could find such a person.

Soon a fisherwoman, accompanied by two other women, rushed in with a deep wound in her hand from a hatchet. The blood streamed from her wound. She stood there, showing him the hatchet and sucking the dripping blood from her hand. Tony realized that in an emergency he didn't need to communicate. He quickly opened the boxes of medical supplies and cleaned and stitched her wound, feeling surprised and elated at his ability to handle the situation. But the elation lasted only until he wrote the name of an antibiotic on a piece of paper and gave it to the woman. She couldn't read. She looked at him angrily and as she walked out she tore the paper to pieces. Tony guessed that she thought he had given her a bill for his service. He picked up the pieces of paper and ran after her, gesturing that she was supposed to take this medication. But the woman walked away, leaving the pieces of paper in his hand.

After the woman had gone, he walked up to the altar and prayed, then sat and continued to pray. But he couldn't still his mind. With every unfamiliar sound he opened his eyes, and soon the desire to pray evaporated.

He stood up and began moving the rickety shelves, which cleared the view from the window. This gave him a little private area for checking on patients. He opened all the boxes and took the stock that had been delivered while noting what he would still need. He started emptying the boxes and then arranging the supplies. Just when he crammed a couple more boxes on the shelves, the fragile shelving gave way. As he watched all the boxes, bottles and packages falling to the floor, he was startled by the sound of laughter. Who was that? He turned, and as he saw the young woman standing by the door, something flickered in his mind and he stared. Then he looked away, trying to connect with the speck of a flickering memory. But, of course he didn't know her; he was very new to this land, and yet he wondered. Did he know her? The young woman stopped laughing. He became aware that his stare might seem threatening to her. To ease his embarrassment, he laughed rather loudly, and now the sound of his own laughter sounded strange to him. But listening to his laugh, she laughed too, and a momentary expression of fright disappeared from her face. Looking at the fallen supplies, he laughed again, and without introductions he started picking up the supplies. She joined him.

As they gathered the items into the boxes, Tony finally said, "I don't know how to do anything here. I knew it would be hard in India. But I never knew everything would be so different." He glanced at her. She was pursing her lips and muffling a giggle. He stopped talking, not knowing the reason for her amusement.

"Did you understand what I just said?" he asked, raising his eyebrows. She shook her head but kept quietly picking up the supplies. If she could understand, Tony thought, then she could also converse in English, and that would be the answer to his prayers.

But, who was she? Had Father Paul sent her? But he hadn't mentioned anything about her in his letter. Suddenly, Tony realized that he had not even asked her the purpose of her visit. Or her name. She seemed different from the others he had met so far. Putting out his hand to shake hers, he said, "Hi, I am Tony."

Instead of shaking his hand she placed her palms together and said, "*Namaste*... Maya."

He corrected himself, "*Na-maa-ste*." He bowed and they both laughed.

"I am very sorry," he said. "I should say Namaste... I forgot."

He stopped as again he saw a mischievous smile play around her lips. "Did I say something wrong again?"

"No. Not wrong. You speak American English. I speak too but, s-l-o-w. Go slow in English." As she stressed the word "slow" they both laughed again. He was amused by her mannerisms, which were childlike and guileless.

Maya had been sent by her father to find a job at the dispensary. She told Tony that as a young girl when her father worked as a medical chemist in a doctor's private clinic, she had learned many things. She learned nursing from the doctor's wife, who was an Englishwoman and that's why she could speak English. "I am a good worker and in this area you won't find anyone like me." Her cheeks turned red.

"I won't find anyone like you?" he asked teasingly.

"No, sir. I have the right qualifications, my father said. He works at the big chemist shop in the town. But if you don't have a job, I'd better go. It's just that this is convenient since I have to help my younger brothers and sisters after school. But it's okay if you don't think you could – I mean if you don't want to hire me, I could go to the doctor a few streets down the road."

"No. I didn't say that," Tony said hurriedly. "It's just I've never done any hiring before. But your verbal résumé sounds good. You are hired."

She laughed at his hurried response.

"The pay—"

"Just pay me accordingly," she said quickly.

"All right, then we can work it out when Father Paul gets back. Fair enough?"

She didn't answer but laughed again.

What was she laughing at? It irked him. Was she going to work or only laugh at everything he did or said? He was worried.

Tony showed her around the house. When they came to the kitchen they found a woman waiting at the rear door. Tony thought he should ask why she was there. "*Kya chhahiye?*" he said, trying his skill at the language.

Instead of answering, the woman pulled her *palloo* over her mouth to conceal her laugh. What's the matter with these people that they always laugh? He shrugged and looked at Maya, who told him the woman was there to claim her old job of cleaning the cooking vessels.

"What cooking vessels? I don't even know how this kitchen works. I don't know how to turn on the gas stove or use the coal stove. I was hoping somebody would bring me lunch just as they had brought me coffee."

Looking at his exasperated face, Maya laughed and asked the woman to bring the items from the corner store. Then on the kerosene stove she prepared rice and a curry dish for him. She used very little chili, only a spoonful, but *wow*! It was enough to turn Tony's face scarlet. He gasped for air and as he drank water it drooled from his mouth and onto his clothes. He stood and paced the floor. She ran to the kitchen to bring the sugar can. When she returned, his whole face was inflamed, his tongue was hanging from his mouth, and he was shaking his head violently as if to shake away the heat. She shoved a spoonful of sugar in his hand, and kept saying, "Eat, eat sugar. *Arre re*… please… eat."

She picked up a fan and again repeated, "*Chuch…ch*… How could I do something like that?" Clicking her tongue, she started to fan him. Then blowing through her mouth, she signaled him to swallow the sugar and breathe cool air through his mouth to ease the burning.

"Don't worry, I am okay," Tony said, trying to smile.

She shook her head as if to say "No, you are not."

"Really, I am," Tony repeated, and he touched her hand for her to stop fanning, "I… *Me, thik hai*." They both laughed at his attempts at Hindi and he repeated, "*Thik*, okay?" He patted her hand.

She looked at his hand touching hers and at once she dropped the fan and ran outside. Tony followed her to the verandah and asked, "Hey, won't you come back? Where are you going?"

She didn't answer but a few minutes later she returned with a loaf of bread and eggs and made him buttered toast and boiled eggs.

"You don't have to do this. I can cook," he said as she handed him the plate.

Again she laughed and said, "Indian men…" Then she paused and continued, "Indian men will laugh at you. Men don't do kitchen work here."

"So, to save me from their taunting, are you going to cook or help with nursing?"

"If you want, I will do both, of course," she said confidently, "for more money." Looking at his red face, she then asked, "You really trust me to cook for you?"

Now it was his turn to laugh and he said, "We will see."

That day she stayed and helped him to plan how the clinic would be set up, preparing the rear space only for women. They labeled the medicines and worked out how to fill the routine charts. She wrote on a board the days and the times that the clinic would be open. When he was putting it up she started to laugh.

"What now?" he asked, puzzled by her laughter.

"The people who'll be coming here can't read." She laughed again.

"Then how do they know when to come and when not to come?"

"They understand Sunday, but other than that we would have to teach them about the times. 'Open till lunchtime' means anytime from twelve till two to them. 'Open after teatime' means anytime after they had their naps and tea. They can't read the time and they don't have clocks. The neighboring industries use the sirens to wake up their workers."

"Thank you," Tony replied, "what would I do without you?"

She blushed.

The next morning, before Tony was up, the milkman rocked the gate. When Tony went out the milkman was sitting by his gate and men and women were gathered to buy the milk. The news was out. The *gora* – the white sahib – had come and people were anxious to get a glimpse of him.

Tony didn't know how to explain that he wasn't a sahib. Moreover, he wasn't rich at all, so he told them, "I am here as a missionary and to work for you. I have no money."

But they didn't understand.

When Maya arrived he had lines of visitors. He was standing in the verandah and talking with a neighbor who had come to welcome him. The gardener was sitting on the ground tying his *pagadi* tight on his head. A street sweeper stood by the gate, hoping to earn extra money by cleaning the latrine. Two fruit and vegetable hawkers were waiting for his attention. The dhobi or laundress sat inside the clinic resting a pack of clean and ironed clothes tied in a cloth on the floor. A boy who sold tea, and was carrying a tea kettle, cups and saucers, also stopped when he saw so many people around. He waited to see if Tony or anyone else would like to buy his tea.

Maya giggled while coming up the steps, looking at the circus of people. Seeing her, Tony breathed a sigh of relief and said,

"Thank God you are here. What do I do with all these people? I don't know what they want."

She quickly assessed the situation: the gardener could stay and clear out the grounds and plant a few things. He needed to purchase some fruits and vegetables. The sweeper and dhobi were not needed at the moment; the maid he hired yesterday would do laundry and cleaning. The boy with tea left without even trying to sell any to her.

Meanwhile, a woman with nasty burn wounds, and a man whose eyes were bulging out, climbed the steps with the help of a young boy.

That's how the clinic began. They sent the man with the eye problem to the hospital and dressed the burn wounds. After that, most of the day was slow, and Tony only had to treat a few children with coughs and colds, yet he had still seen within a day more than he had seen in his entire month of working as a nurse in Iowa.

That night he truly felt that this missionary work was his path. He wanted to help these poor souls. He wanted to cure them, educate them. He wanted to see them prosper in the light of Jesus' torch. He would be a great missionary. With this resolve, he felt a surge of energy, enthusiasm and also a sense of blessedness, as if his existence had acquired a larger purpose. At the thought of serving the naked, starving skeletons of men, women and children, his heart filled with joy.

Then he wondered for a moment about that, feeling guilty about his heartfelt joy. Was he really doing this charity work for the sake of the sufferer only? Didn't he gain anything from it? But he dismissed the thought with a shrug, wanting to enjoy for a bit longer the surge of new joy and energy he felt for what the Church had convinced him was his *selfless* charity work.

Right from the beginning most of the people coming to the clinic followed the scheduled times except once, when Tony was awakened by pounding on the front door. It was his first week. He fumbled around trying to find the light switch as the pounding, mixed with a wailing of a woman, continued.

Reluctantly, he opened the door. A woman stood before him, holding an infant in her hands. A foul smell filled the place. The baby was wrapped in tattered, soiled rags. There were blisters on the baby's face and head. Pus was oozing out from the deeper wounds. The little chest was barely moving.

Tony looked at them both, wondering what he could do.

"Do something... save my baby. Sahib... sahib..." As the woman raised the baby to him, sobbing, Tony stepped backward; he couldn't help in cases like that, he wasn't a doctor. He waved his hands, refusing to help. The desperate mother pushed forward, pushing the baby into his hands. He stood there, looking baffled but the woman shrieked again, "Sahib... save my baby."

He never knew how he had taken the baby and carried it to the clinic, while the woman followed. He unwrapped the baby from the rags; its whole body was covered with infected blisters. The baby was dehydrating and its pulse was going faint.

He gave the baby a shot of antibiotic. Then opening the baby's mouth with his fingers he squirted a few drops of sugar water from a dropper. But the water dribbled out of the corner of the baby's mouth. The life was escaping from the tiny body. His hands shook. The mother collapsed on the floor.

Tony rushed to the altar and put the baby on the floor. Pouring water over the small head he said, "I baptize thee in the name of the Father, and of the Son, and of the Holy Ghost." Kneeling, he prayed as the infant died. Looking at the dead baby, tears fell from his eyes. He shook with a whimper and then fearfully looked at the mother. Beating her forehead, she was crying her heart out. Tony stood up to bring her a glass of water but, picking up the dead baby, the woman rushed outside and vanished in the dark night.

One afternoon during his second week, when Maya had left the clinic, Father Paul came to visit. Tony showed him around. Seeing how much progress Tony had made in a few days, Father Paul congratulated him. Tony told him how crazy things had been, and he talked incessantly of the follies of these illiterate people. Hearing all that had happened, Father Paul apologized repeatedly with an amused laugh.

Father Paul was the second generation of a Hindu family who had become Christian. That day when Tony met him he realized he didn't look anything like the way he had pictured him. Father was much younger looking. He was dark-skinned, short and slightly plump. His thick wavy hair had a woolly appearance, and his eyes reflected his sincere and caring nature. His arms were a little short, and he kept them mostly folded around his chest, his chubby fingers continually drumming on his elbow. His boisterous laugh gave the false notion that the caring expression on his face was not wholly sincere. He was in fact a sincere man.

That day Father Paul took Tony around the city, showing him the pockets of slums where the people lived in mud huts. The huts and a tiny space, which you could hardly call a yard, were cleaner than the streets. There was no running water, electricity or sewer. Any open space around the mesh of huts had turned into a sewage plant where beggars searched for food in the trash and pigs roamed around. Some of the dwellings were not even huts, only shelters of tattered cloth that hung from a tree or a street lamp. Looking at the impoverished ways of living, Tony found himself complaining about how the poverty, the filth, the numerous sicknesses and the misery sickened him. "Father, how can the people tolerate living like this?" he complained over and again.

"Don't go by what you see, Tony," Father Paul said. "Indians are tolerant and timid in most matters but they have the tenacity to live by values, which are ingrained in them by the culture. This culture is what has saved them despite all the foreign invasions."

Tony wanted to argue. "Culture? Hmm! I had read so much about the great cultures but all I see is misery. They live in poverty, filth, and sickness. Their life is a hell. What's so great about any culture where the people are suffering, falling apart?"

Father Paul seemed amused by his outrage. "Take it easy, Tony," he said. "They are not falling apart. You think they are falling apart because they are poor. Sure, they are poor. But most of them are not beggars. Not at all, Tony. There is a different attitude here to poverty. You see, America wants to abolish poverty, which is an honorable thought. You treat poverty like a disease, as if you will find a cure and hope that one day it will go away. And here, in India, it is a way of life. Removing poverty does not solve the problems of society. For centuries of mankind no nation has achieved that, have they? Is America free of poor people altogether?"

Tony shook his head.

"Have you achieved the perfect way of life in America?" He paused and looked at Tony but Tony didn't answer. "America is rich compared to the rest of the world. You have medical care and other benefits, but are you lacking problems in your society?"

Tony shook his head again.

"There are problems in every society, and unfortunately no one can fix every one of them. Since British rule, Indians have suffered more from poverty. But poverty does not have to mean misery. A poor child is hungry and miserable but a poor and fatherless child is a risk to the society. Despite the poverty, we have less social problems than in America, because of the old rooted culture of this country. Here the poor still manage to live a life of values. And you will see that they won't change that easily. You will find out when you want to campaign for conversion."

"Conversion?" Tony said. "Besides baptizing a dying baby I haven't had a chance to talk about it and until I can communicate with them, I am barely staying afloat myself. Though the moment I see an opportunity, I will jump in."

"You will learn. Look for an opportunity and Joseph will bring a few men to introduce to you. We know it's a sudden change for you. Good luck."

As the weeks passed, a routine began to develop at Seva Sadan. Maya started to come in the mornings, from nine to twelve and every afternoon from three to seven. In the mornings, she was sometimes left alone in the clinic while Tony attended to the work of the Catholic school or church. Sometimes they rented bikes for their travel and went to remote villages, where they set up the nursing center either on a porch of a wealthy farmer or in front of a tea shack.

At Seva Sadan, as more and more people started to come, they became more organized. Cases they handled were typical, such as infected wounds, chronic coughs and headaches, high fevers and skin rashes. There were many newborns and infants mainly with stomach and respiratory problems. Sometimes when Tony and Maya couldn't treat the symptoms, they helped the villagers admit themselves to the free hospital.

Though the times they worked together were hectic, whenever Tony glanced at Maya, and their eyes met, she would blush, and he would miss a moment or two gazing at her.

Maya was attractive. Her eyelashes were always darkened with *kajal*, and her big expressive eyes sparkled like crescent of the moon in a dark sky. Her thin lip lines were always open in her exuberant, contagious laugh. Her tiny conical nose was set between her high cheekbones. Her wheaten complexion glowed through her paper-thin skin. The short strands of her curly hair almost always slipped out of her hairpins and fell in an unruly way over her forehead and around her ears. Other than the dangling earrings she didn't wear any jewelry.

Maya's cheerfulness had changed the make-up of Tony's heart. Now, as he walked around Seva Sadan he whistled. He laughed as much as she did. As soon as she entered the place he found himself in good humor. He would make fun of his own way of speaking their language. Her enthusiasm was invigorating to him and to others. Most of the people came to the clinic with an attitude that the world didn't care for them, so Maya would greet them with warm, welcoming words, calling them, "*Kakiji* – Auntie," and asking how their neighbors or in-laws were treating them. "*Ajoba* – Grandpa, you should rest now," she would sometimes suggest to old men, "let your son handle the boat now."

When Tony saw her dealing with his patients with such care he knew he had made the right choice in hiring her.

He found himself looking forward to her arrival each day. In the mornings he stood by the window, waiting. But as soon as he would see her coming up the steps, he would rush to the clinic and pretend to be searching for something. And when she asked if she could help him to find what he was looking for, he would gaze at her, lost for words, before barely whispering, "Nothing... nothing at all." All the time his mind would be saying, Tell her the truth, you idiot, tell her you are happy to see her and she's looking beautiful.

At nights in his bedroom he wrote notes asking her out, but he never dared to give any of them to her. Even in the U.S., he had eyed the girls and been attracted to one or two but hadn't asked a single one out. His feelings for Maya were something different though; he felt they were more persistent, sweeter. More meaningful. And since he couldn't vocalize his emotions, they spilled out silently. His searching eyes, his gestures, gave away what was happening in his pounding heart. Memories of when she had locked her eyes into his, or how the current had surged through his body when he felt the light brush of her fingertips, remained on his mind, arousing his senses.

At night his thoughts turned from his work only to Maya. He talked to her in his dreams, where he wasn't awkward and he didn't fear her rejection or their cultural differences. Holding her hand, he went to the river. By moonlight he rowed with her in a boat. In the garden he strolled with her, whispering a romantic poem while she leaned on his shoulder. Dreaming and wishing to have her in his arms, every night he fell asleep clutching a pillow.

Reality of course was different. Most of the time, behind a curtain, Maya attended the women, consulting Tony at times and also helping him to converse with male patients. For the first time he began to realize how much segregation there was between men and women in this country. Married men and women lived separate lives and played definite roles, without questioning them. Women seemed to spend more time and had closer bonds with other women than with their husbands.

As time went on he realized that running a clinic was an easier challenge than following the real purpose of the mission, which was spreading the gospel. And though he had been told it was difficult finding people to take Christ into their hearts, this began for him in only the third week of his stay at Seva Sadan, when Joseph brought a young man, Biku, over to meet Tony.

Biku was shivering and he held his arms tightly together under his chin.

"Sahib, this is Biku. He needs help," Joseph said in the same indifferent manner he had used when speaking of the begging children at the station. "He's an idiot who's caught in a legal problem. If we could help, he promised me that he will turn Christian."

Tony looked at the shaking young man, who was unshaven and stank. The man refused to make eye contact and kept staring at the floor.

"What has he done?" Tony asked.

"The place of his work was robbed and the owner thinks Biku had something to do with it. So, he ran away from home, and has been hiding. Now the police have sent a warrant for his arrest, and he doesn't know how to prove his innocence."

"Is he really innocent?" Tony asked.

"Sahib, how would I know? But if you take him to the station and tell them his case, they would believe you. Tell them he was here, at Seva Sadan for the whole time when the robbery took place."

"I can't do that."

"Sahib, you have to start helping them this way. Don't we believe in giving a second chance, even if he had committed a crime?"

"We believe in second chances but we are talking of law here."

"Sahib, things are different in this country. Most of the cases don't go to the court. You pay the police and he will be free."

"And you want me to do that?"

"If you want to give him a second chance and make him a Christian. Sahib, you are a missionary, you help." He spoke in a frustrated tone.

"What if I take him to a lawyer?" Tony suggested.

"Lawyer? That's costly. If that's the only way you could help, go to Chitra Pandit. She will give him a free representation. I will give you her address." He wrote the address on a piece of paper and asked, "Sahib, can he stay here tonight?"

"Here? What if the police came here, looking for him?"

"Don't worry. They aren't that smart. Besides, they don't work that hard," he said, scratching behind his ears with a smug smile.

Tony looked at Biku who, for the first time since he had arrived, made eye contact with Tony, begging him to let him stay.

That night Biku stayed at Seva Sadan.

The next day Tony took Biku to the legal office and met with Chitra, daughter of Mr. Pandit, a staunch and rich Brahmin, and a famous attorney in India.

"So you are the new missionary?" she asked, raising her hands.

He shook her hands, thinking she behaved differently from the other Indian women he had met. Her mannerisms seemed more western. Chitra looked different too. She was tall and dark-skinned. Her eyebrows were distinctively arch-shaped and she had a full mouth. Her elegance and her confidence flowed in her gestures and the way she spoke. She looked cultured and dignified.

Tony sat on a chair and said, "Yes, I am the new missionary. But how did you know?"

"It's a small town. Besides I live not far from Seva Sadan. On occasions Father Paul has sent me a few needy people and I was glad to help. But what can I do for you today?"

Tony gave Chitra the information about Biku's problem, the way Joseph had told it.

"Where were you that night?" she asked Biku, her voice changing from friendly to tough.

"*Tai*, I was home," he said reluctantly, still staring at the floor.

"You weren't home. Don't lie." She paused, observing Biku's reaction. She wouldn't fall for any nonsense. This pleased Tony.

Biku fidgeted for a moment then glanced at her. "Please, please," he cried and fell at Chitra's feet. "I will never go and watch the game of dice, *Bai*, I have a family to feed. *Baisahib*, please help me. I swear I will never go again there. This will ruin me, my family. Oh! *Bap*! What will I do then?" he sobbed.

"Who's in your family? And tell me the truth first time."

"My mother," he said, wiping away tears with his hands, "my wife and four children and my sister."

"How in the world these people find money to gamble, one can't even guess," she said, looking at Tony. Tony shook his head, glancing at Biku, who sat on the floor, his arms wrapped around his knees.

"So, can you help?" Tony asked.

27

"And if I did, you would take his soul and run to church?" she asked, laughing loudly.

Her remark reminded him of the old man who had confronted him at the train station and he looked at her with an expression of uneasiness. "Relax," she said. "I am agnostic. Religion is a nuisance to me, and especially in this country."

"Then why would you want to help us? We are a religious organization."

"For me, I look at your organization as a charitable institute. When dealing with me don't bring religion into this. I don't understand why you people can't do the charity without bringing in religion. One can be kind without being religious, you know." She looked at Biku and said, "Look at this, now, if we don't help him there are six other people who would be ruined and have to live on the streets. Does this country need that? No. I say, let's see if he learns his lesson by giving him another chance."

"So you will help him then?" Tony asked.

"I will tell you tomorrow," she said, and shook his hand.

As it turned out, Chitra helped secure Biku's freedom by proving he had been a bystander at a dice game.

After that incident, Chitra and Tony became friends. She started coming to the clinic to lend him a hand or to find him free medical supplies or to give legal advice when necessary.

Biku could have been Tony's first candidate for the conversion, but before Biku had his baptism, another man, Pandu, had become a Christian convert. Again it was Joseph who had brought Pandu, and he had done so because Pandu was literate and could read Bible stories to the other men in the evenings. After the readings, Pandu and other men sang devotional songs, chanting the name of Yeshu, Jesus. At the end of the services, Pandu always became very emotional, and sat praying by the altar or in meditation. On one of those occasions, Tony had asked him if he would like to take Christ into his heart, and Pandu had answered, "Brother Tony, the Lord is always in my heart." Taking his answer literally, Tony had him baptized.

That's how the Christian mission began, and after Pandu, there was Sada. The day after Sada was baptized his wife had come, throwing things around. She threw her black bead necklace, a marriage symbol, on the floor, and accused him of deserting her. She told him how no one in a Hindu family would marry their daughter and that he had ruined them. The following week Sada told Tony that his wife had gone to stay with his parents, who also blamed Sada, and now he was alone.

Even after their husbands were converted, Hindu women refused to change. They held on to their tradition and culture. Tony was told these women wouldn't change that easily. They all had chosen deities to whom they prayed devoutly, so women would be very difficult to convert.

These remarks always made Tony anxious about Maya.

Chapter Two

Immediately after the medical clinic was under way, Tony and Maya began setting up a class for fishermen's children. They went hunting for students in huts across the riverbank but the fishermen didn't believe their children should be educated. Some would take the boys, seven or eight years of age, for fishing expeditions while other boys were employed helping ferrying people from one bank to the other in small boats. The fishermen refused to send their girls, fearing that no one in their community would marry a girl who could read or write.

Still, going through every hut on the riverbank, Maya gathered a few children, and brought them to Seva Sadan. But gathering children wasn't enough. They had hardly any clothes to wear. Those who wore underwear didn't have a shirt, and those who had shirts didn't have underwear. Tony had to send the maid to get some clothing from a bazaar.

In addition to this, the children had not been bathed, and the mission house soon stank. Maya decided to bathe them herself. She and Tony filled buckets of water and lined the children up by the water tap. As Maya started to scrub the children, Tony poured water over their heads, saying, "Well, here begins the process of their baptism," and feeling a sense of accomplishment, a broad smile spread across his face.

"Baptism?" Maya asked. "What does it mean? I hear that word when you talk to the men in your office."

Picking up a child and then holding him in his arms, Tony answered, "Baptism is when a person takes Jesus into his or her heart." Looking at her, he asked, "Maya, would you like to take Jesus into your heart?" The child escaped from his hands. His own heart beat fast. He had never thought he would pop that question so candidly to her.

"So you can pour water over my head?" she asked, giggling and combing out tangles from a girl's hair.

He shook his head, feeling relieved. "No," he said, "Father Paul, the priest, he will baptize."

"Some day we will have enough time when you can tell me all about it," she said, wrapping a towel around a child. "What baptism means and why it matters, so I can explain to people what it's all about."

"Why some day, Maya? This Sunday, Maya, I would like you to attend church."

"Some day," she said laughing, "but right now run and catch that child."

Tony ran after the kid who giggled with delight at seeing Tony running behind him.

Within a few days, instead of Tony and Maya having to search for the children and drag them from their huts, they started coming on their own. A few hopeful mothers even started bringing their children, who were looking cleaner and even managed to arrive roughly on time.

A new routine soon developed. Maya arrived early and after the children's class prepared tea for them while Tony filled out charts for the ordering of supplies, or request forms for patients to go to the hospital. Patients lined up outside the dispensary well before the opening time, and Tony and Maya became busy even before they had a chance to visit or to have tea together.

A little before noon, when Tony was still busy in his office with other men or at times with Chitra, Maya would rush out of Seva Sadan to pick up her youngest brother from his school. Upon arriving home she would start rolling chapatis for her family's lunch.

At times, in the afternoon when she came a bit earlier, she would often find Tony, sitting and reading the Bible. Sometimes with the help of other men, he read the Bible in Hindi or the Marathi language. Every chance he had Tony would show Maya a leaflet about the Christian faith. Flipping through it, she always remarked how Hindus too needed leaflets like these for the temples. Apparently, most of the people didn't understand Sanskrit and no one understood what the priest was reciting.

In their free times Maya would tell Tony stories about the

times she had spent with Dr. Joshi and his Christian British wife. She told him how the British woman had made sure that her two sons got their heads shaven, wore the sacred thread around their shoulders correctly, and recited the Sanskrit mantras every morning. But Dr. Joshi permitted his wife to wear a thick cross with a diamond at its center, which she kept hidden deep in her cleavage under her blouse. When Tony asked Maya what she thought of that, she answered, "Nothing, I was only ten years old. I was only amused by how they were an unusual family."

Maya also told him how it was fun when she listened to the doctor's father comment on how his modern son had changed and become a staunch Hindu. He made a joke that his son had returned to his Hindu path through his Christian wife.

When Tony coaxed her to tell him what she now thought about the doctor's marriage, she answered, "The doctor's wife, Auntie, was a kind woman, and I liked her." When Tony pressed her further, about what she thought of their relationship as husband and wife, she answered, "Their marriage to me seemed more romantic than anyone else's that I knew. But why do you want to know all this?"

"Oh! Nothing – just curious."

But in his heart he knew he wasn't asking only because he was curious. He had overcome many obstacles since he had arrived, adjusting to the food, the weather and the people. But his western attempts at courting Maya had failed. When he bought flowers and put them on the desk with her name on it, she made garlands and put them by the shrine. When he asked her to accompany him to a garden, her brother and sister came along too. Chocolates were distributed to the children or enjoyed by her siblings. When he bought her a personal gift, a pair of long earrings, he was embarrassed when she told him she wasn't that poor. Gift-giving without a reason was uncommon in India and she had insisted on paying for the earrings.

The only progress he had made in his courtship was that when he made eye contact with her now he made comments like, "You look beautiful." When she arrived, he no longer rushed to the clinic but stayed in the verandah. One day, seeing him waiting, she had asked, "Are you waiting for someone?"

The truth had spilled from his mouth, "I am waiting for you."

And in response, as usual, she blushed, but asked, "Am I late?"

Every evening he found excuses for her to stay a little longer and she lingered. Once when she asked if he would show her some photographs of his family and home, he became silent. He couldn't even lift his eyes, and he was embarrassed by his reaction to her natural question. Barely lifting his chin up, he said, "I don't have any." His face was sullen, remembering the morning he had sat in the living room staring at the dull colorless walls.

As far as he could remember about his home in Iowa, there was never anything hung on the walls that could tell a story about his family. There were no photographs, collections of any kind, certificates or trophies, not even unframed posters or travel souvenirs – nothing at all. Along with the walls, the mantel and tabletops also were bare. The only thing that was always there, right above the mantel, was the cross.

On the day of his departure the entire room had looked bleaker to him than a third-class motel room. He had thought that there was nothing there that he would miss, but now the memories of home stifled him.

There had never been any changes in his home. As far back as he could remember, all the furnishings had stayed the same. Over the years they were a little worn perhaps, but otherwise the same. The faded easy chair by the fireplace hadn't been reclined in for many years. Tony had been born just a few months after his father had left. He had wondered if his father had ever lain back in it when he was around. Tony never could form a picture in his mind of his father ever sitting in the chair, or doing anything else for that matter, because his mother, Darlene, had removed or destroyed every photo of his dad.

He remembered the colonial sofa with its tiny green pineapple design, where he had sat and played with toy cars. It was probably collecting dust now. He remembered how by the bay window a rocking chair used to rock by itself as the furnace turned on and off. The lace curtains that hung on the window had never held any charm for him since that afternoon when he had seen his sister, Sharon, peering through it, waiting for her friend John.

Seeing Tony suddenly so silent, Maya said, "I don't have any photographs either. It's not common in India to have a camera, at least not in my neighborhood."

Tony still said nothing. He knew his family had photos that would have kept the memories alive. But they were snatched away from him. He didn't know if his mother meant to protect him after Sharon's death, or was merely driven by her own pain and didn't even realize that she was depriving Tony of a normal family life.

"I don't have to see the photos of your family, Tony, I can imagine them, I am sure they are as kind as you are, and as helpful," Maya said in a soothing tone. "You are helping the poor that you don't even know."

Maya sounded so kind, so understanding, that some block inside him was released. He stared at the floor and swallowed a lump in his throat. "I grew up in a farmhouse," he said, and slowly he began telling her the account of the day he had tried to forget all of his life...

It was a cool but crisp sunny afternoon in the fall. His sister, Sharon, asked Tony to play outside. He was seven years old and loved playing outdoors. For some time he roamed around the empty barn looking for something to do. He threw pebbles on the crawling insects, filled dirt in the hiding burrows of ground squirrels, chased rabbits and tormented his old dog, Sammy. After some time Sammy gave up following Tony and curled up inside the barn.

Behind the barn, in the tall yellow grass, a flock of birds flew in and started making a great noise. Tony took his slingshot out of the barn and looked around for the perfect stones, like a penny – flat and round but slightly heavy so they would cut through the air. His little fingers moved in the gravel scooping out the buried stones. As he found them, he stuffed them in his jacket pocket.

The noise grew in the meadow. He hurried to the side of the barn. The birds were working, their beaks scuffing on the leaves. Then they flew a few feet and again settled on the ground, pitter-pattering. Tony fitted one of the stones on the band of his sling. It fit perfectly. Crouching, slowly he stepped towards the brush. His eyes narrowed, focusing on a reddish-colored bird. He moved slowly, one foot after the other, but with each step the stones scrunched under his boots, alarming the birds. As he neared the meadow the birds went silent. Holding their beaks upward, they were ready to take off.

Bang! The sound of a gunshot cut through the cold silent air and Tony almost fell on the ground. The flock of birds flew away into the sky and the tall tips of yellow grass wavered in the air. Sammy rose on his aching feet and ran about, barking frenziedly. Tony stood for a moment, looking up at the sky and a hovering hawk that had been hunting for mice vanished from his sight.

Someone was shooting!

Excitedly, Tony ran to the middle of a vacant field and moved in a circle, looking around to find the man he imagined must be nearby: a man of forty with a curly brown beard, wearing a baseball cap and a vest over blue dungarees, carrying a hunting gun. Once they met, Tony would be anxious to learn from him all he could about shooting.

Holding his sling up in the air, he took aim, hoping to find a moving target. But through the angles of his sling, he could only see the dried out leaves that flew in the air. He brought the sling down and waited to hear the gunshot sound again, but the only sounds he heard came from the creaking of a chain that held the NO TRESPASSING sign on the eight-foot pole near the entrance gate. Apart from the house and a few bare trees in the front and around the barn, there was nothing to aim at.

The man of his imagination wasn't there.

Again he looked up in the sky, but there were no geese flying across. The sky was empty and the land was silent. Then, when he was about to turn around, he heard it again.

Bang!

This time he heard it loud and clear. The slingshot fell from his hands on the ground. Pointing his fingers in the air, he made the sound, "Bang, bang."

The sound was a gunshot for sure.

It was thrilling; someone was definitely shooting. He had to find him. He ran towards the house, yelling, "Sharon, did you hear that? Sharon?"

Sammy trotted behind him, barking. They ran to the back

door. But the back door was shut. He banged on it hard and yelled, "Sharon, open the door!"

She didn't answer. She could be so engrossed in their talks once John came. Again he screamed, "Sharon, Sharon, someone is shooting around."

He jumped down the three steps, his eyes moving like a bullet, hoping to catch a glimpse of a man. He climbed up the steps again and shook the door. There were no sounds coming from the kitchen, and when he sensed that Sharon wasn't there, he ran around to the front.

John's car wasn't in the driveway.

For a moment Tony stood still, wondering how long he had been playing outside. There was no direct sunlight in the sky; only the lingering, vanishing glow that illumined the spread of their vacant farmland.

He rushed up the steps. The wind had blown the dry leaves onto the porch and they had spread across the front door. Tony shoved the leaves away with his foot and opened the storm door. The front door was open. He pushed it in and Sammy squeezed through and ran to his bowl. Tony stood by the door, calling Sharon. "Did you hear the shots, Sharon?" he asked, and stepped out again, holding the door open, waiting for her to come out. But only Sammy came out. The dog rolled in the scattered leaves, and Tony giggled as he watched him.

When Sharon still didn't come, he looked inside. The house felt empty. He stepped in and Sammy followed. The storm door closed behind them. All the shades were pulled down and inside it had turned very dark. Light came in only through the storm door and at the rear from the window above the kitchen sink. Where was she? He looked outside for her car, even though he knew it was exactly where it had been for days. "Sharon!" he called again. She must have left with John without telling him. "Sharon?" he screamed again.

Silence.

She wouldn't leave without telling him. "Sharon, come down, right now," he demanded. "Or I'll tell Mom that John came to see you, Sharon."

But nothing stirred upstairs either.

Outside, the leaves swirled, the wind groaned, the porch roof creaked, and the door flew open. Gusts of cold air invaded the house. Closing the front door, Tony switched on the lights and stood still, fuming. How could she leave him in the barn? All day, she hadn't been fair, he thought, whimpering as he unbuttoned his jacket. He forgot all about the shots he had heard, wondering only how she could have forgotten about him once John came.

"I'm going to tell Mom," he shouted, going up the steps, "that John came here and you are going to marry him."

He didn't know what could be the big secret about dating John. But Sharon had made him promise that he wouldn't tell Mom about John's visits to their home, and Tony had promised over and over again that he would keep his word.

Sharon had met John when she taught Sunday school. John visited her only when their mother, Darlene, was at work. Darlene worked in the kitchen at the rectory where John was studying to be a Catholic priest.

Today, all day long, Sharon had been inattentive to Tony. All morning she had paced around the front window of the living room. To get her attention he had banged his plastic cup on the wood-grain Formica table, spilled the milk then announced what he had done, and eaten the cheese she had wanted to use for their lunch. But still she hadn't come to the kitchen to prepare his lunch. So he had badgered her, asking, "Are you going to marry John, Sharon?" When she didn't answer, he repeated the question, and answered it himself, again and again, shouting, "I know you are going to marry John. I know you are. And you love John."

"I'll tell you tonight," Sharon had finally answered, peering through the lace curtains of the front window.

At last she had come into the kitchen and stood behind the counter. "Tone," she said, "promise me you will never tell Mom or anyone else that John came to visit me."

"Are you going to marry John without telling Mom, then?" Tony had asked, looking up at her, puzzled.

"Tony, are you listening? Promise me that." Her lips trembled. She was angry even when he hadn't done anything wrong. But he shook his head, mumbling, "You know I won't tell Mom."

He held his cup tightly until the tips of his fingers and nails turned white as he murmured, "I don't tell Mom anything because she doesn't want to know anything."

"I know you won't tell her. I believe you, sweetheart," Sharon had said, bending down and kissing him on the cheek. Pink color had returned to his nails and he had rubbed his cheek against hers.

Now he reached the top of the steps. The upstairs hallway was dark and chilly. Sharon liked to keep the windows open on sunny days like today. He switched on the hall light. The door to Sharon's room was slightly open. As he felt the absolute silence, fear rose in his heart. His lips trembled and this time, instead of shouting, he whispered, "Sharon?"

She didn't answer.

He pushed the door and as it opened he stepped backward. A strip of light fell inside the room. Standing outside, he shuddered with fear. But nothing moved inside. He pushed the door again, and the strip of light widened. Still standing outside, he bent down, peeping. In the dim stretch of light he saw Sharon lying on the floor, facing away from the door. She hadn't complained about feeling sick.

"Sharon?" he whispered, then tiptoed in, looking around.

Blood ran from under her forehead.

He ran out of the room, pressing his arms around his heaving chest. Inside the room a window shade flapped against the slightly opened window. Tony shivered, closing his eyes tightly.

He had never seen death, only lives that weren't happy.

But Sharon wasn't that unhappy, and she was happier since she had met John.

She wasn't dead, maybe just hurt.

Who had hurt her? John? But he couldn't have: he loved Sharon, they were supposed to be married, she was to tell him about it tonight. He opened his eyes. He crept back into the room, his lips trembling, he moved his hands on the wall to find the light switch. He turned on the light. A cool breeze came in from the slightly opened window and the long skirt on Sharon's still body moved. The furnace clicked on and rumbled. Papers from Sharon's desk swept across the floor and landed on her still body.

Tony shivered and leaned against the wall. Slowly, he bent over Sharon's body and looked at her face. Her eyes were fixed and staring upward. A violent sob came out of his mouth. Scared, he ran out of the room. He sat on the floor by the staircase and in muffled moans cried out, "No, no... Sharon, no!"

Crying, he ran into the kitchen, dialed "O" and waited, his hands shaking, his fingers wrapping around the telephone cable. "You ain't dead, Sharon," he cried, "you ain't dead!" Then he began shouting into the mouthpiece, "Operator, please, operator. Help! This is an emergency... help!"

Finally he was connected.

"Operator," the calm voice on the other end announced. Suddenly, Tony was choked up and couldn't speak.

"Operator," the voice announced again, this time a little louder.

In halting words, Tony said, "My sister's hurt." He blurted their address and his mother's whereabouts and then dropped the phone back in its cradle.

As he was coming out of the kitchen he heard the rumbling of a passing vehicle and dashed outside. He ran through the entrance gate and stood in the middle of the road, waving his hands up in the air, running behind the truck. "Help! Help!" he screamed until the red lights vanished from his sight. Turning north, south, east, and west, he jumped up and down screaming, "Help! Help... someone...!" He walked back and was about to collapse on the steps of the porch but he picked himself up and ran back into the house.

He rushed to the bathroom and pulled out the first-aid box. For a moment he looked at the tiny Band-Aid strips and bandages, and then he dropped them on the floor. Instead, he grabbed a towel from the linen closet and ran back to Sharon's room.

Now blood ran below the dresser and up to the door. He crossed the red stream and sat holding the towel over her forehead, saying, "I am sorry... Sharon, I forgot to come in... Why didn't you call me, Sharon... answer me..." But seeing that she wasn't answering, he let the towel slip from his hands and he collapsed like a crumpled ball of paper and sobbed.

After the ambulance arrived he was taken to his room where he watched from his bedroom window as Sharon was carried out on a stretcher. Her face was covered with a sheet. Tony found himself again gasping for air. "She can't... she can't be dead," he cried, then he bolted out of his room and ran down the stairs. But by then they had closed the door of the ambulance and it had left the driveway. He saw Uncle Sam, Aunt Lydia's husband, walking towards him.

"Tony, are you ready?" Uncle Sam said. "You're coming with me for a while."

Suppressing a whimper, Tony asked, "Is Sharon dead?"

"She's... she's er, gone away, Tony."

"Where?"

"Heaven."

"Heaven? She's dead."

"She's with the Lord."

"With the Lord? She isn't dead. She's in heaven? She's in heaven?" Tony kept on repeating his questions, but his uncle didn't answer.

Tony heard that phrase many times over the coming days and weeks. Heaven, heaven, heaven – he heard it till he disliked the word, and he hated the phrase, the Lord's wish, and the Lord who had wished such a terrible thing on him and his sister.

Sharon had left a suicide note but, for many months, every chance his mother had, she asked him to remember who had come to visit Sharon that day.

"No one," he had always answered flatly, without looking at her. Color had drained from his face. To the queries of the police too, he stood firm. Folding his arms across his chest, as if concealing Sharon's secret and the pact between brother and sister, he stood speechless, even when his heart wanted to reveal the truth about John visiting Sharon. Week after week he avoided the questions and eventually they tired of asking.

★   ★   ★

Tony took a deep breath and looked at Maya, who was crying. Her face was wet. He took a handkerchief out of his pocket and gave it to her. "Maya, don't cry, " he said. "This incident carved my destiny and maybe that's how I have reached India. While growing up, I thought only about reaching heaven to find my sister. As a young boy I stared at the sky day and night, hoping to get a glimpse of her in heaven. I sat by the pool for hours looking at the reflection of the unreachable skies in search of heaven. In school I drew clouds and in the clouds I drew a picture of my sister, Sharon, instead of God. Besides searching for Sharon in the skies, I dreamed of her many times. Still in my dreams I talk to her. I plead with her to come back, and sometimes I ask if John, her friend, is with her too, since he had disappeared after her death."

Maya had never heard such a tragic true story. She whimpered, admiring his ability to handle his pain and use it for the betterment of others. In her eyes, he appeared as a hero, superior to any Indian man she knew.

Tony stared at the river, trying to say something happy about his family to cheer Maya up. He thought of telling her about his bubbly aunt, Lydia.

"I am so sorry Tony… I truly don't know… how to express… I – I have been so selfish," Maya sniffled. "I have been telling you nothing but all my petty family problems…"

He wrapped his arms around her and patted her shoulders. "I liked hearing your family stories," Tony said. "And I have been carrying this pain with me for so long that at times I don't even realize how much it weighs me down. Thanks for listening to me, Maya."

She removed his hand from her shoulder and for the first time she held it in hers, pressing it fondly. They sat there silently.

When the clock struck nine, she started to get up, but before letting her hand go Tony lifted it to his lips; this startled Maya, and she hurriedly left Seva Sadan.

That night Tony felt even closer to Maya. Instead of dreaming about courting her he started to think how it would be when they were married. Of course the wedding would be in church, here. But maybe they would go back home for their honeymoon. He was certain she would like that. Then… then they would come back to Seva Sadan and continue to do mission work. Later, as his mind continued to dream about his future plans he was over-whelmed and wanted to go to her home right then and there and ask her to marry him. He got up and saw it was eleven o'clock.

All he did was kneel down and pray.

The next day when she came in he couldn't look her in the eye. She went in the kitchen to prepare tea and he thought for a few minutes: I have to get over this fear. I have to tell her. I can't take this anymore. I love her. But how should I tell her?

He had thought about it all night. In what language would he tell her, Hindi or English? "*Me tumhe pyar karata hun.*" No, not Hindi, she would simply laugh. "I love you" – that's better. But that may… not be so special. Perhaps she would like to hear it in her language, Marathi. That sounds so complex, "*Me tula prem karate.*" He went over it again: *me* meant I. *Tula* was you and *prem* meant love, but then what was this *karate* doing? This would be rather difficult, but he decided he would try it. He tried saying it several times. Yes, he would say it in Marathi. And he would tell her today.

He went to the kitchen. He stood near her, but she ignored him, though he thought she might be watching him from the corner of her eye. His heart raced. "Maya," he said softly.

The sound of his voice must have startled her and the strainer she held in her hand fell on the floor. She went to pick it up. He too bent down and held her hand in his as they both got up. Blood rushed through his veins and she jerked backward as if lightning had hit her. He held her hand tightly in his.

They both stood speechless, hand in hand. She stared at the floor, and he kept staring at her. His heart was pounding. Tell her, *now*! his mind screamed. He took her hand to his trembling lips.

"Tony," she protested, and quickly moved away from him.

He took a deep breath and said, "Maya… *tula.*"

Hearing that, a mischievous smile appeared on her face and she looked back at him.

"I love you," he blurted, moving towards her.

They stood still, their hearts beating fast.

She glanced at him and after looking at his searching eyes, she hid her face in her hands. Softly, he removed her hands from her face but she still wouldn't look at him. She only stared at the floor, her cheeks turning red.

"Maya," he said, "look at me," but she didn't look up. Forgetting he was going to tell her that in Marathi, his lips quivered, his hand shook and this time he whispered. "I love you, Maya, I love you."

For a moment, lines of resistance formed on her face but then they disappeared and she smiled softly.

"Maya, I love you," he repeated.

"I know," she whispered.

She knew? His face lit up.

Yes, she knew, but did it mean she loved him too?

Freeing herself from his grip, she ran outside and stood by the front window. Her heart pounded so hard that she pressed up against the wall. This can't be true, not so soon. She needed some more time to think about this. Tony, please, she thought, wait. Let me only dream a little longer, where we were happy.

He walked quickly behind her, thrilled. He had told her at last! And she wasn't angry. "Maya, I love you, very much," he said, his voice quivering, "I... I've been... I love you..." He fidgeted with words like a musician who sweeps the keyboard with his fingers, trying to create the sounds that he had played in his heart when it was rapturous and absorbed in composing a melody, a raga for his beloved.

Her faced flushed and she rested her head on the window. Putting his hand to her face, he lifted her chin up. She glanced at him and fell into his embrace.

"Does this mean you love me too, Maya?" he whispered.

But she broke away from him, and ran inside.

All that day he couldn't think of anything, he couldn't concentrate on what he had to do. Instead, he thought of her blushing face all the time. His eyes kept following her. His heart sang; he couldn't live without her. Every time their eyes met he would go spinning off into a new daydream about their love, even when there were many people around and he had his duties to attend to.

The next chance he had he didn't waste any time.

"Would you like to come to church with me on Sunday and have dinner with Father Paul?" he asked her.

"No," she replied, avoiding looking at him. "I can't, Tony," she said again.

"Why?"

"Because..." She paused, as he looked at her eagerly. "What would I tell my parents, Tony?"

"Tell them you are going out with me."

"Tony, this is India."

"All right, this isn't a date, tell them this is work."

Her face turned red and tears fell on her cheeks.

"Maya!" he exclaimed. "What happened? What did I say?"

"It's not that I don't want to go with you, but you don't know lots of things, Tony."

"Maybe not. But I know one thing, I love you." He tried to hold her in his embrace. She pushed him away.

He stood, trying to grasp what he had missed. For him there were no barriers in love. But for Maya, it was different, he realized as he saw her tearful eyes.

"Tony, don't try to hold my hand," she said. "Don't tell me you love me... again and again. It scares me. I had a nightmare. Someone might hurt you." She spoke with a whimper.

"Who would hurt me? And why? I haven't done anything wrong."

"No, you haven't. But they might think otherwise. You are different from the men here, and they would think you are being wrong with me."

"But you love me too, why can't you tell them that?"

"Things don't work like that here."

"All right, can you at least tell me that you love me?"

She nodded her head, barely glancing at him.

He roared, "Thank you, Lord. She loves me."

Maya put her hand over his mouth. She didn't want to be reminded of his love and the fact that she too had fallen in love. Their love, the intensity in his expressions, and their emotions scared her. Every day, she tried to convince him that love need not be confirmed in words; only your heart knows the truth.

As the weeks and months went by, Maya was beside herself

when she felt their love would have no happy ending. When she thought of her family, and particularly of her father's strict discipline, she realized that the whole idea of their love was outlandish. To Maya, their love would seem natural and so right when she and Tony were together, but it would seem altogether wrong when she went home. There, she did not want to think that she was in love, though that's all she thought about. At times she imagined them both dying, while yearning for one another like Layla and Majanoo. And her fear increased. The differences between them frightened her and made her anxious about her future. She was sure the love between them would break many other hearts, even lives, and eventually force them apart, only because to the world they were already oceans apart.

That was why she wouldn't allow him to speak openly about how they felt towards each other. Their love remained silent.

As for Tony, it gradually sank in that Maya wouldn't go out with him. But they still spent time together after clinic hours, when they would sit in the verandah together and talk freely. Maya mostly talked about her family life. Initially, she poured her heart out, telling him how sad she had been since she had to let go of her college scholarship. She had to help her parents raise her younger siblings. At times she would tell him about the difficulties of living with so many other members of the family. At other times she would tell him that in many ways life felt complete right here at home when one grew up with a bunch of brothers and sisters. Once she teased him, saying, "Unlike you, I don't have to go across the oceans to find peace or meaning in life."

"I didn't come here to find peace," Tony answered. "I came to find you, and you only happened to be the peace I was searching for. And since I am going to marry you I will have that peace the rest of my life, right?"

She blushed. "Shh! Tony, someone will hear you," she said, looking around.

"So? I love you." He wrapped his arms around her.

She blushed and quickly pushed his hands away. "You may have found me but do you have enough guts to ask my father for my hand?" she teased him.

But when he stood and said yes, he would go to her father

right now, she was petrified. "No, no, Tony, this is wrong. You know that," she protested.

"No, I don't know that," he argued, trying to hold her hand in his. "How can love be wrong?"

"I am not talking about love and I can't make you understand, but—" Her voice trembled. She began crying and ran inside.

Walking right behind her, he wrapped his arms around her. "Maya, what's so difficult? We will somehow convince your father that we are inseparable."

She shook her head, stepping away from him. "It's not that easy," she said. Her big eyes filled with tears. "I shouldn't be coming here, Tony. Our love will cause a lot of problems... to... my whole family... and—"

Crying, she fell into his embrace. He wiped her tears off with his lips, every time, dampening her resolve never to see him again. But every day while going home, she would decide she should look for another job. Their affair was going too far...

For Tony there were times when he felt almost as if he had met Maya before, in some other existence, somewhere. Of course, as a Catholic missionary, he couldn't easily believe in reincarnation but on the other hand he couldn't ignore the connection he felt with her in his heart. He wondered about those close, subtle yet distinct vibrations he felt about her. These matters perplexed him, especially when he was helpless to unravel them. Those were the times his feelings for her became intense and he wished he knew where they had met before. What was it that had kept them apart so long? When she was around him sometimes it seemed as if something would flicker on the edges of his awareness, as if a long-lost memory would illumine a corner of his existence. It was as if feelings that had been lost in the infinite were bursting into the finite vision of his mind. Whenever he felt this, he experienced such joy that everything seemed connected, and he sensed who Maya was to him and who he was to her. He always wanted to grasp and hold on to those precious moments, those feelings; but the flame of unconscious memory would regress as quickly as it surfaced, and Tony could never retrace it, although it always left a distinct impression on his mind, and left him feeling exalted.

He knew that besides going to heaven, this too was what he had been yearning for – love!

Chapter Three

It was the month of August, and in the celebration of their god the whole town of Kulur had gone mad. Singing and dancing, the men threw colored powders in the air. Most were out to purchase a replica of Lord Ganesh, the elephant-headed Hindu god. The road overflowed with horse carriages, rickshaws, and men carrying large-size Ganeshas on palanquins. But most carried their personal, smaller replicas on their heads or hand-held brass plates, jostling for their place in the procession.

At the head of the procession, a marching band in western attire played songs from films; others scattered through the procession playing regional music on *shahanai*, harmonium, and flutes. The discord of all the instruments infused into the rhythms of *dholakis* as every man sang his holy tunes, worshipping the god in the form of clay idols.

The celebration reminded Tony of a scene from a movie in which people made a deity of gold and worshipped it in the absence of the Christian faith. He also was frustrated because the Hindu calendar was filled with many, many festivities, and when they took place, schools and institutions stayed open only half a day or remained entirely closed, which interfered with his work schedule. To him, all the elaborate celebrations of deities were futile.

That morning, caught in the midst of a procession, Tony was concerned about a fisherman's little girl who had been admitted into the hospital at his insistence. He needed to check on her progress and, if she had been released, to know the treatments that had been prescribed for her recovery. So, ignoring the procession and everyone who bumped into him, he walked faster towards the main intersection where he hoped to catch a bus for the city hospital.

The windows and balconies of the buildings along the roads were packed with elderly men, women and young children and as the carriages came closer to them, they threw rice, flowers and colored powders at the Lord Ganesh.

Down the street the crowd clapped loudly, singing praises to Ganesh. A few sat on the pavement blatantly crying, asking for all kinds of things from this god. The voices grew louder in the procession, singing, "*Bappa Moriya re...*" and even louder in one rhythm, "*Bappa Moriya re...*"

Listening to their cries, Tony remembered Thomas, a missionary he had traveled with who had dreamed of converting thousands of souls in India.

Thomas was encouraging to all the new missionaries. If Thomas were here, Tony thought, he wouldn't be intimidated by the size of the crowds. He would run up and down the streets, shaking these people's hands, engaging them in stories of Christ and distributing Christian pamphlets. Before he left he would make sure the people understood that Christ is the only true God and none of this *Bappa Moriya* stuff...

The procession lumbered on at an elephant's pace. Frequently coming to a halt, it blocked all the traffic from every direction. Now it had stopped right in front of Tony. He looked around but he knew he couldn't go any further, so he climbed the steps of a closed shop and waited.

In a few moments his eyes narrowed and he burst out, "What the heck is *he* doing here?" He shook his head. "For God's sake, that's really him," he grumbled, looking at his first convert, Pandu, who was dancing and rejoicing in Hindu rituals like all the rest! With his mouth open, Tony watched Pandu moving swiftly with the crowd and, before realizing it, he lost sight of Pandu. Hurriedly he stumbled down the steps and moved closer to the crowd.

The crowd felt thicker from close up but, once again, Tony could see Pandu who was now reciting mantras. Pandu's eyes were completely closed. Tony could see that Pandu knew the verses by heart; he wasn't acting and there was not even a trace of shame on his face.

Pandu prayed not to please his people but to please this heathen god!

The thought enraged Tony. How could he read the Christian

stories and then do this in the very same week? Foolish – foolish and sad, that's all, Tony grumbled to himself.

Pandu hadn't shown any signs that he was falling out of the faith. He came to meetings regularly, Tony remembered; then why this? And, looking at Pandu, perspiration formed at his hairline. His heart pounded. He can't do that, he should be told... he should be taught... Tony cried. I should teach them... no one can turn away from Christ... Oh, Lord, help... help me to save them!

On the street Pandu continued to dance, with cymbals in his hands. Before Tony even knew what he was doing, he pushed himself into the crowd, thinking he should bring Pandu back to his sense. He moved quickly, shoving people, and seeing Tony, a foreigner, people moved and gave him some elbow room. Taking advantage of their courtesy, he again pushed and shoved with all his might, but he whirled around like a small tow-boat in a fierce sea. He couldn't get through a throng of this size. He stood in the crowd and in few minutes he was crushed like a paper boat and was pushed out into an alley.

On the street a team of jugglers were putting on a show, throwing burning sticks high in the air while people cheered. By the alley, a team of gymnasts were performing complicated somersaults on the rough paving. A group of men in bright turbans, holding *dholakis* in their hands, rushed in front of a carriage. Chanting and dancing with the beating of drums, they picked up speed, and as dust and multicolored powders whirled up in the air it formed kaleidoscopic clouds in the bright blue sky.

Tony again searched for Pandu, who was now throwing flowers at the idols. Looking at his pious face, Tony had a tremendous urge to save his soul. Don't do that Pandu, don't be a fool... he urged silently, but at the same time he felt like screaming, *Pandu, you are a Christian now*. But restraining himself, he stood quietly, watching.

Pandu had convinced Tony that he had taken Christ into his heart. So had he been lying? Why? Unlike the others, Pandu really didn't need any help from the mission. Then why would he become a Christian? And then do this? Who was he fooling? Tony had considered him a good friend; they had good times together since he could converse with him in English.

For generations Pandu's family had lived on an island and had only recently moved back to India. Pandu was a compassionate man, who at times people thought naïve, as he easily mixed with people of all religions, thinking the Lord was in one's heart and not in the way one worshipped Him. For Tony, Pandu's conversion had seemed easy, but what Tony didn't know was that Pandu had never become a Christian in the real sense of the word, because Pandu never saw any difference in the ways God was worshipped.

To inculcate the Christian faith Tony had been advised to break the Hindu clay idols to show that there was no god in them. That would also prove that no bad spell would come over the people if they deserted their gods, and that would help to dispel their fears. Now Tony fretted because he hadn't done that, because he couldn't bring himself to do something so harsh. But now seeing Pandu, still chanting, the veins on his neck stood up, turning his face red. I have been wrong... weak... Oh, Heavenly Father, please grant me the strength to handle these obstacles! Tony prayed.

An announcement came on a loudspeaker – a human-size figure of dancing Ganesh was coming from the south side of the street to join the proceedings. With loud cheers hordes of people ran to the end of the street. As the crowd rushed by, Tony saw Ranga, another young convert, who was waiting to garland the statue. Now I shouldn't be surprised, Tony said to himself. But he held his fists tightly in his pockets as he thrust forward.

Men around him laughed loudly. Their exhilaration angered him even more, and he drew himself out of the crowd, thinking, How could Ranga do that... after we helped him to buy his rickshaw and settled him in a home, when he didn't even have any family, or a home.

The crowd bellowed a tune: "*Bappa Moriya re... Bappa Moriya re...*"

As those words thrashed on his ears, Tony looked up at the sky, searching for answers. Bright sunbeams made him squint. He did not know how to save these converts in this sea of madness. He reached for the cross that hung around his neck and pressed it into his palm. For a moment, he felt peaceful. Holding the cross in his hands he repeated the words from the Old Testament reminding him of his commitment to missionary work. "For all the peoples walk each in the name of their God, but we will walk in the name of the Lord our God forever and ever."

"*Bappa Moriya re… Bappa Moriya re…*" people chanted as they danced.

Tony opened his eyes. The loud chanting continued, "*Bappa Moriya re… Bappa Moriya re…*"

The chants resonated in the devotees' ears. The rhythmic sounds, the scent of burning incense that filled the air and the lure of the colors of flowers and powders hypnotized the minds of the worshippers. All their senses were immersed in the exotic rituals, negating their thoughts, and helping some to be more single-minded. The prayers sifted the impurities from their minds, helped them to focus on the worship of their Lord, making them more devout, and drowned them in meditation, helping them to forget the problems of their routine life.

Though exotic and elaborate, these strange traditions and rituals did not make any sense to Tony. He saw them as chaotic and meaningless – even sinful.

But the devotees' piety, their affection for Ganesh which wafted in the air, and their love for their god, seemed so real that he wondered if *his* God was witnessing this…

Was He listening to their prayers?

Pandu was absorbed in his prayers, unaware of Tony's presence, while Ranga flirted with the girls as Tony stared at him. Right then, as he was teasing a young girl, Ranga saw Tony staring at him and panicked. He bolted away like a frightened deer into a nearby alley. Seeing him so frightened, his friends laughed. Ignoring his friends, Ranga ran down the narrow alley, which contained mainly open gutters, but also was used illegally by the residents to dump their rubbish. The open drains were overflowing, causing an unbearable stench. As Ranga raced through the litter, he tore off the chain with the cross from his neck and threw it to the ground.

Tony ran behind him. A few feet into the alley he shouted, "God will forgive you! *Wapis aa*, come back, Ranga, otherwise you will be a sinner forever. Ranga! Come back..."

But Ranga turned, entering another maze of gutters and rubbish, and was gone from Tony's sight.

Holding his breath, Tony made his way to the chain, which was glittering on the pile of waste. As he bent down, again he looked up in Ranga's direction, into the vacant alley. Swallowing a lump in his throat, he picked up the cross and wrapped it in his handkerchief. He slowly walked back to the procession, wondering if Pandu, if he noticed Tony, would react the same way as Ranga had.

While returning to Seva Sadan Tony saw the entire town was overwhelmed by the celebration of the Lord Ganesh. People offered flowers, broke coconuts on the pavements, lit oil lamps and then circled them around the idol. Right on the streets, even in the tightly packed processions, people were prostrating to this god. This act of throwing themselves before a silly statue disturbed Tony. He was saddened at the thought of these ignorant souls and their false prayers. He felt there was no hope for him or them.

Seva Sadan was quiet. He sat on the verandah, looking at the river, wondering what he was going to do. Was this mission of any consequence? What should he do so he would never have to witness this again? But ultimately his thoughts rested on how he could persuade Maya to become a Christian so that he could marry her.

Maya hadn't come to work that day because of the Hindu holidays. He remembered her excitement as she told him how it would be a treat for him to see the festivities, how it would be so colorful and how she had helped young girls to choreograph dances in her neighborhood. She had invited him to join her at home, so he could see the dance drama.

But thinking about how Pandu and Ranga had turned their backs on their adopted new faith, enjoying going back to their roots, he became concerned about Maya. He wrestled with the thought – what would he choose if the time ever came: his love for Maya or his faith?

The choice would be agonizing.

No. He hoped he never would have to face it.

Up to now he had convinced himself that Maya would convert to Christianity, but now he was unsure.

He stood up and paced the verandah, thinking how he would bring this up to Maya. He should ask her to start Bible study and join the services at the church – at once, at least on Sundays. If she did, he thought she would take a liking to the Christian teachings. She would see how wrong it was to pray to the idols. He knew she revered the mission work of helping the poor. She would understand, he hoped. The sooner she started her studies the better it would be. With that, he stopped pacing.

But the thoughts of baptizing Maya, converting her to Christianity and taking her away from what she loved, made him uneasy. On the other hand, their sharing of the Christian faith would surely elevate their relationship to a different dimension. But doubt kept insinuating itself. He blamed himself for not raising the topic earlier with Maya. Had he somehow betrayed her by not giving her a complete account of the activities of the Seva Sadan, the house of service?

Every evening at around nine the men gathered to read Bible stories or sing devotional songs about Jesus in the Marathi language, but it all happened when Maya had already gone home. Most of the other religious activities took place in the church, which was in the inner part of the town. Now Tony felt he should have talked to her openly about these activities, and the purpose of the mission. He hoped it wasn't too late, because he didn't mean to betray her. In fact, they... these people... Pandu and Ranga had betrayed him, and the Christian faith.

Again, Pandu's peaceful invocation in front of a clay idol replayed in his mind. Just then he saw Pandu rushing up the steps, overflowing with joy, happy as ever. Tony realized that the whole incident in the procession had left no mark on him. Tony looked at him, his eyes searching Pandu's for signs of remorse, but Pandu seemed unperturbed, and was as jolly as usual.

Is he naïve? Tony thought, or stupid? Or a conniver?

He did not know what to think. He decided that he would ask for an apology from Pandu, and if he didn't receive one he would tell Pandu to leave Seva Sadan and the Christian faith at once. But an apology seemed to be the last thing on Pandu's mind. He happily bounded up the steps, holding the *prasad* – the offerings for an occasion he had come to share with Tony.

"Brother Tony," he said, and then stopped for breath. "They told me you were at the procession. You left without taking the *prasad*. Here, I have brought it for you." His behavior appalled Tony; he has been expecting a sincere apology. But Pandu was behaving as if he had done nothing wrong. Pandu brought two plates from the kitchen and was opening the package of *prasad* carefully, so not even a morsel would fall on the floor. If it fell, for him it would be a curse!

"Pandu, don't you think you need to confess? Don't you think you have done wrong?" Tony asked.

"Wrong? Why, Brother Tony?"

He wasn't even aware of his sin! Pandu's innocence was touching but Tony wasn't going to fall into his trap. He ignored Pandu's guilelessness.

"Pandu, let's kneel down and pray."

"*Han, han,*" said Pandu. Nodding his head, he left the plates on the counter and continued, "Let's pray before eating the *prasad*. Prayers make me happy. Prayer is like a bath for your mind." He looked at Tony's expressionless face and teased, "Oh! You Americans, you don't take baths. For you, Brother Tony, prayer is like a shower." And he laughed loudly, pleased with his own banter. But Tony didn't join Pandu, feeling that his loud laugh was like a roaring ocean, fearless and shameless, that swallowed everything, even his faith.

Stern-faced, Tony walked to the altar, lit the lamp, and asked Pandu to join him. Pandu quickly walked to the altar and kneeled, closing his eyes.

"Our Lord, Jesus, Yeshu," Tony prayed, translating the prayer of reconciliation, "I am heartily sorry for having offended Thee. I detest all my sins, because I dread the loss of heaven and the pains of hell; but most of all because they offend You, my God, who is all good and deserving of all my love." Tony opened his eyes and looked at Pandu, who was lost in his own world. Tony continued, "I firmly resolve, with the help of Your grace, to confess my sins, and…" Tony again paused, then repeated, "I firmly resolve, with the help of Your grace, to confess my sins." He looked across at Pandu, who was not joining in. "Pandu, please say it with me," Tony urged. But Pandu didn't respond. His eyes were still closed. Tony murmured, "And to avoid the near occasions of sin. Amen." No words came from Pandu. Tony saw that Pandu was oblivious to his words; he was again absorbed in his prayer.

Gazing at Pandu, Tony noticed that he didn't look any different than when he was standing before a Hindu deity. This frustrated Tony. What could he make of Pandu's behavior? How could he make an impression on a man who could be so easily absorbed in any prayer, whether Christian or not? Pandu was just silly, he concluded.

But looking at him, Tony remembered a story which a missionary had told him about his attempts at kindling the Christian faith in his mission in India. This missionary had converted a Hindu woman. But when she came for the services she was obviously frightened. She shook violently, squeezed her eyes shut, and foamed at the mouth. As the service went on she continued to shake, faster and faster, as though possessed by some spirit. She made grunting noises, as if fighting with herself, and said in snarling words of contempt that the goddess Kali planned to kill her, that Kali was angry at her betrayal. This happened every day. It was disturbing to all the new converts who feared to come to the service. Other people were deterred from converting. The missionary became angry with the woman, telling her that he planned to attack her goddess, Kali, with the help of Satan. At nights he visited her home to tell her stories of Satan and wicked witchcraft. After that, the woman never misbehaved. Tony had later found out, however, what the missionary had never told him: some time later, the woman had become psychotic. She now walked the streets, fighting either with Satan or the goddess Kali.

The next day Tony went to visit Maya at her home as she had invited him. As he got off his bicycle to ask for her house, half a dozen children ran to him, asking, "Maya… Maya?"

Tony laughed at their enthusiasm and nodded his head. Seeing his cheerful acceptance of them, they clung to his hand and all tried to climb on his bicycle, pulling him in the direction of Maya's home. Someone had already gone ahead, to tell her of her

American visitor.

She stepped out of her house and stood looking at the alley from which Tony would be coming. Her face turned red. He was really coming to her home! What should she tell her parents now?

Her bashful look contained fear. Her parents would suspect that something was going on between them. Her long eyelashes flickered, hiding her awe about this visitor. With an extra spring under her feet, she didn't know how to stay calm. She stepped down from the verandah, then climbed back up again and waited, anxiously looking at the end of the alley.

When their eyes met, he smiled and waved. She had been thinking about this meeting since the previous night. But now that Tony was here, she didn't know how to hide her feelings. She felt overwhelmed. Overjoyed, she ran back into the house and to the kitchen, where she whispered to her mother, "*Aai*, Tony, American, American is here!"

"Maya, don't joke around. It's already late," her mother said.

But Maya's younger brothers had already heard the children outside and ran out to see Tony. The moment they saw this strange white man they knew he was their guest. They rushed back in, shouting, "*Am'erikan, Am'erikan* is here!"

By now Maya's father had put his newspaper down, and was asking Maya why Tony was visiting their home. Was everything okay at her job? Blushing, Maya whispered in her mother's ear, "*Aai*, I don't know why he is here. But I had asked him to come for *prasad,* so may—"

Her mother relayed this information to Maya's father, who gathered up the newspaper and said, "Have you gone mad? He is a Christian. He doesn't believe in *prasad*. Or, for that matter, anything we do—" He stopped as he saw Tony at the door. Getting up from his chair immediately, he asked Tony to come in.

While removing his shoes, Tony saw how tidy and clean the two-and-a-half-room house was. Lack of money was evident but the home displayed order despite the peeling paint. The tile floor had just been washed as it showed wet spots in the dimples of the surface. A storage loft was draped over with curtains made of old saris. There was a cot, two wooden chairs, and a tall wooden cupboard, which was covered with an embroidered cloth. A radio and a few torn, faded books perched on top. The bed was covered with a faded bedcover mended in several spots. The chairs showed bare wood. Under the loft was a small teapoy, covered with a new red cloth with a gold border. The wall around the teapoy was decorated with garlands of flowers and leaves. Although there was some attempt at a festive look, it all appeared odd to Tony. The tiny replica of Lord Ganesh was placed on a raised platform covered with beautifully embroidered fabric. A small unframed mirror was placed behind Lord Ganesh and there were flowers, powders, and incense in a copper plate. The room was filled with the smell of the incense. The idol and everything around it looked better than the family's entire possessions.

Why were the images of Hindu gods all laden with ornaments and other expensive items? Tony had often wondered since coming to India. After all, these people had barely anything to eat. But someone had tried to explain it to him. A man is always praying for bounty, went the explanation, but if the images of gods had none, what would be the point of praying for something that even the deities didn't have?

But taking into account this family's lack of material things, it was clear that their god wasn't blessing them much with anything.

Maya's father came forward, slipping a T-shirt over his bare chest. "Come, come," he said, motioning to a chair. "We... poor, but I happy... you come," he said ruefully.

Tony reluctantly sat down. Maya's father, forgetting he had just reminded his family that Tony, a Christian, would not be there for *prasad* or *pooja*, asked, "You wait? *Pooja* and *prasad*. Soon."

When Tony did not answer, the father stood and gestured to Tony with his fingers that the rituals would start in five minutes. At once Tony stood, not wanting to relive the earlier experience of the procession. But Maya appeared from behind the curtain and he sat down again. The father rushed inside and a few moments later reappeared with a yellow-colored cloth wrapped around him. He started chanting and preparing for afternoon *arati*. Maya's younger brother helped him diligently, as he knew that, some day, as a man, he would take over this family tradition.

A small group of children had already entered the house and

they were all sitting on the floor, waiting to sing the *arati*, beat the cymbals and eat sweets afterwards. Tony couldn't relate to this; he stood and turned to the door. But again he stopped, afraid of hurting Maya's feelings but feeling uncertain about the observance of these customs and how they would square with the proprieties of his own convictions and religion. He walked to the door but then lingered. He couldn't leave without telling Maya. The ringing of the small bell reminded him of the procession in the streets of Kulur. Again he looked for Maya, and saw that she and her mother were bringing out the offerings and setting them on the table. All of them had their eyes closed, including the children, and the room wore an air of piety that he felt was hard to ignore.

Standing awkwardly in the center of their room, Tony was again assailed by conflicting emotions. He walked back to the door facing outside, thinking, What right do we have to come all the way across the world to tell these people not to conform to the religion and customs they have observed for so many generations? Quickly he came up with the answer, soothing his doubts. Because this was all false. It was not a true faith or the God!

In a few moments he was roused from his thoughts when he saw Maya before him with a bowl of sweets. Her brother was behind her, showing him how to rest one palm over the other to accept the offerings. Tony was puzzled. Waving his hand, he stepped backward, denying their *prasad*.

He did not know that one never denies the *prasad*. One must accept it with no objection, since it is meant to help develop an attitude of acceptance in life. Surprised at his denial, Maya insisted, "You must."

But he hurriedly picked up a Christian book he had brought with him and gave it to Maya. He asked her to read it since, starting tomorrow, he wished to start teaching the fishermen's young children. By now Maya's mother had wrapped the *prasad* in a banana leaf and Maya pushed it into Tony's hand.

On his way back to Seva Sadan, Tony passed their *prasad* to a child in the street.

Part Two

Chapter Four

Mr. Pandit, like a caged lion, paced the verandah of his estate home the entire afternoon. He paused every few minutes to listen for the sounds of the iron gate opening, but no one was even around the courtyard. The only sound he kept hearing was of squirrels rushing around in the vines covering the verandah arches. Looking at the squirrels running carefree on his railing, he stopped pacing, watched them for a moment or two and then said, "Shh... shhh..." and thumped his hand on the wall. They vanished but moments later reappeared, and he ran at them, grumbling, "Lowly rats!"

As they disappeared he rubbed his sweaty palms against one another and leaned against the arch. "Lowborn ignorant fool!" he grumbled. "How could he do this to me?" He shook his head as he walked down the steps, where he stood, waiting.

Even the green moss on the center fountain had dried up in the heat. Canopies of vines were laden with exotic flowers, and their scent had spread all around the garden of the estate. The tall iron gates, with "P" inscribed on either side, were newly painted, but the brass finials of the top rails had been left tarnished. On one of the two marble pillars of the gate there was a gold plate with black etching that read, "Built in 1863". Underneath was the inscription "For H. H.", which meant, for His Highness. The letters after that had been scratched off, as maharajas had never occupied the estate. The ruling British officials of that time had lived in the house before Mr. Pandit inherited it from his grandfather in 1942, and he been living there now for fifteen years.

The previous evening when Mr. Pandit received a telegram from one of his clients, saying a signed contract and the large sum of cash had not been delivered as expected, he concluded that Ram Sable, a "lowborn", was out to destroy him. He remembered that when he had asked, "When would you be returning?" Ram hadn't answered.

"If today's the seventh," Mr. Pandit counted, looking at the calendar, "you should be back on the tenth."

"Eleventh, sir."

"Tenth," he had insisted.

"I don't..." Ram had tried to explain, but Mr. Pandit had looked at him in such a way that by the time Ram had escaped from his office he was saying, "I will try."

Now Mr. Pandit was convinced Ram was up to something. "Cunning fellow," he said in a ludicrous tone.

Today the twelfth too had passed. Such incidents outraged Mr. Pandit because he felt that no Indian, except himself, was fastidious about the importance of time.

Mr. Pandit upheld the British virtues of punctuality as well as knowledge of science and technology. Trained at Oxford, Mr. Pandit thought like white men. Since he thought that the British sort of respected the Brahmin caste, he tried to live as a staunch Brahmin, though he didn't understand the real meaning of being a Brahmin. To be Brahmin, according to the scriptures, was more a matter of attitude than of caste. A person of any caste or class could be virtuous and dutiful enough to be considered a Brahmin. But Mr. Pandit had never read the scriptures or understood the subtle meanings behind these things. He wasn't a very religious man.

He was five feet ten inches tall and stood out among Indians as a tall man. He kept his hair very short – a crop cut – and he wore a khaki, sahib-style hat. His bushy eyebrows were fierce-looking, but his straight, snow white, petite teeth somewhat softened his appearance. But he rarely smiled, and the creases of a frown were always deep around his full mouth and on his short forehead.

A highly intellectual man, Mr. Pandit suffered and made others suffer with his own suppressed self-worth when growing up and working under British rule.

Chitra watched her father through the etched glass panels of the dining hall. Seeing his furious pacing, she asked her mother, "*Aai*, you know Ram wouldn't run away with his money." Taking cups and saucers from the hands of a maid, she continued, "But he thinks everyone is like him, who values nothing but money."

"Chh... chh!" Her mother only clicked her tongue, scowling, conveying her annoyance.

She was always like that, Chitra thought. When she's with him, she's non-existent, she has no voice of her own, but the mere suggestion of a harmful word about him and she'll hiss at anyone like a cobra, protecting him. Yet, when Chitra was younger, watching her mother's loving behavior towards her father, she had thought how wonderful it would be to love a man that much! Now, Chitra had outgrown such notions and, as she looked at her mother, she wondered whether her mother really loved him, or was it all a pretense? Was it because of the pressures of old traditions? Chitra was convinced that no one could love a man like her father. She didn't love him anymore, not as a person, definitely not as her father. She believed one can will to love or not to love someone.

A peon tiptoed in from the side entrance of the verandah and stood silently looking at the floor. Then he announced, as if it was his fault, that Ram Sable was again not at home.

"You idiot," Mr. Pandit shouted. "You probably only saw the lock on his door from a distance and came back." Advancing towards the peon, he screamed, "Didn't you?"

The peon stepped backward.

Every time the peon had come back saying Ram Sable's door had a big lock and no one knew where he was, Mr. Pandit had scolded him.

"You came back without asking someone about his where-abouts, didn't you?" he asked again, advancing still closer.

The peon rushed away, gliding down the steps.

"Idiot," said Mr. Pandit, looking at the man's running feet. The disgust on his face clearly showed that the world was full of ignoramuses like these, and how unfortunate it was that a person of his intellect had to put up with them!

Coming down the steps Mr. Pandit slipped into his *chappals*, and walked towards the gate. Although it was late in the afternoon, the intense heat was still in the air. There was no one on the street. Through the iron bars, he looked towards the river. A few fishermen were talking idly while mending their nets by the riverbank. Behind them were their huts where the women were cleaning leftover pieces of fish. A mother was picking lice from a little girl's hair. An old woman was dozing on a cot and half-naked children were playing marbles in the dirt. Mr. Pandit hated the scene. He believed the poor people lived like that because they were lazy and stupid. He never helped them or even wasted his energy pondering their unfortunate situation, and he never appreciated Chitra doing so either.

He turned his gaze to the other side of the street and saw a cyclist pedaling in his direction. He noticed the cyclist was wearing a uniform. Since it was a little after four, he would have to be the express delivery postman. Mr. Pandit hurriedly opened the gate and stepped outside, smiling pleasantly. But the postman stopped a few feet away, barely looking at him. Then he threw Mr. Pandit a glancing look and turned, ready to cycle the other way. Nervously ringing the bicycle bell, he checked his pencil behind his ear. Mr. Pandit, firmly planting his feet on the ground, stood watching him with a steady glare, as if the postman was his bait.

Again the postman looked curiously at Mr. Pandit, and cautiously waved to him. Mr. Pandit advanced a few feet, ready to pounce at him. But trying to sound normal, he said, "Do you have express delivery mail for me?" His voice was loud and the postman was startled by the question. Mr. Pandit laughed as if to suggest, what a timid fool!

Express deliveries were very few and the postmen usually knew those delivery addresses before leaving the post office. However, fearing Mr. Pandit, the postman pretended to search his bag.

"If you knew I had an express delivery letter..." Mr. Pandit said, waving his fist in the air and walking a few feet further. "Your job... you hear me *ae*, madman, I am talking to you." The postman barely looked up. "Your job was to deliver my mail first. How dare you turn around and go to others before me, when I am waiting?"

The postman's knees wobbled as with an effort he rested his bicycle on its stand. He brushed a little patch of cement walkway with his hand and emptied his bag on the ground. Frantically, he shuffled through the papers in search of a letter he knew he didn't have. Mr. Pandit rushed to him, swearing. He pushed the postman away with his *chappals* and he plopped himself down, forgetting the layers of filth on the ground. In the hurried but systematic manner of an attorney, he read each and every address on the letters from the postman's bag.

There was nothing for him.

Standing up, he kicked at the scattered letters with his feet, and when he turned back, he was further annoyed seeing his wife, Sita, lingering at the gate.

Sita was short, almost a foot shorter than her husband. She was a fair-skinned, pretty woman, with a tiny nose set between deep black arched eyebrows and long eyelashes. Her dark curly hair always veiled her deep forehead, which was decorated with a deep red, huge kumkum. As a young girl, Chitra had always thought that her mother looked like a pretty Indian doll.

But she was more than just pretty.

Her heart was big and she refrained from saying anything that would hurt not only her husband and children but also the servants. She idolized her husband, and receiving her adulation, Chitra knew, made him more powerful. It irritated and also saddened her to see that in return he couldn't love her in a way she deserved.

Seeing him coming back empty-handed, though she couldn't see his shadowed frown, Sita felt it. She made it appear as if she had come only to push the goats away from the gate. Annoyed by her behavior, Mr. Pandit rubbed his head, and she dashed inside the gate and then disappeared. He left his *chappals* by the steps and, striding across the verandah, sat on the divan in the sitting room, rapidly fanning himself with his hand, wondering how he would manage if the money was gone.

Would he let the client suffer, allowing him go to court where the trial could go on and on for years? Or accuse the client who had entrusted him money without a receipt and tell him that the money was never received? His mind cooked up many options, although none of them included facing the truth and taking the loss himself.

He wouldn't be ruined, he thought, but he would have to sell the house, and he might lose business in that particular circle. His entire achievement would be spoiled because some low-class cheat had succeeded in fooling him. He stopped fanning himself and banged the fan on the teapoy. He wouldn't let it happen, he wouldn't let Ram Sable ruin his entire life's work. He would find an underground agent to search for Ram Sable and ruin the plebeian fool.

Soon Sita appeared with a tea tray and lingered at the door. The tinkling sounds of the cup and saucer made him stop fanning and he gestured for her to set the tray on a teapoy. Slowly walking towards him, she set the cup down on the teapoy, casually glancing at him. She handed him a new fan, and said, "You know Ram is an honest young man, you needn't worry…"

"You call that lowborn fool an honest man?"

"He is ethical, Brahmin by attitude…"

"Why do you always take other people's side?" He tossed the fan across the room. "The thief should have been returned by now. My whole life will be ruined and you want to tell me how honest he is?"

She shook her head and walked across the room and picked up the fan from the floor.

"Then," he roared, "stop telling me how to run my business and manage your kitchen and teach your daughter to do so."

Putting the fan on the teapoy, Sita went inside, silently.

The despair remained on Mr. Pandit's face. His wife always but unexpectedly peered into his conscience and that reminded him of his father, another very conscientious person for whom he had no respect.

His father – everyone had called him Bappa – was only a postmaster in a small town. Though intelligent, Bappa never had the ambition to accomplish more in his life. He did his job, and lived a simple life. During the terrible epidemics of malaria or typhoid, when postmen could not make their deliveries, he had carried all the mail to every home with little or no help. And no matter how many hours he worked, he never missed his religious rituals.

Nana, Mr. Pandit's maternal grandfather, always ridiculed his son-in-law, Bappa, for working at a menial job and spending his time every day in the worship of idols. Seeing his son-in-law's fish-tank ambition, Nana always regretted that he hadn't spared enough time to find a better match for his daughter. When she had turned seventeen, and he could not find the deserving match for her in a big city like Bombay, he had rushed into arranging her marriage by going to his village and seeking Bappa, a nice Brahmin boy. Nana had hoped that he would be able to mold Bappa, send him for a law degree, perhaps even to Oxford, and then have him as his law partner. But Bappa never left the small town, and Mr. Pandit, as a young boy, was influenced by his grandfather and had stayed with him in Bombay.

As a well-known barrister of the British Empire, Nana was a man of modern thinking. A simple son-in-law like Bappa was not his equal. Every chance Nana had he picked on his son-in-law. How could he spend his time in counting stamps all day, in a dumpy one-room post office? Or how could he spend all that time in front of those stone idols? How could he be so naïve to think there was god in those odd shapes?

Never losing his temper, Bappa had answered every time, "Nanasahib, I am sorry I have turned out to be such a disappointment to you, but I like my job, and your daughter has never gone hungry." And when he talked about his faith in the idols, he said, "It's not a worship of statues, but if I learn to see God in the stone statues, how difficult is it for me to see God in every man? It is not the worship of idols but an attitude. It teaches me humility, you see. If I can bow to stone figures, how difficult is it for me to bow to a conscious creator in every living being?"

Without fail, after hearing Bappa's justification of his asinine religious thoughts, Nana became outraged. He would get up from his chair and walk away, waving his arms in the air. Then standing by the front door, he would shout loudly so the whole alley could hear, "This is what's wrong with Indians. They are too eager to bow to everyone. The cowardly rascals don't have the guts to stand up for their self-respect and they are trying to realize the God in every human being. I am telling you there is no God in heaven or here. It is about time the Brahmins, the only people of intellect in this country, should seek other professions; otherwise there is no hope for India. It is all washed up!"

The memories of Mr. Pandit's childhood ran through his

mind, but he took no notice of them. That night he hardly slept.

Chitra knew Ram Sable wasn't even thinking about his delay in delivering the money or her father's business matters. Chitra wondered if he had been waiting for her for the past four full days. The day before leaving he had given her a letter, making sure that he had explained to her everything that was on his mind:

Dear Chitra,

I am going to Madras. I am not coming back to work for your father. As you know, this is something I have been thinking of doing for quite some time. I think the time is right. I need to make a move to practice law to protect people's right, and not to use it to extract money by wrongdoings. I need to get away from his unethical practices of law. The one thing I don't wish is to be away from you! You are the only reason I have stayed as long as I have. You know how I feel about you, and I would like to think that, although you don't reciprocate my feelings, you do find me somewhat worthy of you. Chitra, I want to marry you, today – "right now". I don't think there will ever be a right time for your father's approval, because it may never happen, because I will never be able to change my birth status. In his eyes I will always remain a lowborn. Why not escape the whole infuriating situation with a fresh beginning? As you know, my family is not rich but they will welcome you. Chitra, please don't disappoint me. Living without you will be nothing but misery. If you decide not to join me I have no idea what I would do. I may run away with your father's money (!) and live off it as a bum. Ha!

Dear, as idealistic as you are, I am sure you don't approve of running away from your family but I have no other choice because I am running out of my wits and patience. I wrote my resignation letter to your father months ago and have been waiting for the right opportunity to give it to him. This way, I will be gone and he will not know my whereabouts to make my life miserable. Chitra, my dear, I hope you won't disappoint me. I will be waiting for you at Babu's house for twenty-four hours. Once you come there, I will have all the things planned so we could be married right away. You won't have to live with your father's name anymore. Chitra, I know how pleasing that sounds to you. You will be my wife and we will be free to do as you please. I would love to have you as my partner in our law practice. Chitra, dear, can I count on you coming?

Yours, waiting,
Ram

After reading Ram's letter, Chitra had put it away. She would have married Ram eventually, but not this way. Eloping wasn't for her, though running away would have been a great way to offend her father. But she did not want to hurt her mother, or subject her to her father's abuse by eloping with Ram, not when her mother's heart condition from diabetes had worsened.

For the last couple of days Chitra had stayed in her room, saying she was feeling sick and avoiding any confrontations with her father regarding Ram. But by the sixth day Chitra too became worried about Ram when she stood behind the door, listening to the conversation between the police inspector and Mr. Pandit.

"What do you mean, you can't do anything about this? What kind of a police officer are you?" Mr. Pandit screamed.

"Sir, it's been only six days. Two days—"

"It has been three days more. And tell me why can't you issue the warrant when the crime is suspected?"

"That's not it, sir, I know Ram personally. He's a good man, though you may not think so."

"Get out. Get out of here." Mr. Pandit jumped out of his chair and walked towards the door. The police officer sat patiently, tapping with his baton on his hand. Mr. Pandit stood by the door, holding it open. The police officer didn't move, and Mr. Pandit came back and sat in his chair and picked up the phone to call his superiors.

Before he could dial the number, the police officer said, "Sir, let me take care of it as I know it. We will wait for a day. I will report to you later."

Mr. Pandit dropped the phone back onto its cradle. "You know at the end you are dealing with me," he said.

"Precisely, sir," said the police inspector. He then got up and left.

After the police inspector had gone, Mr. Pandit stormed out of the house, and Chitra decided to visit the address Ram had given her, but only to check if Ram's friend, Babu, knew anything regarding Ram.

Chitra had mentioned to Ram that they might elope when the time came. But that would have to be a joint decision. He wasn't to assume. She wasn't like other women who would automatically follow the man when he asked.

She was the first generation of women graduating from the law college. And her great-grandfather, barrister Nanasahib, had made sure she would have all the opportunities that women in England did.

But while walking along a desolate alley, Chitra certainly did not feel she had the same opportunities as women in England. The rickshaw had dropped her off before the cluster of shops and nearly collapsed buildings. She walked swiftly, passing huts, which had cow-dung walls and no windows. Pigs, goats and cows all scampered around the street trash. Every other step Chitra had to jump over puddles of drain water or the flies that gathered on the excrement of children and animals. At every breath she took in the stench of open gutters; at every glance in which she saw belligerent women and heard offensive words from ignorant men, she became acutely aware of Ram's struggle and how far he had advanced in his life.

Avoiding the eyes of anything that moved on the street, Chitra walked faster, holding her starched and ironed sari in her fingers, avoiding the filth on the ground while trying to find the address Ram had given in his letter. The buildings all looked the same, drab and barely standing erect. People seemed to move in slow motion as if human life had suddenly changed its character and become more stoical.

At last she came to a cross alley and spotted the building Ram had mentioned. As she came closer, she noticed a staircase that was secured by a rope. She asked a boy, who was gargling outside his home, if he knew where Babu lived. The boy pointed to the only closed door of the building.

Chitra knocked. From inside a groggy voice questioned, "Who... is... it?"

Not knowing how to introduce herself, she didn't answer. Seeing her puzzlement, the boy rushed to the door and rapidly pounded on it. There was no answer. Shaking the open padlock on the outside of the door, the boy called, "Get up! Oh, Babu! Your happy day has come. A lady-sahiba is here for you." And he giggled.

At once the door opened and a man stood before her in his wrap-around, stained lungi and sleeveless undershirt. He was unshaven and his hair had not seen water in several days. Chitra introduced herself and asked if Ram Sable was there.

The man shook his head, speechless with embarrassment at seeing her at his door. He kept staring at his overgrown toenails and the dirt that was packed underneath them. Tilting her head, Chitra glanced into the room and knew that Ram wasn't there.

"Are you Babu?" Chitra asked with a friendly smile. "Ram has told me you two have been friends since you were four years old."

A faint grin appeared on Babu's face. He opened the door reluctantly and Chitra stepped inside. Aware of all the eyes behind her, she stood in the doorway and whispered, "Do you know where Ram is, right this minute?"

Babu reluctantly nodded his head, scratching his unshaven chin. To make him aware of the urgency, Chitra said, "He may get in trouble. If you could tell me where he is, I can help him."

Babu's forehead wrinkled and his eyes narrowed in doubt, but he didn't look up. Noticing his changed expression Chitra realized that he knew more about Ram's affairs than she would have liked him to know.

"Listen," she said hesitantly, deciding to reveal something of her personal life so he would be more understanding of her inquiries, "I could not go with Ram even if I wanted to."

He looked up from his toes and raised his eyebrows in a way that conveyed, Ya? Why is that?

"It is not because of my father or *his money* that I didn't go with Ram." She emphasized the money to make Babu understand her intention. But he did not respond.

"It's my mother," Chitra explained. "I could not leave her in her condition. It's her heart." She paused, but she couldn't tell if he understood what was she trying to get at. "She is sick, you see.

I can't even think of marrying Ram because no one knows what it will do to her and how my father will be with her."

Searching her eyes as if to make sure she was telling the truth, Babu said, "I don't know, *Taiji*, when Ram left. I was on a night shift. I did not want to come here when he was waiting for you, and when I came back he was gone."

"When was that, yesterday or the day before?"

He looked confused, trying to figure out on his fingers when his night shift had started.

"*Taiji*, I am not sure. It could be more than two days ago."

"Two days ago, perhaps it is correct…"

She reached some conclusion in her head about Ram's whereabouts and was ready to leave when Babu cried, "Where is my friend? He was saying he was going to go to you, *Tai*. But you didn't come and now I know, he didn't come to you. But then where is he?" She shook her head. "Hey! Ram, he never should have left his own people and joined you." Shamelessly, he picked up an end of his lungi, exposing his thighs, and dabbed his eyes. "He wasn't like me. He was smart," he cried. "Ram dreamed big," Babu continued. "Now he is in big trouble, isn't he?"

Again his eyes filled with tears. His emotional display didn't offend her, though she felt how different it would be if all the elite men expressed their emotions that openly. Even as a woman she knew she couldn't have openly shed tears for Ram. She looked away and he went inside.

She waited for a few moments, then standing behind the door she assured Babu that since Ram had left only two days ago, they would hear from him today or no later than tomorrow. And she would send a message with Laxman and let him know as soon as she knew Ram's whereabouts.

Around noon, Mr. Pandit returned home and found a person from the telegraph office waiting for him outside of his office. The man held a letter in his hand. When he saw Mr. Pandit, he walked in and put it on his desk. Mr. Pandit gestured him to wait outside while he read the letter from his client.

Mr. Pandit,

It was a great pleasure doing business with you. Your assistant Ram Sable was very cordial in handling all the details of the contract; the sale of this industry would benefit all of us. The total sum of money has been received and as per the contract the work of building the chemical plant would start as per schedule.

Sincerely,

He placed the letter on the desk and, initialing the return receipt, he called the peon back in and handed the letter to him.

He had not heard from Ram Sable, however, and wondered if he would be coming today. Now aggravated by the casual delay, Mr. Pandit planned on reprimanding him on the importance of punctuality. He planned to curse Ram out for taking ten days to do a job that could have been completed in matter of three, at the most four.

When his office clock chimed, Mr. Pandit opened the office door and noticed Sita lingering there. She looked pale but he didn't inquire about her health or if she had a doctor's appointment. He ignored her. Most of the time he was not sure what she expected from him, but this time he knew that she wanted to know about Ram Sable. It irked him because he had never approved of Ram Sable's friendliness with his daughter and his wife. But as she walked behind him he assured her that everything was okay and, when Ram Sable came to work, he would chastise him about the problem he had caused.

"I am glad he's safe," Sita said. "I was worried about his safety since he carried the money."

Dismissing her worries about Ram, he said, "There is a long envelope on my desk that contains a marriage proposal for Chitra." Then, avoiding meeting his wife's eyes, he scornfully added, "And please remind her, she is twenty-six years old, almost twenty-seven. She may become an old maid. It is becoming more difficult to find a suitable match. I know how she has made herself known as an unruly woman." He paused, then with his typical "Hmm" sound, he pitched his concerns about his daughter into the air.

Sita was proud of her daughter but her husband's remarks always made her anxious. Hiding the shooting pain that went through her spine, she leaned on the door. "You need not worry," she said. "I will have a talk with her. She will listen to me."

When the pain receded, she again walked behind Mr. Pandit, enthusiastically asking for details of the proposal. Mr. Pandit had no patience to dream or drool with his wife over a marriage proposal. He shook his hands, dismissing her enthusiasm, and mumbled, "You and that girl... total opposites!" and went out.

Chapter Five

Ram didn't return to Kulur as Chitra had expected, but his tall, dark figure remained on her mind. Whenever she went to the city she wanted to stop at his place or ask Babu if Ram had returned. But she had held back; her mother was visiting doctors more often and she didn't want to stir things up between her father, Ram and herself.

Now, while going to Seva Sadan, Chitra wished her brother, Chandu, was around. When she stopped at the intersection she looked around for a rickshaw and saw that all the eyes of the street were on her. Men! Shaking her head, she wrapped the *palloo*, the end of her sari, tighter around her body. Chitra wasn't beautiful, but there was something distinct about her appearance, like a wild flower attractively arranged in a crystal bowl.

There was no rickshaw on the street and she became increasingly uncomfortable with the stares of the men.

Chitra missed Chandu. She knew he would have helped in the search for Ram Sable but would have stayed neutral regarding her concerns about their father. Chandu had always swallowed their father's faults. He loved and admired their father without much deliberation about his nature. He lived like a fruit that hangs on a tree without reflecting on its origin. To Chandu, love was natural, a given between a child and its parents.

When he saw how she suffered by trying to alienate her father from her life, many times he would say, "Let him be whatever he is, Chitra. You hurt because you choose to ignore that love you feel for him. You want to prove you don't love him because he isn't the ideal image of a father. You want to show him that you don't need him. And you know that's not true. Everyone needs parental love."

But Chitra was never convinced. She didn't feel that love was a given between relatives. She believed we love a person because he or she is fair and good-hearted. "By nature we love who is noble," she would argue. And then she challenged Chandu to find anything that was good in their father so she could love him too. To Chandu their father was a man of a different purpose; he was trained to be businesslike. He argued that Chitra only needed to understand him.

But Chitra always defied their father's rule and Chandu did not blame her for that either. He loved her as she was. He accepted everyone, related or unrelated, as they were. Chitra thought that was because Chandu was too timid, too tolerant. To her he was lazy. Either that or he didn't have enough strength to bring about a change in a person or in a situation. But what bothered her the most was how their mother would often sing songs that implied how *guni* – virtuous – her son was.

Chitra shrugged her shoulders. How could their mother think that accommodating their father's erroneous behavior was a virtue?

Finally, she spotted a rickshaw and, looking at her wristwatch, she gave the rickshaw driver the address of Seva Sadan, where she was to pick up the list of medical supplies and try to find a donor.

Since Ram's disappearance she had drowned herself in lots of social work. She was receiving praise from the outside world and had been written up in the newspapers, but Mr. Pandit never read any of it. Only that morning when Sita pushed a newspaper before him that contained an account of Chitra's victory in court on behalf of an abused woman, he said, "Don't throw that in my face, she can't earn a penny. Charity workers are many and they are nothing but a nuisance. It's a machine that makes lazy more slothful."

"If anyone is making the poor slothful, it's people like you." Chitra took her stand and the two of them had ruined the breakfast. "If you treat the poor as if they are brain-dead, then what do you expect?"

"I expect nothing from these fools," Mr. Pándit said. To ridicule her even further, he added, "I didn't expect anything better from you either."

Chitra excused herself from the dining table, after which Mr. Pandit turned to his wife, and continued, "After all, she's a woman. She can only show her intellect in breeding children.

What was I thinking when I sent her to law school? Now she is turning out to be an old maid. Do you know Judge Sathe was telling me how she argues to save the wretched women..." And he went on and on and only stopped when he heard a long sigh from his wife.

But when Chitra was young, he had encouraged her argumentative nature, and expected her to behave like a boy – *beta*. It was when she turned thirteen that she discovered there were definite boundaries for girls. Her skirts were made longer. She was expected to answer politely, looking at the floor while talking to elders. But she never bothered to do that, and every day, when her foreign-made dresses were replaced by ankle-length Indian ones, she tormented her mother and maids. Later, when her mother insisted that she wear a sari, she locked herself in her room. She didn't understand how girls were expected to behave as ladies, at once, at the stroke of their thirteenth birthdays. But even when she had turned thirteen, Mr. Pandit continued to treat her like a *beta* – so much so that she had wondered if he wished she was one.

But now, having openly defied his rules, even when Chitra graduated from law school, Mr. Pandit ignored her accomplishments and took more pleasure in advancing Chandu. He sent him to England for further studies. Mr. Pandit now wanted to turn Chitra into a *beti*, as she was too much for his bloated ego to handle. But despite all his accusations and the tribulations she went through, she never shed a tear.

As Chitra's rickshaw slowed near Seva Sadan, she saw Laxman, Mr. Pandit's driver, waiting on the street. He ran to her. "Chitratai, Chitratai, where have you been all morning? Aai-sahiba fainted and was rushed to the hospital almost an hour ago. Barrister-sahib has asked you to come at once."

Chitra got into the car and they reached the hospital in a few minutes. She searched for her father but he was not there. Chitra did not expect anything else from him. She would have been surprised if he had remained in the hospital until she arrived. She rushed to the intensive care unit.

Knowing Chitra would be arriving at the hospital, Mr. Pandit had dashed out, avoiding the glances of various familiar people. Once he was out of the hospital gate, he realized he did not have any particular place to go. But his legs took him to a place he had visited with his wife many a times. It was a ritual. On evenings when he worked at home, Sita would wait by his office door. He could hear the tinkling of her glass bangles. When he was in good spirits he would say, "Oh! You ready to go to the temple? I envy those gods. I should be standing in a temple like them, so I too could have beautiful women at my feet."

"You should come to temple not to see women but to have some quiet time to yourself," Sita would reply.

Whenever his mood and time allowed him, he went with her. They would walk in silence. And when they reached the temple, he always remained outside.

Now, while walking, Mr. Pandit felt very lonely. His wife gave him only what he asked for. In return, she never asked for anything. She was aware of his faults, but she chose not to mention them to him or to others. She trod the path laid out by her elders, which required tremendous self-restraint, one of the virtues she possessed. The problems only started when Chitra grew older and talked about his faults openly to her. Mr. Pandit never liked Chitra to speak about his faults to his wife. He expected her to be as devoted to him as his wife was.

Now she was in the hospital for the third time in the last few months, and he wondered if this time she would pull through. His doubts made him very uneasy, and with his cane he shoved a stray dog that had been following him. The dog yelped and ran away. As Mr. Pandit walked further, one of his clients saw him from the balcony of his house and rushed down to meet him. "*Namaste!* Barrister, Mr. Pandit... sir."

Mr. Pandit was wrapped up in his thoughts but when he heard the respectful tone in the voice of a person calling him Barrister, "Barrister", Pandit stopped.

The client approached him. "Oh! Barrister, I never thought I would see you walking here and at this time of day." Looking around, he added, "Where is your car? And the driver?"

Mr. Pandit merely raised his eyebrows and said nothing.

"I am in need of your services," continued the man. "Again,

sir. Sorry, sir, to... and I wondered when I can come to see you."

Mr. Pandit stared at him in disgust; the man obviously was disregarding Mr. Pandit's powerful position in society. Apologetically, the man fumbled with his words. "I am very, so... very sorry to detain you, sir. Sir, may... maybe today I will call your office and... and schedule an appointment with... with you, sir?"

Mr. Pandit gave him a nasty look. "Have you prepared a file?" He expected all his clients to be disciplined and organized, like the British.

Trying to convey a positive impression, the client mumbled, "Yes, yes, of course, sir. Yes, a file, when I come to..."

"Never mind. Let's go."

"To your office, sir... Barrister?" He was nervously fingering his trimmed mustache. "But, I have no app-app..."

"I said, *never mind*," Mr. Pandit growled. "Where is your office?"

"Third... third floor, sir." The man raised his hand to indicate the location.

Mr. Pandit quickly walked to the building and started climbing the stairs. The man lagged behind him, babbling words that barely made any sense. "How... Thank you, sir, thank you, but..."

Mr. Pandit glared at him and the man cringed and led him upstairs silently.

As they stepped onto the open balcony of the third floor, all the pigeons flew away from the balcony into the sky. Mr. Pandit looked up. Sunrays glimmered through the clouds. After making a gentle circle in the air, the birds flew out of sight. Mr. Pandit nervously swung his cane in the air to dismiss his thoughts.

Until late into the evening, Mr. Pandit worked with this new-found client, altogether forgetting that his wife was in the intensive care unit.

Over a week later, while Mr. Pandit lay awake in the early morning, a crow pecked on his bedroom window. He wondered if the crow had been there when his wife was alive; for the first few days after her death he had hardly noticed it. Now he could not even remember if Sita had kept the window closed or open in the mornings, or even at night. Were the curtains always drawn or left untouched?

Sitting up in bed, he thought his whole life needed to be rearranged.

New contracts, new files, and new depositions. That's how he started his new cases. He wondered how he should start his new life at home. Who would look after his needs?

His older aunt, who lived with him, had gone blind. Laxman was of a low caste and Mr. Pandit didn't even like him to prepare his tea, etc.; the Brahmin cook was arrogant and wouldn't do other work. The only other person was Chitra, and he couldn't think of dealing with her every morning and at nights.

Opening his wardrobe by the window, he started looking for his own clothes.

The crow kept tapping steadily with its beak. Mr. Pandit raised his hand in the crow's direction, making shushing noises to drive it away. The crow kept pecking. Mr. Pandit thumped on the wall by the window, which startled the crow who flew a few feet away from the window, shrieking, 'C-aw... C-aw...'

After a few moments, more crows gathered and flew around his window before settling on the ground beneath it. Mr. Pandit bent forward only to find his son, Chandu, feeding cooked rice to them. Bothered by his grown son's behavior, he shouted, "Chandu! Have you gone mad? What are you doing? Why are you feeding those ugly birds?"

Chandu looked up. "One of them could be my mother's unfulfilled, departed s-soul." His voice choked. Clearing his throat, he tried to convince his father. "Bappa used to say that the soul keeps coming back for thirteen days in the form of these birds. I am hoping this can help her rest in peace. She died alone, Baba..."

Disdainfully, Mr. Pandit shook his head. Turning from the window, he said aloud to himself, "He is another fool." Then, standing and appraising his image in the long mirror, he asked himself, "These fools are born to me?"

Walking back, he sat on the bed.

Although he felt repulsion towards his children, something stirred in his heart. He wondered, was there anyway we could connect to a departed soul? No. He tried to convince himself there could be no truth to these myths. There was no proof about the existence of a soul, no evidence.

Sita was gone.

But again he wondered if the crow had been around before. Had the window stayed open? He could not pin down any recollection in his mind. It was as if someone had erased his memories. When he tried harder to remember, the only thing that came to mind was that, before he even opened his eyes, his wife would be up. Every morning she handed him the newspaper and any new messages the peon had brought in from the telegraph office. She attended to his every need and he managed to be human in her congenial company. She lingered around his office door only if she wanted to ask something and he always responded according to the law of his mental state. At times he chided her, at other times he completely ignored her, but he managed to display his annoyance in physical or verbal language.

It seemed she took everything in her stride.

Mr. Pandit left his bedroom reluctantly, not knowing who would be around, so he could ask for Chitra. He stood on the balcony, in the already blazing sun, trying to remember the names of the servants.

The crows had brought a chunk of rice to the edge of the balcony and were busy feasting on it. This time trying not to disturb them, he tiptoed to the rail. But holding their find in their beaks, they flew away anyway. "Rascals," he mumbled, "stay and eat!" As the flock flew off, a gardener looked up, and Mr. Pandit asked him to send Chitra to his bedroom.

Chitra entered the bedroom, having managed to stay away from it for the past decade, during which time she had seen him only at his office or at the dining table. When she came in, he asked her if she was ready for "the thirteenth-day rituals". Without looking up, she shook her head and didn't say a word. He also avoided looking at her. He repeated the question more loudly. Startled, she raised her head and noticed her mother's garlanded photograph on the wall, which she knew was Chandu's doing. Tears welled in her eyes and for a moment she wished she could climb up on his bed and cry like his little girl. But pushing these thoughts away, she asked, "Something special in Baba's mind?"

Her respectful tone soothed him. "Chandu said... in the hospital." For the first time in his life, he did not know what he was saying, which was also something new for Chitra. "She... she was alone. Maybe we can... you..."

Embarrassed by the way he stumbled over the words, he could not face her and he turned away. She took a step towards him but couldn't go any closer. Going to the wardrobe, he grasped a handle, trying to stop the gathering tremors. Looking at him holding on to a support, alone, like a defeated warrior, Chitra's heart sank but no words came to her and she was unable to commiserate.

Slowly, he said, "Call all the Brahmins... I mean the priests, and do what is needed." He felt more comfortable giving these commands than speculating on his feelings. "Do what your mother would have done under the circumstances. She loved all the rituals and..." Staring at the crows flying by the window, he continued, "Let everyone know I intend to look after all the details of the day." He again felt powerful, dominating, as if in these new waters he had found his course.

Surprised at his desperate attempts to make it up to his dead wife, Chitra said quietly, "It is too late now."

He was standing by the window staring at the crows. "What did you say?" he asked.

She heard the dissatisfaction in his tone. "Nothing," she replied. "I will do whatever I can."

On other occasions, vague answers like "whatever I can" would have enraged him. And to Chitra it was always a game. Conversations with him were always calculated, measured in words chosen to wound one another. She waited for his counter-response, but there was no reaction. Walking away, she softened, and to dispel his anxiety, said, "Whatever pleases you... I will take care of everything."

Next day, on the morning of the thirteenth, Mr. Pandit woke up early, at four o'clock. Everyone was asleep. For a change, he fetched water for himself. Instead of causing an uproar over not having the right temperature water for his bath, he bathed in cold water. After his bath he walked about the house. Though every room breathed with human presence, the house felt melancholy. Dismissing his nervousness, he went over the things he needed to do: call the newspaper; send a driver for the prominent people from the town; announce a scholarship fund in his wife's name for the poor Brahmin boys. The thought of paying tribute to his dead wife in an ostentatious manner strangely excited him.

He paced the verandah, but stopped at times, thinking he heard his wife's glass bangles behind the curtain. He stood by the curtain, feeling her presence. A tear fell from his eye. It startled him and he looked around to make sure that no one was near before wiping it with his sleeve. "What do I do?" he asked himself, pacing nervously. "What do other men do?" He did not have any friends. He hated feelings of helplessness, loneliness and isolation. He breathed heavily to stop any sound that might betray his uneasiness. In an effort to dismiss these emotions, he cleared his throat constantly.

All his life he had known only two emotional states: triumph at winning in court, and anger. His inflated ego was provoked easily by incompetent people and incomprehensible situations. It helped him think he was better than others. But now, losing his wife aroused emotions he did not know how to disguise. At home, his wife had made things better for him. Now she was gone. This was something different, disturbing, something he had not known. What was he to do? He was helpless to dispute these feelings. He wasn't in a courtroom now. He couldn't sentence his emotions to a lifetime behind bars. Instead, the tears flowed freely, shamelessly.

Hearing the milkman by the gate, he quickly walked up the stairs to his bedroom. A few minutes later, he shouted down, "Are the Brahmins here or not?"

No one answered, but he heard feet rushing by his bedroom. At the door, he again shouted, "Are the cooks in yet?"

No answer.

Someone dropped the newspaper by his door and ran away.

A Brahmin cook, with Chitra behind him, carried the tea tray. The cook placed the tray on the table and ran out.

After he left, Chitra said, "There are lots of guests in the house." She paused. "And the cooks and priest will be here shortly."

That did it!

She was not really surprised when he shrieked, "What do you mean, lots of people in the house? Are you asking me to be quiet in my own house?"

"No."

"*Then what*?" he roared.

"Nothing," she said quietly.

"Nothing?" He had become a time bomb ready to explode at any moment. Chitra stepped backward and Chandu came to her rescue by walking in the room.

"The priests are here," he said, "and want to know where they should set up for the pooja rituals."

No one had the answer. The three of them stood in silence.

Without looking at them Mr. Pandit slowly responded, "The verandah. The verandah is what she would have preferred."

When he came downstairs he saw that the priests were standing on the verandah watching a gardener wash the floor before they could begin to set up for the rituals.

"Well, well. The great Brahmins of the town." Mr. Pandit's greeting was sarcastic.

"*Namaste*, Barrister-sahib, sir," a couple of them greeted him, undermining his ridicule.

He ignored the greetings and instantly exploded at the gardener for being inside the house. He walked up to the man, angrily kicking at the puddles of water on the uneven tiles. Scared by Mr. Pandit's reaction, the gardener dropped his broom and jumped from the verandah.

Mr. Pandit kicked the bucket with his foot. It flew in the air and landed on one of the flower beds. "Idiot! *Kamchor*!" No one knew what was wrong. He turned around and said to the priests, "You… you should be ashamed of being Brahmins." The power of his money spoke. "Why are you standing there with your hands idle? I want everything *shuddha*, completely clean, pure for this occasion. Brahmins will have to do everything, even cleaning." He made it an order as priests stared at the floor. "Don't the priests clean the sanctum of the temple themselves?" No one answered or even made eye contact with him. "Then you should clean the place before the rituals. Why should we have this idiot washing everything?"

The priests looked at each other and shook their heads in disapproval. That made Mr. Pandit angrier. Shoving his hands at their faces, he said scornfully, "*Wah. Wa.* The holy priests."

The priests stepped back. "Come on," Mr. Pandit demanded, "clean the place and then bathe yourselves again. I will give you new dhotis. I say, clean the floors."

But no one moved.

Stepping forward, he screamed, "I said, *clean the floors!*"

The priests shrugged their shoulders and looked at each other, amazed at his irritation. They stared at the floor, without moving.

"I know how you're thinking – why should we clean? It is not our job." He took one step further. "Listen," he said, then paused, but they barely raised their eyes, "I am asking you because I know better." Two of the priests glanced at him, but as he stared at them they looked outside.

Still no one moved. Mr. Pandit kicked the broom again and again until it fell off the verandah. The two older Brahmins walked down the verandah and slipped their chappals onto their feet.

"Where do you think you are going?" Mr. Pandit shouted. "*Wa!* What cheek! What ego! You take one step out of this house and I guarantee you will be ruined."

Both paused for a moment, reading each other's thoughts. The older one took his cap out of his bag and, putting it on his head, walked out. The other followed him a little slowly but as he reached the gate, he also walked out with the same determination.

Mr. Pandit ran to the gate. "Go, go! You will see, I will ruin your three generations!" he screamed.

As he strode back, he saw the rest of the priests still standing and staring at their toes. Chandu had started cleaning the floors.

"*Wa!* I send you to England so you can work under these penniless, mediocre Brahmin priests?"

Chandu looked up. "Baba, please. I missed my mother's funeral. At least let me help do whatever is needed. You want Brahmins to clean the floor, I am a Brahmin, am I not? I will obey your wishes. Please think of my mother, she made all occasions happy by including everyone."

Tears rolled from Chandu's eyes. Ignoring his son's tears, Mr. Pandit walked to the kitchen, looking indignant.

The kitchen was busy. Three cooks had lit the big *chulha*s in the outdoor kitchen. The flames licked the huge pots and sparks from the fire flew into the air. The cooks stood, half bent, over the boiling pots of curried vegetables or cooking oils for frying. Two assistants followed their instructions, but never touched the cooks as they wore sacred, wet clothes for the special cooking. Mr. Pandit noticed they had set the garlanded picture of his wife on a chair at the center of the kitchen, as if she was overlooking everything. His blind older aunt was seated on a raised wooden platform in an effort to recapture her long-lost authority in the kitchen. In a far corner, by the water tap, Mr. Pandit's driver, Laxman, was washing rice in huge brass pots, unaware of Mr. Pandit's presence.

Laxman was the only person who was always around Mr. Pandit and was accustomed to Mr. Pandit's threats and abuse of others. Nevertheless, he was loyal and had served him without any reservation.

Mr. Pandit walked past Chitra and, reaching Laxman, hollered, "Laxman, you low-class butcher, and in this kitchen? You better stop whatever you are doing. Who allowed you?" Laxman did not answer. "You listening? Get out. Go. Just do your job."

Holding the pot of rice in his hand Laxman stood, with a questioning look at Chitra. Mr. Pandit screamed, "Out! Out!"

Chitra came to Laxman, took the pot from his hand and gestured him to move. As she put the pot down, Mr. Pandit kicked it hard enough so all the washed rice scattered to the floor.

"I don't want anything that this butcher has touched," he roared.

Chitra couldn't control herself. "I would rather not have anything that *you* have touched!"

Mr. Pandit was about to yell a reply when Laxman quickly said, "*Taiji*, Barrister is right. I shouldn't be in the kitchen." By then, a few of the house guests had gathered outside the kitchen, listening to the quarrel.

Chitra said, "Laxman, Baba shouldn't be in the kitchen. He doesn't know you always helped Aai to get things ready on time. She welcomed everyone and loved everybody." Looking at Mr. Pandit, she said, "He didn't even know how graciously she managed the affairs of this house."

Mr. Pandit's blind aunt screamed, "Watch your tongue, girl, he is your father. *Han*."

But ignoring her, and stepping right under Mr. Pandit's nose and looking at him directly, she shot at him, "You didn't even know what she was really like. You even left her on her deathbed..." Her voice broke before she could finish the sentence.

"Of course you have to bring that up!" he shouted back. "But since we are on that subject, where were you when she died? You were joining hands with those Christians to help them ruin whatever is left in this country."

"I don't expect you to understand being useful to any charitable institution, so let's leave it at that. But, for today, please let's finish what's needed to be done to rest Mother's soul in peace."

"None of you know what's needed to be done. You're all illiterate idiots, trying to preach to me about the existence of soul."

Walking out of the kitchen, he was pleasantly surprised to realize that he sounded exactly like his grandfather, Barrister Nanasahib.

As Mr. Pandit came out of the kitchen, he heard the priests reciting mantras. The two priests who had left before were back and were chanting in loud voices. Their return offered Mr. Pandit an opportunity to ridicule them further. He was about to march towards them but was seized by Chandu, who handed him his saffron-colored dhoti and requested him to get ready for the ceremony.

Part Three

Chapter Six

The monsoon season was over but torrential rain fell fiercely and there was no sign of it stopping in the near future. The clouds hung densely in the black, infinite space. With each splash of rain, branches bowed, and crops drowned. Flowers withered, buds died in the onslaught of nature. Cows and goats claimed their space with beggars in the porticos and verandahs of buildings. Birds crowded under the edges of the tin roofs and lived in the cramped spaces like the people in the *chals* of Bombay.

The flooding waters made the streets increasingly impassable. Street dwellers and vendors piled up like soiled laundry at the bus and railway stations, making the already dirty platforms disgusting. Very few buses ran through the scattered routes, and as the floodwaters rushed like venom through the veins of the city, it gave up its usual activities.

Across from Seva Sadan, the River Aruna swelled beyond its limit, viciously swallowing the boundaries of that part of the town. The mud huts collapsed. The fishermen gathered their belongings and vanished from the riverbank. Animals disappeared. People talked about drowning incidents, and rumors spread on moist winds.

Standing by the front window of Seva Sadan, and seeing the coconut leaves that once were the roofs of the huts now floating in the water, Tony was dismayed at how nature had worsened the conditions of the poor people.

There was no one in sight and Tony knew no one would dare to come to this part of town since it was flooding dangerously. It was around five o'clock, long past Maya's arrival time, but he hated giving up on the hope of her coming to the house. While standing by the window, Tony imagined her coming up the steps and bouncing onto the verandah – as she always did – her eyes searching his. He imagined their eyes meeting, Maya smiling, then giggling without any reason, like a sudden splash of raindrops falling from a lone cloud, pleasantly surprising people underneath it. Remembering her image, and pacing back and forth in longing for her, he thought it would be nice if she were to come when it was this quiet; finally they would have the peace to talk over things they had been waiting for.

The clock chimed five thirty and Tony resigned himself to the fact that Maya would not be coming that day. He stepped away from the window, walking through the dining hall and into the kitchen where he searched the shelves for the matchbox. The matches were damp and after several tries still refused to light. He gave up lighting the stove and walked listlessly back to the window.

His melancholy did not last long and his eyes widened as he spotted Maya coming up to the gate, wading through knee-deep floodwater with an umbrella in her hand. He froze for a moment in fear for her safety, then a smile lit up his face. At last she was here! He ran outside. Seeing him standing outside, she too trudged faster. He rushed down to the verandah and in no time he too was soaked. They both laughed as they walked to the verandah, as if the flood was another paradox they had to overcome in their relationship.

Seeing her shiver, Tony ran inside to get a towel. When he came back, she was squeezing water out of her clothes. Maya's sari was pulled up to her knees. Her blouse was soaked and clung to her skin. As she squeezed her petticoat under her sari, it hugged her body more tightly.

"Oh, Maya, there's a ton of water in your dress. You are soaked," he whispered. Bending over, she pulled her sari down, and when she looked up, she caught him gazing at her. That was nothing new, she thought, and she blushed. Still holding the towel in his hands, he stood a few feet away, glancing outside, avoiding looking at her while she was squeezing the water out of her clothes.

The sounds of the iron bolt opening at the gate startled both of them. Maya snatched the towel from Tony's hands and quickly went inside the house. Tony walked to the front steps of the verandah. A neighbor from a few houses away was approaching, and he announced he was there simply to chat; he was bored with the rainstorm.

Behind the partition of the dispensary, loosening her long braid Maya spread the towel under her hair, then went to the kitchen to prepare tea. As she filled the pot with water, she thought, I never should have stepped out of the house. Now this man, who is only here to chat with Tony, will wonder what am I doing here in this storm. And how did I come?

Coming to Seva Sadan hadn't been very difficult; she only had to take a little longer route. The water was only deep when she came down the hill near the house.

As she listened to the man's chatter from the kitchen, she decided that if he stayed to have a cup of tea with Tony, she would say that she had come to help in case of emergencies! With that thought she took a deep breath, shaking her head. She couldn't believe her own swiftness in coming up with excuses. And how easily of late she had come up with stories to cover her tardiness in returning home from Seva Sadan. She was tired of her lies. She wished she could say to her parents that she loved Tony. But even the thought of telling her parents about her love affair made her break out in a sweat. "What's wrong with me?" she said aloud.

Then she stood surprised, realizing how she was losing herself, how she couldn't give a straight answer to her mother anymore. But her mother still trusted her. Thinking about how she had deceived them even now, before coming, made her uneasy and she dropped the matchbox without lighting the stove.

What was she to do then? Leave Tony? That had been impossible. Every time she thought seriously about leaving him, it had made her feel that her life wasn't worth living. Loving another man was impossible and she shuddered at that thought. "No," she murmured, "I couldn't even dream of loving anyone else. And what about him?" She remembered how he talked about how happy he'd been ever since they had met. How his life had changed for the better. How he had overcome the disconnection he had suffered within himself since the death of his sister, Sharon. How he had told her it was all because of her. She had become the cause of his existence, his mission. He also told her he had written about her to his mother, and how his aunt was anxious to meet her.

Maya lit the burner and put the pot of water on it.

Maya had never talked about Tony to anyone at all. Her mother was busy making ends meet and completely trusted her. Her father would never even have thought that Maya would fall in love with a foreigner, a Christian.

She knew their love was not only unacceptable to her family, it was even worse than that. They would regard it almost as an act of suicide for the entire family. Her parents would never hear about how she and Tony felt; they would never understand that, despite the differences, they felt naturally connected with each other. They were soul mates!

Love! Soul mates!

She sighed at the thought.

There was no room for the word "love" within the strict confines of her tradition and culture. You don't fall in love; you marry and then you love whom you marry. That's what everyone was taught. Indulging in romantic ideas of love before the wedding was immoral.

Trying to solve the conflict between her family and her love, the only thing she had come to realize was that her love wouldn't be fulfilled; it would be dragged out on the streets of Kulur and talked about in the corners of every alley. Her parents would be ridiculed and her family would not survive in the community.

Her love would have to survive only in her heart.

Thinking of all this, she stared blankly at the boiling water, forgetting to add tea leaves and sugar. She decided that as soon as they had tea together, she should leave. Yes, and without a moment of delay, she told herself. This was all wrong. She must not be selfish. She must end this affair, today. Now. With that resolve, she turned off the stove, leaving the pot of boiling water on it.

Seeing the rapidly increasing water level outside and listening to the visitor's stories of old floods, Tony worried for Maya. As the neighbor left, he wanted to alert her. He hurried to the kitchen to tell her that she should be going home. But when he saw her in those wet transparent clothes, he forgot why he had come. He stared at her profile. She stood engrossed in her thoughts and didn't move.

Her thin sari was still hugging the contours of her hips and slightly exposed legs. Her long hair had fallen loosely over the towel she had wrapped around her neck. Looking at her midriff exposed almost to the navel erased Tony's thoughts of sending her home. Puzzled by his own emotions, he slowly stepped towards her; softly he held her in his arms. His touch startled her but she did not move. Only her heart beat fast and she closed her eyes, thinking, This, I need to resist.

But she felt she was glued to the ground. Again, something inside told her to move away. Move, quickly... But before she could, his loving embrace became tighter around her waist and her breasts were crushed on his chest. She had never experienced exultation like this. Even then, for a fraction of a moment, she wavered and tried to shake off the intoxicating feelings. She bent backwards to free herself from him but her defense had no force as the elation grew in her veins and the sensation that shot through her body quickened her heart, and thought of resistance evaporated from her mind. His kisses and tender touches mesmerized her, aroused the exceptional thirst, her body pulsating with vigor. She became eager to be one with him. Exhilarated, she was losing control in his arms, and their arms became tighter around each other.

Feeling her in his arms, Tony felt as if the thirst from every one of his senses was being quenched. He lacked nothing feeling whole. The irresistible feelings captivated his mind. Thoughts evaporated and his mind existed only to glow in the flames of his sensuous joy. For him and Maya, time stood still, and an inexplicable emotion and the tender touches of their skin made them forget the drowning world outside.

She awoke at dawn. The rain had slowed. Tony was fast asleep. She drew herself together without any conscious thinking, and slowly walked out of Seva Sadan. Pulling up and tucking in her long damp petticoat with the sari around her waist, she looked around. There was no one on the street or beyond the river. Walking down the steps of the hill she came to the street and walked into water which reached to her knees. Though the rain had slowed, the water on the street was flowing with great speed. It gushed into the gutters, and this was the only sound breaking the silence. The river water had calmed down but, with no signs of human life, the early morning light appeared mystical with shades of fog over it.

As Maya stepped deeper into the water, her body shivered. Water struck her rhythmically. Stroking it away with her hands, she tried to gather back the lost pleasurable sensations of the previous evening.

Somewhere in the distance the temple bell started to ring with the sounds of early morning worship. Hearing the sounds of the bell she instinctively closed her eyes. That very moment the familiar rhythmic sound of temple bells broke her spell. The realization of what she had done the night before dawned on her. The sharpness of reality at once startled her. Every chime of the bells made her fully aware of what had happened. It couldn't be true! She put her hands on her ears to stop the sounds of the temple bells. Although it was usually her favorite sound, now she wanted it to stop. But covering her ears did not help; the ringing bells mined the depths of her soul. Tun-tun-tun.

With every ring the bursting emotions became unbearable. With every thought of what had happened and how she could have gone this far, her body swayed back and forth, like a wind-shaken tree at its roots. She felt she was losing strength in her legs. Her soft whimpers broke into a loud cry. But there was no one around to hear her sobs or help her walk through the floodwater.

The rhythm of the temple bells and the chanting of mantras became louder and louder. The floodwater gushed quicker and quicker. She started losing her balance. With every step she tried to take forward she fell deeper into the water. Then she found another set of steps going up the hill, which she climbed quickly.

As she reached the top of the hill she thought about what she was going to tell her mother and father – if her father had returned from work. The memories of Tony's touch now began to tear at her. She began to rub her hands on her body to wipe off his touch and what she had lost.

Far away the sound of bells increased its tempo and started to thud in her head. With every stroke her thoughts became louder and clearer. She was a fool and a hypocrite. She wasn't a good woman. She wished she were dead; she did not want to be reminded of what she had lost in the rain, in Tony's arms.

A woman should be in control. It was her fault.

Again she slid down the hill and jumped in the water, desperately trying to let herself go under. Holding her hands on her eyes, she started to slip under the water.

There was nothing left anymore to live for. She had ruined herself. This flood was a good chance to let go and end this maddening existence. His love and her family's fate – it wouldn't work. If she knew that, then how could she have forgotten it all last night? Moving towards deeper water, she kept wondering how she could have got lost in passion just when she had thought out everything.

Guilt and self-hatred gripped her mind and she began to submerge again and again, sinking deeper and deeper. Every time she went under, she stayed for longer periods before surfacing again and again. She tried to remain below the surface, desperately wanting to let herself go; yet, suffering, she emerged again. One moment she was above water and the next she was swallowing it. Finally she was going under... under. Then she felt a big thrust and it was over.

The next day, when she opened her eyes, she was at home. She saw her mother bending over her, anxiously looking at her. Maya smiled softly at her mother's kind, loving face. Seeing the smile, her mother at once became ecstatic. "Children, she is up. She is up," she announced.

Maya's younger brothers and sister ran into the room and, climbing on her cot, they started shouting, "Maya is alive. Maya is alive. She was only sleeping, like a sleeping princess."

Pushing them aside, Maya's mother cupped her hands around her face, mumbling some words with a name of a goddess, then pressed her folded palms around Maya's ears in the belief that the bad spell was over for Maya. As she threw her arms up in the air, all the children clapped their hands and jumped up and down holding each other's hands. Maya laughed at them. Her mother lovingly embraced her and the three youngsters piled onto them. Then the eldest boy entered and pushed the younger siblings out.

Her mother sat by Maya. "What a rain we had!" she said. "And what a night it was. Without you, it felt as if the sky had fallen on me."

Hearing that, Maya looked through the window at the still drizzling rain. The dreary sight and the sounds of rainwater falling from the roof brought back the memories she felt she had ended forever. At once she became sullen, the smile disappearing from her face.

Someone saved me. God! Why? She drew herself away from her mother's embrace and crept under the bed sheet. Tears fell under the cover. Everything tumbled in her head: I broke my parents' trust... I will be a disgrace... to them... Do they know?... They will be so hurt... so humiliated in society. Obviously they didn't know, as her mother was so loving and happy the moment she was awakened. If they don't know, do they have to know?

No... no.

Maybe.

No.

Oh God, it wasn't meant to be like this, she thought. What happens to me now? It was bad enough when I was only in love with him, but where do I go from here? How can I live with myself? How could I be so stupid? Baba would be so disappointed. Yes, but... but only if he knows, besides how would I tell him this thing, anyway?

Thinking of her father at once made the whole occurrence grotesque before her eyes. Under the covers she shook with whimpers.

Now alarmed by Maya's unusual reaction her mother pulled the sheet away from her and pressed her palms on Maya's arms and hips. Maya turned to the wall to get away from her mother's glance that was probing her mind. Her mother asked anxiously, "*Han... han...* what... what's the matter, Ma-ya? Did anyone hurt you?"

Maya pushed herself further towards the wall. Mother and daughter tugged at the sheet, and Maya tried to cover up her face.

"Tell me, Maya, where were you? I was told you went to see your girlfriend, what's her name?"

Maya wouldn't answer. She held the sheet tight over her face.

Her mother knew something was amiss; her motherly instinct told her that her daughter was keeping something from her that she wasn't proud of. She kept asking, "Maya. *Ae'*... Maya," and then, suspicious, she whispered, "You are never like this. What's wrong?" She sat by her bedside, wrapping her arm across Maya's body. "I know something is wrong. I can tell."

Just then Maya's younger brother walked in the room and said, "*Aai*, why you always worry about the worst happening to her? She didn't try to drown herself, like the man who saved her was trying to say. She's fine. She is upset that her best friend is going to be married, and not her. Remember that's where she went last night and the girls must have spent the night talking about it. That's why she rushed home this early in the morning."

On any other occasion Maya would have given him a piece of her mind for acting like her grandfather, but this time she was happy he had confirmed her lie. Looking at her son, their mother kept pressing her arms on Maya's body, as if her body would tell her the truth, even if Maya would not. When her brother left the room, Maya broke into a loud sob. Her mother embraced her but they both became wary when they heard the sounds of her father entering the house. Maya's mother instructed her to keep quiet about her absence from home last night, and then went out to see her husband.

Lying on her cot, Maya could hear how her father kept going on about the storm and the flood and the hours he had spent in the pharmaceutical shop the night before.

Maya was the last person on his mind.

Chapter Seven

Even two months after the flood the signs of disaster were scattered everywhere. Many roads had caved in and were left without repairs. Buses, trucks and other vehicles slowed down every few yards and drove around the huge potholes. Trees had fallen and were left across the streets where now cows and other animals sat chewing their food. The exposed electrical wires were tied to poles, and when sparks flew from the wires a few regarded it as a curse from the skies, while others blamed the government and walked away. Neither God nor the government nor the people themselves tried to make any difference in the surroundings. For the most part, life in Kulur went on as before, except that now there was great enthusiasm because of the Diwali holiday, the festival of lights, one of the most important holidays of the year.

In the mornings, young girls drew colorful designs on the ground in front of their homes; at night, oil lamps decorated their balconies. Day and night women were busy in the preparation of fancy foods. Wearing new sets of clothing, the people visited each other, tasting foods and renewing family relations and friendships.

Shopkeepers tried to recoup their losses from the flood by featuring more displays in their windows. The fashionable saris and jewels from the shops in the bazaars tempted the women, young and old. Tailors worked hard and long hours before closing on the third day of Diwali, which was an auspicious day to pray.

At home Maya quietly helped her mother in the preparation of food but didn't participate in the activities of Diwali holidays; they couldn't lift Maya's spirit. But on the evening of the third day of festivities, when the youngsters were quarreling over each one's share of firecrackers, she quietly walked out of the house.

Hiring a rickshaw, she went to the old temple of Shiva. The temple was deserted. Maya sat on the steps, remembering past

Diwali festivities she had enjoyed with her family. Every year, although her father couldn't really afford it, he would buy a new garment for each member of his family. Those were pleasant times, she thought. She had felt special. Her father would take only her to the bazaar for the holiday shopping spree. Now things will be different. She chewed her lips, slowing down the onslaught of whimpers. She looked around making sure no one was watching her and, with tearful eyes, she observed the idols from a distance.

The stone statues were beautifully decorated with ornaments and new clothing for the Diwali celebration. The signs of festivities were significant even on the deities. At her mother's insistence, Maya too was wearing a new light blue sari with a small *jari* border and a gold choker that her mother had taken out of her special jewelry box. Feeling the choker with her finger, Maya remembered how that morning, her mother had tried to tease her about finding a match who would decorate her in gold jewels, and about the different proposals her father had received. Not noticing the tears gathering in Maya's eyes, her mother had kept telling her, "Do you know the property owner, Mr. Gade?" Maya shook her head. "His son has seen you and his father has sent his proposal. And another good one is from Mr. Patil, the one who owns the big farm, and I have heard they have a refrigerator, Maya…" Then, noticing tears in Maya's eyes, she told her how proud her father was of her, thinking no one was worthy of his daughter.

Maya pushed her mother's hands aside, restraining her from fastening the old choker around Maya's neck. Doing it herself, she said, "*Aai*, I don't want to get married."

"*Ahn*? Don't say something inauspicious like that on Diwali day, Maya."

Her brother, who had been listening to his mother's excitement over the proposals from families in a higher economic class, barged into the kitchen. "You want to get married," he said, "the whole world knows that." Stroking his freshly growing mustache, he sat on the barrel of wheat flour, trying to hide his *phoophi* laugh behind his fingers.

Maya turned her face to the side. "Tell him to go away," she said.

Her mother signaled her son to get out of the room, and began to talk. "Look at yourself, Maya, you look beautiful in simple things. I keep dreaming about how beautiful you would look as a bride, of course for a very worthy man." Knowing that something had been bothering Maya, every chance she had she would assure her that her father was not going to give their daughter to just anyone. "No unworthy man is going to claim our daughter, *han!*" She used her reassuring tone of voice. "You needn't worry about it, Maya, you know your father isn't like that and besides…" She stopped, painfully aware that tears were now falling on the floor from Maya's eyes. Her mother's face creased with anxiety and then with anger. But a visitor had walked in and it provided a welcome distraction to their conversation. Wiping her tears, Maya greeted the guests, leaving her mother in the kitchen.

Now, sitting at the entrance of the temple remembering the scene at home, she rested her head on a column and closed her eyes. The image of Tony holding a towel in his hands and looking at her flashed into her mind. She had not seen him since the day of the flood, having stopped working at Seva Sadan to avoid further temptation. In this hopeless state of mind, trying to find a clue to solve this puzzle, she had come to this temple every evening.

The temple had become her refuge.

It was in the outskirts of the town and was dilapidated. The steps going up to the main temple were split at their base and shook when people stepped on them. The floor, which was tiled with a beautiful mosaic design, now had missing stones in many of the motifs, making it look like an old person missing every other tooth. Originally, the carved caps of the columns were decorated with precious stones, but those had been stolen, and the gaps had been crudely patched with cement. The gold filigree had been scraped to its bare mortar after ransacking by the Mogul invasions.

The center door at the far end wall of the temple led to a few steps going down to the sanctum. Both sides of this door were surrounded by the images of deities sculpted in stone. Deep down in the sanctum was the altar of Shiva-Lingam, of Lord Shiva. And

Hari, the priest was always there, if he wasn't teaching the seekers outside under the tree.

No one knew if the temple belonged to him or he had only taken refuge there to assure that the worship and the teachings of the scriptures were carried out properly. For many years now he had lived in a hut back of the temple.

Hari was sixty-eight years old, a thin, kind-looking man. His light-skinned face wore many age spots, but a certain spark in his eyes made his face distinctive. His ears were large compared to the size of his face and he made fun of this, calling it a blessing of Ganesha, the elephant-headed god. The most extraordinary thing about him was his deep voice. When he spoke he held people's attention by the sheer gravity of it. The purity of his heart and tranquility of his mind touched anyone who came to his temple.

The very first time when Maya had entered the dark sanctum and stood still, trying to adjust her eyes, Hari had told her the darkness of the sanctum symbolized the ignorant mind. When she had asked him what having an ignorant mind meant, he had explained, "The ignorant mind is the mind that is blinded by the problems of everyday life. And, as a result, we are unaware of God's presence in our day-to-day life, within every part of His creation." He had paused, as if he was assessing whether she understood what he was telling her. Then he had continued, "And, since we are part of His creation, He is within us."

"He's within us," she had said, not understanding fully.

A water container hung over the Lingam, dripping in a continuous, rhythmic flow. One evening while filling the container with water, Hari had explained to Maya, "Don't think this water is here only to clean the deity every moment of the hour. It is there to help you clean your mind. With every drop."

"How could the water falling on Lingam help me to clean my mind?"

"Just observe the drop." Closing his eyes, he had said, "Drop... drop... drop, Maya, recognize the silence between the two drops." Opening his eyes, he had said, "Drop... silence... drop... silence... drop." Maya repeated with him, "Drop... silence... drop."

For a few moments they had listened, watching the falling

drops of water. Maya even felt a moment of relaxation as she observed the falling water without any other thoughts.

"You see," Hari said, "the drop represents a thought in your mind. But the fraction of a second – the time between two drops – is a silence." He closed his eyes. "Try to be aware, to know that silence that's between the two thoughts. The time between the receding thought and the next thought is the silence and the nature of our soul. When you can distance yourself from your thoughts, you can recognize yourself independent of thoughts. That is meditation. The peace to us, *Om! Shantih, Shantih!*"

He had stayed in meditation for a long time.

"*Shantih,*" Maya shook her head as she murmured. Peace was far away from her. She had sat in the temple for hours, pleading with deities, waiting for their forgiveness, hoping to find a way to tell her parents the truth and asking for their forgiveness. But today she couldn't make herself even enter the sanctum. She sat in front of the idols and watched the luminous figures in the dim light. The burning oil lamp flickered at times in the breeze. A moth circled around the flame, at times almost entering it then returning back and continuing to circle around it. For a few moments she watched the flying moth burn itself into the glow of the flame. Then she stood and walked over to the feet of the deities. Falling at their feet, wetting the statues with her tears, she requested, "Hey, Ram, you are the kindness. Couldn't you forgive me?" She looked up at his beautiful face with hopeful eyes.

Silence.

She looked for a sign. But the oil lamp did not flicker, nor did any flower fall from the hands or crown of Lord Ram. She rested her head on his feet, determined not to rise from them until she was forgiven. "You are the personification of kindness, *Deva,*" her heart cried. "Help me. Where are you, Lord, when I need you to guide me, forgive me?" Her tears fell on the flowers. "Have I been that distant from you? Please, God, understand me, after all, I am helpless. How could I bear what I have lost?" She sat on the floor sobbing, dropping her head between her knees.

A few moments later, she heard footsteps at the entrance. The visitor couldn't be Hari, who was out visiting his daughter in town. Maya quickly slid behind a column, pretending to be engrossed in prayer. Through her half-closed eyes she saw a young couple strike the temple bell and walk inside, musing with each other. They became silent as they approached the altar. There were designs of henna on the girl's palms and feet and her new gold jewelry sparkled in the dim light. Dozens of green glass bangles tinkled as she covered her head with the end of her sari. They were newlyweds.

The young man came forward. Placing his offerings he prayed, "Hey Ram, I am grateful for your kindness. Our love grew right here, in front of your eyes. Now Shobha is my wife and my friend. It is all your *kripa*. *Bhagawan*, shower us with your blessings, and every Diwali without fail we will come for your *darshan*."

Closing their eyes, they fell to the floor in prayer. A few minutes later they silently left the temple.

Maya's silent sobs became more intense. "Hey, Sita Mai," she said as she moved closer to the feet of the goddess, "why did my beloved have to be born in a strange land? And why has he found me here, in India, the country of strict and ancient traditions? Tell me how to cope with my fate."

Holding her plea in her eyes she stared at the goddess, but the goddess only stared back obliviously, unmoved by Maya's pleading. Maya pounded her head again and again at the goddess's feet but there was still no response As her stifled emotions became unbearable, she went from one foot to the other, hitting her head again and again like a trapped bird flying against a glass to escape. She pounded her head.

She sat up. The deity's aloofness made her feel no one cared for her anymore. Even a goddess.

She sobbed violently, hopelessly pounding her head on the stone deity. While pounding she hit a broken part of the altar and blood dripped from her forehead, mixed with her tears. Ignoring the hurt, she pleaded, "Help me. Help me. Please, God, help me…"

The stone gods remained placid, unruffled.

These were the forms she had loved and trusted all her life. Now, they had abandoned her. She stood up, blood dripping from her face onto her blue sari. She looked at the red stain, it reminded her of the kumkum on her mother's forehead, and the pain she was causing to her mother. More blood fell onto her sari and the stain grew wider. She wiped the blood from her forehead onto her palm. It looked as deep in color as her guilt… and her father's anger. She stood next to the deities, staring at their aloof faces.

Her eyes caught fire. She jolted like lightning. She looked at her blood-drenched palms, then, clenching her fist, she leaned forward and smeared her blood on their faces. She hissed at their necklaces, ripping them off. Pearls and beads scattered to the floor. The flower garland fell on the burning lamp and the altar darkened before her eyes. Crying like a child, she said, "There! Now I don't have to see your smiling faces that don't care for anyone."

Maya turned and walked away from them, but she collapsed by the entrance. A few moments later, barely raising her head, she looked back. The faces of the images looked frightening, and she became aware of what she had done. She hadn't behaved like the Maya she knew; once again she had forgotten who she was. She looked back again and saw that the faces of the gods were still smiling. She stepped backward, and the fallacious smiles on their faces scared her. She collapsed on the floor. She was afraid to look up. But nothing changed. No image burst out of the deities and advanced towards her. No energy from them came to crush her.

She looked around and then at the deities. She couldn't leave. She walked back, took a clean cloth, and as her tears fell she wiped their faces clean and gathered the beads in a bowl.

She did not know how long she remained in the temple after that. But it grew very dark and she knew it was late. On the way she decided she would never return to the temple. She had deserted Tony and betrayed her parents, and as if that wasn't enough, now she had lost faith in God, because of the stone deities.

That night, when her mother questioned her about the wound on her forehead, she laughed, hiding her emotions. "I tripped on the steps of the Old Shiva temple. I believe He punished me for something," she said.

Her father looked up from the game of Snakes and Ladders he was playing with his son. "Don't blame God for you not paying any attention to where you were going," he said.

"Really," her mother agreed.

Her father made a move with his dice at his turn, and said, "Maya, your mother tells me that every chance you get, nowadays you go to the temple instead of visiting your friends. What's going on? It worries your mother, you know? And what happened to your job at Seva Sadan?"

Maya knew he wasn't expecting an answer. She watched them, father and son, engrossed in a board game, and she felt a stab of envy.

"Do you know, Maya," her father went on, as he watched his son kiss the dice to bring him luck, "when girls forget their friends, and worship Lord Shiva, it is very obvious that they are praying to find a good husband."

Maya was sitting on the floor, resting her head on the wall, while her mother mixed turmeric powder, a home-made antibiotic, with water in a dish to prepare a paste to put on Maya's forehead.

Maya knew her father had always enjoyed teasing her but she couldn't respond to his friendly jabs. She sat silent.

"I know, I know it's time for me to search for a good man for my daughter," he said, sounding somewhat guilty. "Otherwise you might turn into a god's devotee like Meerabai, who let her husband suffer because she thought she was wedded to Lord Krishna." He laughed loudly, but the mother and daughter were not amused.

Maya suspected that her mother had given up on finding a clue to Maya's suddenly changed behavior, so she had asked her father to seek a groom for her as soon as possible.

But it wasn't that easy.

According to her astrological charts, the auspicious time for a wedding was blocked by some stars and he preferred to wait a few more months. Maya knew her mother was uneasy with the idea of waiting, but was relieved at least for a few months from the talk of marriage.

Tony had waited a couple of days for her return but she didn't come. When there was no word from her, he feared the worst: her family had found out and now she was either locked up in the house or sent away somewhere and forced to marry someone else. Any chance he had he walked around her neighborhood, seeking a private meeting with her.

But when he couldn't wait any longer he went to see her. It was noontime and Maya was the only one at home. She stood by the door, tears welling in her eyes. She did not look him in the eye.

"Maya, what's going on?" he asked.

She ran in and pulled a hidden book from underneath the bed. She took a letter that she had hidden in her cleavage, and slid it inside the book. Running back out to the door, she handed it to him and closed the door immediately, shutting him out.

Tony knocked but she wouldn't open the door. By now curious eyes were peering from other doors, and Tony knew he had to leave without talking to her. He walked to the riverbank and read the letter.

Dear Tony,

I don't know how to tell you this but I think it's best that we don't see each other anymore. I am sorry it had to end this way, but I knew that sooner or later I would have to bury my feelings for you and accept the realities, the responsibilities of my life. So, here I am, living with the memories of our love and these will live in my soul for the rest of my life.

Please, try to forget and live happily… perhaps we will meet again, somewhere, in the next life. Goodbye, my love.

Maya

She can't be serious, he thought. The next day and for many days after that Tony went back, wanting to plead with her, but she avoided him. She found a new job in a nursery school, telling her parents she liked it better. When he did manage to see her he gave her a book with a letter apologizing for his behavior. She wrote him that it wasn't his fault. He should forget her and never come to see her again.

People had started to talk about his frequent appearances looking for Maya, and, after a while, to stop arousing any suspicions, Tony stopped coming. He spent many hours in doing penance. He wrote a letter of confession to Father Carlos back home, telling him about his guilt and that he had vowed to convert Maya to Christianity, then marry her.

In his heart of hearts he didn't care about anything. His work became mechanical, his life meaningless. The sufferings of the poor didn't concern him as much. He couldn't even pray for the souls he had devoted his life to. Then he thought of returning home, though he had agreed to stay in India for a minimum of three and half years. But even if he were to let the agreement elapse, what would he do at home?

He knew that either here or at home, he would be lost for answers and a lonelier man.

Diwali was over, and once again the normal weekly schedule had begun.

Every night on her way home from work, Maya would plan to tell her mother the truth and that she no longer was interested in marriage. She wished to attend college the following year, when she had saved enough money. She would like to become a teacher.

But as soon as she came in through the door, she would have chores to do, the younger siblings would be running about, and she would put her confession off for one more day. She also knew that if she didn't marry, her parents would never live in peace and accept her decision. They would worry about her for the rest of their lives and she would remain a constant cause of pain to them.

Day after day, listening to the bickering of her younger siblings, the endless teasing of her younger brother, her mother's nagging, and her father badgering her with the names of suitable boys, Maya felt suffocated. Once again she was drawn back to the temple to which she had sworn she would never return.

When she reached the temple, she could only stare at the crumbling floor. Slowly she came up the steps of the temple and saw Hari.

"Where have you been, Maya?" he asked. "Without your help, these poor deities are wearing unsightly flower garlands every day." He smiled and his old face wrinkled further, but there was compassion in his eyes.

She looked at the deities out of the corners of her eyes, with the guilty feeling of a child who knew she had been bad to her mother. But when she glanced up she perceived the serenity of the place. She realized the deities too were the same as before: pleasant, kind, smiling, not mocking. They were unaffected by her outburst.

Walking inside she stood next to Hari. He was busy fixing the altar for the next ritual time. "Harikaka, how can you devote your life to these idols?" she said. "They don't do anything. They don't feel our sorrow."

"Why do you say that, Maya? They always hear whatever we want to tell them."

"Hear?" Maya exclaimed.

"Of course they hear you but if you think they should perform some miracle to remove your pain, that may not happen. But if you think differently, they do help. And help in relieving us of our pain. Think, Maya, where would a person go to pour his heart out? No one will listen to our sorrows without blaming us. Or without feeling we are blaming them. These kind images don't show any reactions to our outcry or to our anger. They remain same, always."

Pouring the flowers from the basket into the brass plate, he took some thread from a spool, holding it in his hand. Admiringly, he looked at the idols. "That's how they symbolize the steady, sublime force that underlies this ever-moving creation."

Slowly she walked to him, took the needle and thread from his thin hand, and started to string flowers into a garland.

"Do you think," Hari continued, "that even your mother would listen to you without feeling the hurt? Or without being hurtful to you?" She shook her head. "I guarantee you, when we want solace there is nothing like these idols. The idols are what we can turn to. Without these idols, in the image of the Almighty, even relating to God, for an ordinary mind is difficult." He held the other end of the garland in his hand and Maya pushed the flowers on the thread.

"I understand what you are saying but what about their so-called powers which make us think they can grant wishes?" She dropped the completed garland in the basket. "Harikaka, so many people have such strong faith in these deities that they fast for days for their desired goal or remain speechless for weeks. And they do all this in good faith. But if there is no such thing as power to bless the devotees, what's the use of images?"

"Every deity represents a subtle power in this creation. Shiva is for knowledge. Laxmi is for wealth, and so on. That subtle power is what we invoke through our prayers for our desired gains. If you have devotion in your prayers you will see the results in keeping with what we call the law of karma. Taking a penance, such as fasting, etc., is a form of prayer and since prayer is a good action, naturally it will produce a positive result."

"The law of karma," she murmured. For a few minutes, silently they sat stringing garlands; then Hari stood and began cleaning the deities.

"Harikaka," Maya walked up to him and said, "I need to admit something that I did. I know it was wrong, very wrong. I don't know what came over me…" She wanted to confess everything to Hari, about Tony and her, about her outrage in the temple, but she didn't know how to begin.

"Go ahead, *beti*, tell me what's on your mind."

"I… I… Oh God! I can't… I don't know… how," and she began crying. Hari came and patted her head.

"Maya, you need not explain," Hari said. "I can see you are a good girl, and good at heart. I also can tell something is bothering you terribly. You are doing the right thing; you are coming here, to God – to find right answers and to find peace, and *beti*, I certainly hope you find it here. If I can help you in any way, I will." He went back to the altar and began decorating the idols, singing a *bhajan*, which he explained to Maya:

> "A bird who is in the cage is so used to being in the cage
> He doesn't even try to find the way out to fly.
> He's so attached to living and groping in the cage,
> He's totally unaware, even when the door opens.

For a man the door is always open,
But he behaves as the caged bird, and
He too, dies in his cage of pain and sorrow.
Hey, devotee, look within.
Open the door by knowing thee, within.
Set yourself free, to eternity."

Hari added, "You have to open the door, Maya, there is no other savior. You are the savior of the self."

Chapter Eight

It was still dark outside. Even the sparrows hadn't started chirping when Maya awoke feeling sick in her stomach. Holding her head in her hands, she sat on the edge of the drainage hole in the kitchen to retch. In a few minutes her mother walked in and, seeing Maya sitting by the drain, said, "Are you feeling sick again? Did you eat anything outside from a *lorriewala*?" Maya shook her head. "Let me give you some warm water with lemon in it, maybe it will help you." Her mother squeezed the lemon while murmuring her morning chant.

The next day she gave Maya a paste of honey and ginger but nothing seemed to help.

The next day her mother came into the kitchen and stood holding her hand to her cheek. Maya looked back. In the kitchen it was still dark. She could only see the outline of her mother's body. But she felt her mother looked very suspicious. Maya knew that her mother had noticed her condition morning after morning for several days, and she was sympathetic towards Maya, but now her mother stood, realizing that something was "terribly wrong". Maya whimpered in fear. Her mother came near her, and Maya cringed. The next moment she bent down her head to the floor, spilling from her guts the fate of their family.

This time her mother didn't offer any home remedies for Maya's sick stomach. Instead, grabbing Maya by her hair, she shook her viciously. "What have you been doing, Maya?" she whispered.

The words pierced through Maya's body, and she shivered. Then pulling Maya's head back, her mother held her face against Maya's, "*Hn*? I trusted you," she said, raising her eyebrows. "My firstborn, the oldest." Her voice became louder, and Maya held her palm on her mother's mouth, "Shh!" she said, tearfully glaring at the front room.

"Don't *shh* me," she said. But as she pushed Maya's hand aside she lowered her voice. "I have been trying to find the clue to your sadness and had suspected many things, including you falling in love with that American." Maya looked up. "But I thought you weren't that stupid and thought you were disappointed for not being able to attend college – but you could have talked about that freely. So I even thought that all your friends were married and gone and we still have no prospect in sight. But, this –" she shook Maya, "– I hadn't even thought about this from my daughter. Not at all."

She hit Maya with her fist and then slumped on the floor, sobbing. Stunned by the sudden blow, and seeing her mother crying like that, Maya felt she should leave; instead, hiding her head between her knees, she whimpered.

"We were so proud of you! And now look at this, you have gotten your head in cow dung. Rotten girl." She held her *palloo* in her hand, wiping her eyes with it; she paused and then whispered, "Or someone forced himself on you? *Hn?*"

Maya didn't answer.

Her mother shook Maya's head like a cloth bag but no words came out of Maya's mouth, which made her mother shake her even harder. "Who forced…" she asked repeatedly, "Who?"

"No one," Maya finally said, shaking her head.

"No one? So, you did this… willingly?"

Her mother yanked her, holding her shoulders in tight fists. Maya closed her eyes and chewed her lips, whimpering. Looking at Maya's face, her mother didn't know what to do with her grown-up daughter. She fell on the floor right beside her and started smothering her whimpers.

Her father was asleep in the front room. But he would be up soon. The hazel glow was creeping from the front window. The neighboring people were up and Maya could hear the pumping sounds of kerosene stoves and sounds of the milkman dipping the ladle in his metal container.

Ignoring the waking world, her mother shoved Maya to the rear corner of the kitchen, where it was still dark, and they stumbled on some kitchen utensils that had been left to dry. She held Maya's hand tightly, and waited, making sure that no one had been woken up by the noise they had made.

"I thought you were a good girl," she whispered. "But you are a cheat! You cheated every one of us with your sweet talk and laugh. Oh my, that... that smart brain of yours, where was it, Maya?" Maya took her *palloo* and jammed it in her mouth. "Who, who is he, Maya? Is he going to marry you? I hope it's not that white man you worked for. He is here today, but he'll be somewhere else tomorrow. What are we to think of those foreigners?"

Maya still did not answer.

"It can't be him. As per your dad, he's a Khristi, and a very religious man. Then who, Maya?"

No sound came from Maya.

Her mother held Maya by her hair again. Maya put her hands over her face. "If you don't tell me, then what's next? Are you going to become a street woman? *Hn*?" As she slapped Maya's face, her glass bangles broke and fell onto the floor.

Pushing the broken pieces aside with her foot and pausing for breath, she threw the back of her head on the wall. "Why, why don't you go away and not show us your blackened face? You, a whore, a wicked, rotten... loose girl," she said.

Maya's father stirred in his bed and they sat still. After hearing the sounds of his heavy breathing, her mother's fists became tighter around Maya's wrists.

"You are not worthy to be my daughter. You are nothing but a witch. You were born only to destroy my home." Maya winced with pain and her mother eased the pressure on her wrist. "Oh! How I want to kill you. You don't know, you stupid girl. I wish you had died before you were born. I wish you had died in that flood. Why did God keep you alive?"

Whimpering, Maya pleaded, "I know, I made a mistake but... but... I... I am not a bad girl, *Aai*, and you know that. I... am... not a bad... girl."

"If you are not bad then who is this man? Why can't you tell me his name? Come on, *tell me*." Her eyes widened, firmly stabbing into Maya's. "Who is he, Maya?"

Maya looked away.

A strip of light grew around the kitchen window and every object became clear before her eyes, but to Maya her home suddenly looked strange, and the feeling grew that she didn't belong in the family anymore. Every object seemed to push her out the door. Maya held her breath, gathering courage. "No one forced me," she blurted, glancing at her mother. "I am at fault, *Aai*… I – I… love him."

She had pleaded long enough like a child but now she sounded like a grown woman. She was ready to own up to her love.

Her mother shook her like a piece of cloth. "What love? What are you talking about? Have you gone mad? People will kill you and me both. And him, the skunk."

Maya raised her hand and pressed it over her mother's mouth. Tony wasn't a skunk.

Shoving her hand away, her mother demanded, "Who is he? *Hn*, Maya? I want to hear it from you. Why are you protecting him? Don't you understand that skunk has ruined you? He can't be good." Outraged by Maya's silence, she slapped at random on Maya's body.

Maya heaved in pain, but still refused to answer.

"I… am going to find out… who destroyed my daughter," her mother announced, "then and only then can I rest."

Her mother wrapped her arms around Maya, who was heaving, and held her to her bosom. Wiping her tears with her *palloo*, she softened her voice. "Who is he, *beti*, tell me. *Hn*? No one can ruin my daughter as long as I am alive. Who is he?" She held Maya tight and stroked her hair. "Men know only one thing, Maya. Don't protect him."

Maya's embrace became tighter but when she offered no reply, her mother pushed her away, again slapping and shaking her for answers.

Maya bore all the physical and mental abuse but refused to divulge Tony's name.

In the front room, sitting up in his bed, Maya's father called out, "Maya, what's going on?"

They didn't answer. Her mother let go of Maya's hands and held her *palloo* over her mouth, muffling the sounds of her cries.

"Maya, what is going on?" he asked again.

"Nothing," Maya's mother tried to answer. "She is ill. You go back to sleep."

Holding her head in her hands, her mother sat on the floor, mumbling, "Hey, Ram! What has she done? What is going to happen to us?" And for a while, they both cried uncontrollably with muffled moans.

Finally she whispered to Maya, "You decide what you are going to do with this – I mean the man you are involved with. But I will have to tell your father before it's too late. I can't ruin our whole family because of you." Looking at Maya's heaving belly in disgust, she said, "I have to get your younger sisters married. I have a pretty good idea who this man is."

Then she sat there motionless, staring at Maya by her side. Maya sobbed, wrapping her hands around her knees, hiding her head between them. Finally, her mother stood up, and in a firm voice told Maya she couldn't predict what was ahead of them.

A couple of days later, when Maya served a cup of tea to her father, he pushed it aside. But she lingered by the kitchen door, her eyes filling with tears. Anger filled his face. Maya gazed at the face that had showered her with love and happiness when she was growing up. That face suddenly looked stern, as if all the love for her had been dried out of it. Her father had become distant, as if he had found out she was not his daughter. She belonged to someone else. Sniffling, trying to get his attention, she said, "Baba—"

"Don't even call me Baba!" he shouted. "I don't wish to be a father to you. You died for me when you blackened your face with—"

But her mother cried from the kitchen, "No need to announce our troubles to the whole world."

Maya's father took his cap and, without eating or drinking anything, walked out of the house.

Every day there was a blow-up in the family, and they eventually stopped communicating altogether. The whole family lived in a mysterious silence. The two younger siblings sought every opportunity to smooth things over, but their innocent efforts of finding games that would include their whole family had started to feel pitiable as no one wanted to play. For the next couple of months Maya's parents took to fasting and they avoided Maya completely.

Her happy and noisy home had turned into a tomb. No one talked, the children began to whisper and they welcomed very few visitors. Those who were admitted left thinking, What is wrong with these people? At times, she heard her father discussing with male visitors that he was finding new work. There were new pharmacies in the bigger cities and he would like to try his luck there.

None of Maya's younger siblings knew what was amiss, except that something was wrong with Maya. The eldest boy detested Maya so much that he started to stay out more and more. When she looked at her younger brothers and sisters she felt she should leave, so they could all live happily as before.

Maya couldn't tell anyone about Tony because she knew that the people in her community in such instances were almost always vindictive towards the guilty person. They feared to support the guilty person because it would reflect badly on them. Morality was not open for discussion; it was ingrained in the fiber of the culture. When incidents such as this occurred, people took it upon themselves to decide the victim's fate. Justifiably, Maya feared for Tony.

Thus, even on Sundays now Maya went to the Shiva Temple.

Two months passed and that particular Sunday morning when Maya was ready to step out, her mother came to the door and held Maya's hand. Maya put her head on her mother's shoulder, and tears streamed from the eyes of both women.

"Let her go," her father said. Her mother let go of Maya's hand, but, turning her head to the wall, she whimpered. Her father shouted, "Now, will you stop making a scene at the door."

The other children came and, crying, clung to Maya and their mother. "Children, let her go," the mother said. "She's going to the temple as usual." The children let go their embrace and silently stood aside.

Her father grumbled, "No visits to the temple are going to wipe off…"

"Why do you start?" said Maya's mother, pushing a few rupees into her hand. Then taking a rupee and one quarter wrapped in a red cloth, she said, "Offer this to the Shiva, he…" But she choked on her words.

"I said, let her go!" her father called out again.

Maya hurried out the door and her mother went back inside.

All day, that Sunday, she helped Hari in fixing and cleaning the temple, while wondering about her mother's sudden loving and caring behavior: was she feeling bad for alienating her so long? Was she ready to accept her? Thinking that her mother still loved her, Maya wore a smile on her face. When Hari asked about it, she said it was nothing; she just needed to go home early.

She would try to make things better between them, she thought. Tell them the whole truth. But then what? The child wasn't going to go away. She put her hand on her belly. She thought of Tony. What would he do if he knew that she was carrying his child? What would he do when they moved away? After she made things better within her family should she go see him, once, to tell him goodbye? Tell him that he was the father of the baby, and that she'd chosen to raise it alone? Perhaps, she thought, she could live as a widow, along with her family, somewhere in a different city. She suspected that was what her parents were planning, move away.

She shook her head; she knew that seeing Tony wouldn't be that easy. She knew that he still loved her: her siblings told her that they had seen him walking around their neighborhood, even until last week.

She looked at her wristwatch; it was nearly one o'clock in the afternoon. She knew her family was all going for a wedding in town and wouldn't be back until late in the evening. She decided she would return after the evening worship. Around three o'clock she went to the bazaar and bought some trinkets for her brothers and sisters. She bought a blouse piece for her mother and a white cap for her father. His old one had turned so gray.

After shopping she returned to the temple and helped Hari. She felt light-hearted. In the late afternoon, when Hari was getting ready for evening worship, he taught her a new song:

"O, Lord, you are my refuge,
I am even in surrender to you,
For you are the most compassionate,
You are known as the savior of the Fallen,
For you alone hear their voices.
Lead my boat through this storm,
For I am lost here in eternity;
Destroyer of delusion, remover of grief
Is this not what people know you as?
I, Tulasidas, cast at your feet,
Will you shower your mercy on him?"

As Hari sang, Maya saw Pushpa, a twelve-year-old deaf and dumb girl from her street, hastily coming to the temple. Seeing her rushing in, Maya left Hari to finish the rituals and hurried to the entrance. Pushpa dragged Maya away from the temple and started gesturing with her hands – *Your Aai and Baba. Packed...*

"I know," Maya replied. For the last couple of weeks they had been packing and they would be moving to another city or town; she didn't know where. And she didn't care. She was going away from Tony and she had lost every wish for living.

Pushpa shook her head – *You don't know. They left without you.*

"They left, without me!" Maya shook her head, disbelieving what Pushpa conveyed.

Pushpa gestured again – *They went without you.*

"They went without me? Where?"

They went in a horse-cart and also in a rickshaw.

For a moment, Maya thought that her parents must have sent Pushpa, and there had to be a reason.

"Did they want me to go to the station?"

No.

"Are you sure?"

Pushpa pinched her throat, conveying she was only telling the truth.

"When?"

Pushpa didn't know. She told Maya she had been given a trunk and a box for her. But her parents had told the neighbors that Maya would be joining them a little later. For a while she would stay with her friends.

"Friends? What friends?"

Pushpa shrugged her shoulders.

Maya wrapped her *palloo* around her shoulders tightly. "They left for good," she whispered.

Quickly, she walked back to the steps of the temple and slipped on her chappals. "I have to find them, wherever they are going," she said to Pushpa, and started walking.

Pushpa held her hand – *Where are you going?* she asked. Then, repeatedly she gestured – *There is no one at home. There is no one at home.*

There... is... no... one... at... home. The phrase echoed in Maya's head as she walked a few feet and stumbled. She didn't have a home. Deep down she knew that she didn't have a home, not anymore.

The empty house stood before her in her imagination.

She saw the empty rooms. Empty walls and peeled paint. Seeing the empty shelves of the kitchen and the discolored, smoke-smeared walls brought tears to her eyes. She saw the empty door frames where her brothers and sisters bounced in and out all day long. She heard their laughter and their screams. She saw the spot, now empty, where her father had sat in his chair, reading the newspaper, chatting with visiting men. She saw her mother haggling with the *lorriewalas*, then banging brass pots and pans in the kitchen when she was angry.

Suddenly the banging sounds faded from her mind and the puzzling silence that filled the air of her home penetrated her heart. Imagining the hollowness of her home left her breathless and made her pale, even while she stood outdoors in the court-yard of the temple. She gasped for air.

It can't be true, they wouldn't deceive her. But she too had deceived them.

Her mind froze. Icy chills went through her spine and her body trembled as if she were caught in a whirlwind. She held on to a shaky tree for a moment and again started running towards her home.

Pushpa ran behind and grabbed Maya's hand. Maya slowed down and then slumped to the ground like a punctured balloon.

Hiding her head between her knees, she rocked, frantically repeating, "I am deserted. I am alone. What am I going to do? How will I have this baby?"

Pushpa put her hands on Maya's shoulders.

She stopped rocking. "What am I going to do?" she repeated. "How will I raise the baby?"

Pushpa held the end of her long skirt and dabbed it on Maya's face. Again, Maya felt a strong urge to catch up with her family. She tried to get up but Pushpa patted her shoulders and Maya collapsed in her thin arms.

My family has really left me, she thought. To deal with my fate… to deal with society's scorn… to take care of my child. They have tossed me aside as if I was a piece of rotten fruit. Just so they could save the other fruit in their basket! Didn't they care for any part of her?

Was this the only way they could have dealt with this? It would have been better if they had asked me to leave. Is this their way of telling me that they would have nothing to do with me anymore? Why did they leave without telling me? Why couldn't they do it differently? In a new town I could have lived like their daughter, as a widow who had to raise the child all by herself. Why didn't they think of that? How could they stop loving me?

She felt like a lonely bird in a barren land. Thoughts about her family and her desperate longing for her mother, father, brothers and sisters spun in her head. She stood and started walking, but as she came to a turn she didn't know which way to go. She collapsed. A huge black cloud covered her mind and everything seemed dark and bleak. She trembled as the cloud darkened, covering her mind. She looked like a cadaver. Her stillness scared Pushpa, who ran back to the temple.

As Pushpa left, tears streamed down Maya's face. She shook like an empty, tiny boat that had lost all its passengers. The emptiness gripped her heart and she blankly stared at the evening sun that rolled down the land, and then at Hari, who appeared before her.

Part Four

Chapter Nine

It was after eight o'clock in the evening. The moon was rising in the gray sky and the air was cool. The riverbank was empty, except for a few evening walkers and worshippers sending oil lamps over the water. Shadows of moving boats faded in the twilight. Smoke smoldered in coal *chulhas* of every hut, and hungry infants wailed, sucking the dried-out breasts of their mothers.

That Sunday morning Tony had ridden his bicycle to visit a clinic at a nearby village; now he carried the bike in a rickshaw. As his rickshaw reached the foot of the hills, he noticed the light was on in the back of the Seva Sadan. He wondered, why would the maid remain this late? Or did he have an unexpected visitor? Anxiously, he pushed the bicycle out of the rickshaw.

A man standing at the foot of the hills hurried to Tony. "Sahib," he said, bending down and eagerly touching Tony's feet with his forehead.

Tony questioned him and the man said Tony had saved his son, and now, after having rituals at the temple, he was here to give him *prasad*. While paying the rickshaw driver, Tony asked, "So, now would you make your son a Christian?"

At that, the rickshaw driver giggled.

"Christian?" The man again fell at Tony's feet. "Sahib, don't make fun of this *garib*, sahib. Please. Forgive me. *Bhagawan* be good to you."

"Whose *Bhagawan*? Yours or mine?" Tony teased.

"Everyone's *Bhagawan* is one, sahib," said the man, staring at Tony's feet.

"If *Bhagawan* is one, why won't you come to the church?"

"My… my heart isn't there, sahib. *Maf karana*, sahib."

Before taking his bicycle towards the steps, Tony handed his *prasad* to the rickshaw driver. Looking back, he said, "Isn't it good to share? Rickshaw-wala wanted your *prasad*. *Maf karana*."

Excusing himself, he carried his bicycle up the steps to the verandah.

The front door was slightly open. The familiar cooking aroma had filled the room. A trunk was sitting by the front door. As he came near, he read the name on the glued-down label: Maya Tarap. There was no address. Oh God, he thought, what's going on? Is she here? After all this time? He could hardly believe it, and yet his heart leaped all the same and before anything made any sense, he excitedly shouted, "Maya, Maya, is that you?"

Maya stood at the door frame of the kitchen barely looking at him, but wishing she could share his eagerness. A surge of emotions ran through her body and, as the doubts arose in her mind, her knees shook. He seems excited now but how would he feel when he came to know the truth... She looked up: he looked thin, he hadn't shaved and he also looked as if he hadn't slept. But he was smiling.

He could have forgotten her, she feared.

She stood still. He came near and as he looked at her his face fell, the excitement died.

She was not wearing her usual bright-colored sari. Instead, she wore a white one, and she seemed withdrawn. Her face looked older, more serious. She looked withered. Seeing him, her face softened but its remoteness did not change. And not a single giggle spilled from her mouth to accompany this unexpected meeting.

He reached out to her and she burst out into sobs, rubbing her head on the door frame while looking down at the floor.

"Maya? No!" he exclaimed.

She looked at him and seeing his worried face she fell into his arms. He lifted her chin up and kissed her troubled face.

"Oh God, what's wrong? Don't, don't cry like this, Maya, I can't bear it."

She hugged him tighter. He held her tight and she cried for some time as he stroked her hair.

When she calmed a little he held her face up, and said, "I missed you, Maya." Tears fell from his eyes and he gazed at her face. Holding her tight in his arms, he whispered, "I love you, Maya. I love you." Holding her chin in his hands, he searched her eyes.

But she closed her eyes. She couldn't look into his eyes. She swallowed the lump in her throat to speak but couldn't say a word.

He pleaded, "I love you. I can't live without you, Maya. Please, don't ever go away like that. Don't ever, ever leave me!" And for a long time they stood, silently, in each other's embrace.

When she recovered, she pulled herself away and stepped back. Now, standing a few feet away from him, she whispered, "Tony..." but again she began crying, holding her head between her hands.

"What, Maya? Tell me..." He moved closer to her but now she held him away, saying, "*No*." Then with as much determination as she could muster, she said, "Don't come near me, it was a bad thing." She pushed him away from her.

"What's wrong, Maya?" He stood a few feet away, pleading. "I want to help you. I want you to stop crying. I can't bear it... What has happened to you, Maya...?" he cried.

He walked to the door and said nothing. She couldn't see his face, only the popped-up veins on his neck. Then she heard him sigh. "I am sorry, Maya..." he said, without turning, "but you have no idea how hard it has been for me..."

"I know... I am sorry," she said. "But I can't believe I could be that foolish and let this happen."

He turned and looked at her, as if to say, what happened? You left me. That's all I know. But noting the sadness of her eyes, he didn't say it.

"We both... how could we... Tony?" she wailed, shaking her head. "Everyone hates me."

"Why?" His face was agitated. "Why should anyone hate you?"

"Me, I... I am pregnant... Tony." Her voice fell. She looked at him, smothering the desire to spill out all her anguish in one terrible outburst.

"*What*?" His eyes narrowed and his forehead wrinkled as he stepped back.

"You are pregnant?" he asked. "But... but..."

He didn't believe it.

Her lips moved but the words were lost in her whimpers. Her

body heaved with sobs. Tony choked back his own tears. He stood there, trying to grasp what she had said. He heard another whimper, but he was afraid to go near her because she might push him off; yet wanting to hold her in his arms, wanting to stop her from sobbing, he stood away from her, feeling guilty, not knowing what to do.

Turning her face away, crying, she hugged the wall, thinking that now he too wouldn't want her, as she saw he seemed puzzled, troubled.

Tony went to the chair in the dining room and sat there, speechless.

Seeing him so troubled with the news, Maya went into the kitchen and placed lids on the pans. She washed her face, and filled a glass with water and waited. Harikaka was sure that Tony would marry her – that he really loved her. When she left the temple she too was sure he still loved her. How could he forget in a matter of a few months what they felt for each other? That wouldn't be like him. She liked him because he was so sincere and kind. He was a gentleman. She valued what he revered. He was a good man.

But now she had doubts. He was sitting in a chair, not saying a word as if it was all her fault. She was pregnant and he had nothing to do with it? Everyone was holding her responsible, even him. Men are skunks – her mother had said that.

He wasn't like that.

Or maybe he didn't believe that she was telling him the truth. Maybe he thought it wasn't his child. She took a deep breath, her face turning red.

Where would she go from here? Her mind was blank and she waited. Tony hadn't moved from his chair. It was getting late and she had told Hari she would come back and spend the night there. The temple was on the other side of town. She needed to go or she might not find a rickshaw… clearly he needed to think about this, make a decision… maybe he would stand by her.

She saw he was still sitting in a chair, holding his head in his hands, resting on the table.

A few minutes later she walked into the dining room, in complete control over her emotions. She placed a glass of water on the table.

"Maya!" he said, and took her hand. She brushed it away and walked into the front room and picked her trunk up. Opening the door, she lingered. Should she say goodbye one last time?

Hearing the creaking of the front door, Tony jumped from his chair. He bolted out, shouting, "Maya, where are you going?" When he saw the trunk in her hand, he asked, "Are your parents sending you away? Are... are... do they want you to get rid of it?"

Without answering, she stepped out. Why should she bother to tell him anything?

He rushed out and held her hand. "Maya, you can't leave like this."

She looked up. Was he telling the truth? His face was troubled, but care was in his eyes and in the tight grip of his hand.

He pulled her inside, taking the trunk from her hand. She picked it up again, but he said, "Maya, where do you want to go? I will go with you. I don't want you to go alone." He stood by the door, barring her exit.

"What were you thinking, Tony? That it's not your child?"

He saw she was angry. He lifted his hands from the door, and approached her. "That didn't even cross my mind," he said, shaking his head.

"But you seemed to act as if it was my fault."

"Maya, it just overwhelmed me. I can't think straight. It's such a sin, no repentance would wipe—" His voice broke. He sat on a bench in the clinic, shaking his head.

She waited a few moments, then said, "I am going to a temple."

"Why are you going to a temple this late?" He stood up and went over to her. "Give me the trunk..."

She held it away from him.

"Oh, no," he said, looking at her. Something had just dawned on him. "Did your parents throw you out of the house because you are pregnant?" He took the trunk from her hand and pushed it away. "I can't believe your parents would do that, Maya. Or you left them. For heaven's sake, will you tell me something?" Holding her in his arms, he shook her, but she got away from him. "Maya..." he cried, feeling frustrated.

She stood leaning against the window, clutching the iron grid. Beyond the street, she glared at the water ripples which sparkled randomly in the lights of the passing vehicles.

"I have no home… none," she said staring at the floor, hiding her own river of tears gathering in her eyes. "They all left me. All I have is this trunk and a box… I have nowhere to go," she cried, holding her face in her hands. "What am I going to do? How am I going to raise this child by myself?"

He took her in his embrace, and she didn't resist. He made her sit on the bench, and he sat next to her. She sniffled.

"Maya, you have a home with me, I swear," he said, looking at the shrine. She held his hand tight. Stroking her hair, he said, "I am not letting you go again. Everything will be okay, I will make sure…" He wiped her tears with his kisses and when she peered into his eyes he gave her a reassuring smile.

The next morning, when Tony was riding his bicycle to a first-aid class at the Christian school, he passed neighborhoods like Maya's. Many women were sweeping floors or were busy in cleaning vegetables or grains. Men were shaving outside in the verandahs or reading newspapers while sipping tea. As he passed them they tried to avoid making eye contact with him, but he knew they thought it strange for a white man to live as if he was poor. Over the months he had tried to greet them with a wave or *Namaste*, and they were intrigued by his friendliness. Although they seemed reluctant to respond, he knew they enjoyed his friendly approach.

But today, looking at them, he could not help but think, What sort of people are these? Compared to Americans, they seemed so reticent. They were dirt poor yet proud. And their morality troubled him. How could Maya's parents be so afraid of being shamed by the society that they would abandon their own daughter?

Despite the poverty, her parents were kind, cultured people, very hospitable. But did they really value morality more than the love for their child? How could they do this to her – just leave?

As he rode his bicycle Tony thought about the story Father Paul had told him about the nature of Indians and how one of his maternal great-uncles had remained a Hindu. Father Paul described this Hindu uncle as a wise old man. Once, when he was a young boy, they were on a fishing trip together, and when they spotted a floating log in the water, his uncle had said, "We are all born like these bare logs. Initially we float with the current, enjoying riding with the waves. For most of the Indians still have the same mentality. But an Englishman will fix a motor on his log. He will go farther, enjoy the speed and go to faraway places. Thus they capture more things and places. The English are empirical by nature, they build on their practical experience. But the Indians have a log mentality. They go with the flow. Foolish, I suppose, because now the English have captured these Indian logs and have installed motors on them! It's a shame. Indians will be destroyed in this process."

Remembering this story, Tony thought, They certainly don't go with the flow or show any compassion when one of them has failed according to their standards. Even someone they love and who needs them the most. Certainly Maya's parents had failed her.

He shook his head. It was hard to believe what had happened to her. He had not slept a wink, he had felt so guilty. He had put her through this ordeal. He remembered her happy face. The face he loved once had suddenly become older and frail. She was like a flower that had been plucked in an untimely manner and trampled on the ground. Now, he would protect her even from a gentle breeze.

Turning onto the main road, he decided to make her feel secure again. As he was pedaling his bicycle on the bumpy road, he held the handles tightly and pledged to do what was right for Maya. He would give her the honor she deserved for loving him, for saving him from people's threats and abuse. He felt he loved her now even more.

Only a year and a half ago, he did not know what his life would be like and what the future held for him. He had been drifting like a cloud in a vast space. Now he felt he had a purpose, a destination.

Happily whistling a tune that shrieked from the radios of the tea stalls, he thought that soon Maya would be a Christian. She would be his wife. They would be happy together. Then he thought of his mother and Aunt Lydia, and realized that he should let them know he was getting married.

He stopped at the telegraph office to send them a telegram. Also he needed to meet with Father Paul to give him the news; it was Father Paul who would have to marry them. He had so much to do. As soon as the class was over he decided to meet with Father and discuss his wedding plans.

After the class, Tony went to Father Paul's quarters. It was a bungalow on the grounds of a church, behind the Catholic school. A gardener worked in the yard, tying bright-colored flowers on the posts of the verandah. A peon sat on a stool on the verandah outside of Father Paul's office door. He announced Tony's name, nodded Tony to go inside, and left to chat with the gardener.

The front room of Father Paul's home was used as his office. It was sparsely furnished with a metal desk, his chair and visitors' chairs and a bench against the entrance wall. A few photographs hung with yellowed matting around them. A wooden cross hung above the back window.

"Come, come, Tony. What brings you to visit me this early morning?" Father Paul welcomed Tony with his hearty laugh.

"Am I disturbing you?" Tony asked.

"You westerners are very mannerly. By now you know we people just drop in on you. You see, we live with all kinds of disturbances. Besides people, everyone else drops in on us, flies, goats, cows." Father Paul lauged. "So," looking at Tony's expressionless face he asked, "what's new at Seva Sadan?"

"New? Nothing new at Seva Sadan."

"So, things are going well, I take it."

"In most parts. But... but, Father, I am here for a personal reason."

"By all means. Have a seat, and tell me what's on your mind."

"Father, I want to get married," Tony announced, looking away.

"Wow! Splendid! So you engaged the bride of your choice?"

Tony nodded, a faint smile appearing on his face.

"Well, is she from the U.S.? Or have you charmed one of our girls?"

"Yes, Father. She's Indian."

"Oh!" The priest raised his eyebrows. "Who is she? I suppose she is Christian."

"No, Father. But I want to tell you something."

"What is it, Tony?"

"Father, I hope you understand…"

He paused and looked at Father, who nodded.

"She… she's pregnant with my child."

"What?"

Tony did not respond and glared at the floor.

Ignoring Tony's guilty expression, Father Paul rose from his chair and paced the floor. Tony watched him, feeling certain he wouldn't understand.

Tony cleared his throat. "Father," he said, "I… am very ashamed that this has happened."

Father Paul glanced at him.

"I have confessed in a letter to Father Carlos at home. I have taken a penance to help me heal my sin. And marrying her would help me correct my mistake."

Father Paul stopped pacing and stood by the window, turning his back to Tony.

"I love her, Father. I know this doesn't mean anything in this culture, but it's not the same for me. I love her. I'm sorry for not coming to you before, Father, but I didn't think you would understand how I felt."

"Have you met with her parents?" Father Paul asked.

Tony held the edge of the desk. Leaning forward, he whispered. "Father, they left."

"What do you mean, they left?" Father Paul turned around.

"They deserted her. Her parents, her whole family, they all left this town. Leaving her alone."

"What?"

"Yes, Father. They left, so she had to come to me."

Father Paul slowly walked back to his chair. The distress in his face made Tony uncomfortable. Closing his eyes, Father Paul shook his head. "Does she know what is ahead of her?"

"What can be ahead of her, Father? I love her. Love has no boundaries, no distinctions. It would dispel all the differences. And I'm going to marry her. Soon, very soon. That is—"

"It couldn't be soon enough, for her sake, Tony," Father Paul cut in, ignoring Tony's passionate ideas about love.

"I'm sorry," Tony mumbled.

"You are sorry! You have no idea what these things mean here. It's not only a sin, it's a death penalty here for that poor girl!"

"Father, I am truly sorry," said Tony, staring at the cross.

"Anyway," Father Paul said, softening his voice, "did you tell her she will have to be baptized and become a Christian? Perhaps what's more important, and what she should know, is that after her baptism she can no longer worship other gods."

Remembering the gaiety of the religious holiday at Maya's home and her desire to give him *prasad*, Tony fell into silence.

"Prepare her for what's ahead of her. Being pregnant and alone, I can understand that she is desperate. I know, now, she has no place in this society. These people would not forgive such behavior. So, she may agree to whatever you say. And it may not be a bad idea if you ask someone to help you, perhaps another woman, who can be with her and help her."

"I don't know anyone, Father."

Father Paul rested his chin on his hands, thinking for a few minutes. "How about Chitra, Mr. Pandit's daughter?" he said, looking up. "She comes to help you, doesn't she? She also helps some of the women at the center." Leaning back in his chair, he went on, "If I understand correctly, I hear that, since her mother's death, things are quite shattered at the Pandits' estate. Have you passed it lately?"

Tony shook his head.

"In any case, ask Chitra to talk to your… Oh, what's her name?"

"Maya."

"Oh, Maya, the nursing assistant… Why didn't I think of her? So, this may not be that difficult since she works there."

"I hope not, Father."

"Congratulations, Tony!" Father Paul raised his hands in Tony's direction.

"Thank you, Father." He turned and walked to the door, then turned back again. "There is one more thing. She says she won't – shouldn't – stay with me at Seva Sadan until after the wedding. Late last night she went to some temple outside of the town and I don't know what to do about it."

"Well, we can see if they have a place at the girls' hostel in the city, but it is far from Seva Sadan. Besides, in her condition…" He got up from his chair. "Perhaps Chitra can keep Maya at her estate. She might be able to find her some work, if helping you at the house has become difficult for her." Walking back with Tony, he asked, "But for Mr. Pandit's sake, what is her caste? Is she Brahmin? I guess not."

"I don't know what her caste is, Father, but I don't think she is Brahmin."

"You don't know? You are in India, my boy. You should be aware of these things. You should know, especially who you are going to convert. Conversion is the whole purpose of your mission. Isn't it?"

Absorbed in his own personal mission, Tony didn't answer.

The next day, at Tony's request, Chitra went to see Maya at Seva Sadan. Tony wasn't around. Chitra and Maya had seen each other on occasion but had never spoken; Chitra had always arrived after Tony's morning clinic hours.

It was a little before the afternoon clinic hour. Maya was cutting labels to put on medicine bottles when she heard the front gate open; she rushed to the kitchen from the dining hall and stood behind the door, watching as Chitra entered the front room.

Chitra wore a mint-green sari with an elegant white embroidered border. Her short, silky hair was tied in a ponytail above the nape of her neck. Her pearl earrings, with heart-shaped emeralds, shook in rhythm with her elegant step.

Seeing Chitra's elegance, Maya shrank behind the door. She looked at the back door, but couldn't think of anywhere to go. When she saw Chitra coming towards the kitchen, Maya quickly walked to the stove and stood with her back to the door. Chitra waited at the door for Maya to turn around. But Maya did not move and only stared out the window, as if engrossed in watching some birds on a branch, though she could hear what was happening behind her.

"Aren't you going to offer me tea, Maya?"

The words startled Maya, even though she knew Chitra had been waiting for her to acknowledge her presence. She turned, at once facing Chitra.

Chitra stepped into the kitchen. "I am Chitra," she said. "Tony asked me to visit with you. So, now, are you going to offer me tea?"

Maya nodded, still staring at a corner of the floor. "Why don't you sit in the dining hall, *Tai*?"

Sensing her hesitance, Chitra declared, "No, I am staying right here in the kitchen, so we can talk."

"No, no," Maya said hurriedly, "*Tai*, please go and sit outside. I will be there with your tea." She turned the stove on.

Chitra waited, then, walking to a kitchen counter, she stood facing Maya. Maya did not know what to say. She wasn't this speechless person before, she thought as she poured water into a pot. What's happening to me?

"Maya, Tony didn't tell you about me, but do you know me?"

Looking at the blue flame of the stove, Maya nodded. She was fully aware of who Chitra was. The whole town of Kulur was aware of who Chitra was. Why was she asking, then? And where was Tony? Why has he sent her to embarrass me? Creases appeared on Maya's forehead.

As Maya prepared tea, Chitra took the cups and saucers from the shelves. Maya rushed to stop her but Chitra ignored her and set them on the counter. Maya put a cup of tea on a tray, and carried it to the table in the dining hall. Chitra filled another cup of tea, and as she brought it to the table, Maya glanced at her. "Here, you sit down with me so we can have tea together, *hn*?"

Though Maya began to like Chitra, she was hesitant to sit. She stood rigidly, gripping the edge of the chair tightly. Chitra patted Maya's hand and waited for her to sit down. Maya did not move. It had been so long since someone had talked to her as if nothing was wrong. Maya feared that she would cry. "*Tai*, have your tea," she said, and started going back to the kitchen, feeling intensely awkward in Chitra's presence.

Chitra got up and, holding Maya by the hand, gently pushed her into a chair. "There, now we can talk," she said. But Maya wouldn't say anything. Since Chitra wasn't in the habit of coaxing people to talk, they both waited in silence. Maya fidgeted with her cup and saucer, wondering what was wrong with her, and thinking that she should say something. But without saying a word they both stared ahead of them.

From the corner of her eye, Chitra saw that the girl was not ready to make eye contact with her, so to encourage her she said, "Tony tells me you two are going to be married soon."

Maya blushed.

"He also said, that, after the wedding, he would like to find your parents."

A string of tears swept down Maya's face and she quickly turned her head, getting up from her chair. "Oh! I forgot to bring you some biscuits," she mumbled, without hearing Chitra saying she didn't want any.

While Maya was gone, Chitra picked up a booklet about the Christian faith from a stack that was lying on a table. Flipping through the pages, she wondered why she should help Tony in this personal matter, since it obviously involved religion too. But when Maya returned, Chitra said, "Tony would like you to study the Bible. What do you think about that?" Maya didn't respond. "You know you will have to learn everything about the Christian religion before…" She saw tears forming in Maya's eyes, and paused. Then she asked, "I know things have been hard for you but did I say something that made you cry?"

Maya shook her head.

Putting the booklet back on the table, Chitra said, "Tony wants me to buy a fancy white sari and a blouse for you, Maya. I am sure you would like to do that with me."

For the first time since Chitra's arrival, Maya looked directly into Chitra's eyes, but she didn't respond to the question. "He is going to see if his mother can send a veil," Chitra continued, glancing at Maya. "Veil is a fancy piece of white cloth they sew together to cover the head of a bride. And he said you will be a beautiful bride."

Veil, and a sari? Maya raised her head. Gathering courage, she said softly, "But, *Tai*, I don't want anything very fancy, not in my condition. And, white?" She paused, looking at the neatly folded pleats of Chitra's sari. "*Tai*, he doesn't know, but you know we don't wear white. White isn't a happy color for a bride, not here."

Chitra was going to explain to Maya about Christian traditions, but Maya continued, "I always dreamt of wearing a red sari, with a big, gold *jari* border, and dots of gold all over the sari for my wedding."

Chitra knew most girls thought of these things. Then she wondered how long it had been since she had thought of herself as a bride. Ram had never written to her again. Nor had she ever gone to Babu to find out if he knew anything. After her mother's death she had just thought of herself as "not the marriage type".

Seeing Chitra lost in her thoughts, Maya said, "But, now, in my condition, plain red will do."

People started gathering in the clinic, as it was time to open. Getting up from the chair, Chitra assured Maya that she should bring this up with Tony. Perhaps it wasn't that important to him, and she could wear red if she desired.

While they both were taking their cups into the kitchen, Tony arrived. Chitra handed her cup to Maya and walked into the clinic.

"How did it go?" Tony asked.

"How did it go? I didn't get the chance to ask anything." Then, looking inside, making sure Maya wasn't coming, she said, "She won't open up to me, Tony, at least not yet."

"What did she say? Did she say anything about the baptism before the wedding at church?"

"You know the wedding won't be a problem. But I couldn't get to her." Again lowering her voice, she whispered, "All her ideas of life, I feel, are according to the Hindu culture, naturally." Then, feeling unsure, she confessed to Tony, "I am even surprised that she has gone this far with you, since she is so..." Noticing Tony's worried expression, she stopped herself, then continued after a moment. "But, didn't you two talk of these things before?"

"We tried. But she was petrified talking about love and marriage openly to her parents. She lived as if she was in denial of her own feelings. So you see I couldn't figure out what she believed. I knew she loved me and somehow I thought we would manage when it came to that."

Chitra rolled her eyes.

"And don't go by how you see her now. She was different," Tony said, when Chitra looked at him questioningly. "She grew up under a British woman's influence while her father worked at their clinic. That's why she speaks English. But…"

"The British woman was probably more of a Hindu," Chitra said, "Then, there were many of them around. But here you are talking of making *her* Christian."

He looked at Chitra, wearily, and said, "I don't know, what will I do as a missionary if my wife isn't of the Christian faith?"

"Well then, you become Hindu." She laughed, but watching his changed expression, she said, "It hasn't come to that yet… and—"

As Maya entered the room, Chitra stopped. Looking at both of them, but ignoring their questioning expressions, Maya said, "I will be back tomorrow. Will you go to the bazaar in the morning?"

Tony nodded and she handed him a slip of paper with a list of things to buy. At the end of the list she had written, *Tony, would you come to the temple in the evening?*

Tony read the message and looked up. "Why?"

Maya did not answer.

Chitra reached for the piece of paper, and without thinking, Tony handed it to her. Raising her eyebrows, Maya looked at him and he pleaded with his eyes. After reading her note, Chitra returned it to Tony and turned to Maya.

"Maya, sit down," she said. "We, Tony and I, would like to talk about some things." Like an obedient dog, Maya quickly sat on the edge of a chair. Standing in front of her, Chitra looked down at Maya's face. "Maya, it's different now. You shouldn't go to the temple anymore, or…" Or any other place of worship, she wanted to say, but, looking at Tony's eager face, she stopped.

"Why, *Tai*?" she pleaded. "That's the only home I have left." As her voice broke, Tony put his arm on her shoulder.

"That's not true. We are here for you, Maya," Chitra said. Pulling a chair to her side, she softened her voice. "And tomorrow, why tomorrow? Tonight, you come and stay with me so you won't have to go to the temple again; Tony told me that's where you went last night."

Surprised at Chitra's sudden authoritative manner, Maya looked up, then looked questioningly at Tony.

"Chitra is right," Tony said. "In fact, Father Paul suggested the same thing. You should stay with her." Then, suddenly feeling excited that things were going as he had hoped, he went on hastily. "Since you will be a Christian soon, why not start now? I mean by going to church?"

"Can you do that, Maya?" Chitra asked, sympathetic.

Maya stood up, feeling confused but wanting to talk privately to Tony about all this. "So, will you come to the temple this evening?" she asked again.

Suspending all his thoughts at the sight of Maya's bewildered face, Tony looked at Chitra, who shook her head and hands impatiently.

"Maya," she said, "Tony can't come to the temple. Church is where he would like you to go."

Maya nodded like a marionette.

Tony rushed in, suggesting, "Yes, and Jesus – I mean Yeshu – you would pray to, Maya."

Maya held her trembling lip in her teeth.

"For our baby's sake, she should, right?" he asked, looking to Chitra. Chitra shrugged her shoulders.

Maya felt numb. What did all this mean? She looked at Tony like a lost lamb, and he smiled reassuringly.

"Do you object to going to church, Maya?" Chitra asked.

Maya didn't answer and Tony repeated the question. Avoiding looking at him, she said to Chitra, "I don't mind going to church, *Tai*. But—"

"You don't mind; that's good," Chitra said, finishing the matter quickly. "That's settled, then. Traditionally, a woman automatically takes whatever her husband's name and religion are. And since Tony is a Christian, so should you be." Chitra tried to give Maya some reasons to feel happy about what was happening.

That was true! Maya knew it. Even Hari had advised her that. And just for a moment, Maya was relieved at the idea of being married to Tony, having a father for her baby, having a home, and ending this unhappy episode in her life.

Chapter Ten

The beautiful gardens at the Pandit estate had turned into a
barren wasteland. Children vandalized them and stray animals
roamed the grounds. Those who witnessed Mr. Pandit running
like a madman through the yard after the animals or children
spread rumors that Mr. Pandit had gone mad! The people who
knew Mr. Pandit laughed and wished that they too could witness
the scene. But aside from the gossip, no one cared or helped.

After the death of Mr. Pandit's wife, his son, Chandu, had left
for England to complete his studies. Chitra spent most of her
time doing social work at women's centers or at Seva Sadan. Mr.
Pandit's nearly blind elder aunt was the only person around the
estate. She, too, possessed Mr. Pandit's temper and the habit of
classifying everyone who was not Brahmin as a person of low
caste. She feverishly washed the sacks of sugar, and even salt, to
wipe off the contamination generated by such persons. As a
consequence, she had lost the entire staff at the estate.

When Maya arrived with Chitra, she was overwhelmed at the
splendor of the place, despite the dried-out gardens. As they
walked through the courtyard, she whispered, "*Tai*, I never
thought I would be at this palace. And we will be friends."

Relating to Chitra as a friend seemed out of place to Maya, as
did the fact that she was walking on the grounds of the large
estate. Apologetically, she said, "Am I crossing my boundary by
calling you my friend, *Tai*?"

"Friend?" Chitra laughed a curious laugh as she stopped by
the fountain. It made Maya even more uneasy.

"I am sorry if I offended you. I was just admiring—"

"Don't be silly," Chitra interrupted, "we can be more like
sisters." Glancing at Maya, she repeated, "Sisters. That's what I
meant."

"*Tai*, you are too kind," Maya said, still feeling uneasy. She
lingered by the fountain, wondering how to accept Chitra's

graciousness. She stared at the enormous building in front of her. Besides standing as an elegant structure, the building also seemed imposing, like Chitra, who had flown up the steps and had reached the verandah.

Maya stood in the center of the courtyard, watching the wind blowing dry leaves through the air. She felt as if her life too had become like a dry leaf, drifting, aimlessly wandering in the wind of misfortune. I am here today, she thought; where am I going to land tomorrow? Only God knows.

Chitra looked back and saw that Maya was lost in her thoughts. "Maya, are you feeling okay?"

"I am fine." Maya took a step towards Chitra. "Only I don't know how am I going to repay you for your kindness."

Chitra hurriedly stepped down from the verandah. She grabbed Maya's hand, and pulled her forward. Maya managed to smile, holding back her tears. "I hope some day I can repay you for your kindness, *Tai*."

"Don't worry about that. I have promised Tony that you will be safe here. But please avoid my father, by all means. All the time." Maya noticed the troubled expression on Chitra's face. "Then everything will be all right."

Turning back to Maya, Chitra laughed a mirthless laugh, which Maya felt only expressed the sadness in her heart. Maya had heard many things about Mr. Pandit but now she realized that even his own daughter didn't like him.

Entering the guest room, the first thing that Maya noticed was the huge balcony overlooking the gardens in the rear. She went to the window and saw that these gardens also were in disrepair.

"Chitratai, can I water the garden?" Then she realized she wouldn't be there very long. "At least as long as I am here. Hopefully, I can bring these flowers back to life."

"Sure. If that is what you'd like."

"I never had a garden. So it will be nice." Looking at the enormous size of the room, she added nervously, "I never even had a room to myself."

My whole family could fit on this bed, she thought, then remembered how she had slept with her younger brothers and sister on thin mats and spreads on the floor of the front room of their home. And how every night the younger siblings gathered around Maya for ghost stories. Even now, she could feel their tiny arms around her and she felt their goosebumps.

There would be no one around to cuddle on this huge bed.

She stroked the empty bed and said, "Why, we all slept in one and a half rooms." Her voice dropped as she spoke slowly. Chitra was busy trying to open the rusty top latch of a shut window and responded without thinking, "Really? *Han!* That can be fun."

"Yes. That was fun," Maya said, sighing.

The latch finally loosened and hot air blew in. "But looking at this estate," Maya continued, "I wonder why you would say that."

"Why not? I would give up all these riches to sleep among brothers and sisters. Like I tried to do with our maid's children when I was a girl…" Chitra's eyes darted around the room to see if anything was missing in the room. But Maya felt she was deliberately avoiding eye contact with her, as if she was embarrassed by the affluence she enjoyed. Chitra's eyes finally rested on the corner of the bed.

Maya tried to coax her into elaborating. "Maid?"

"*Hn, hn,* maid," Chitra replied, shaking her head. "I always used to sneak into the maid's cottage in the back and sleep with her children. Later, after I was asleep, she would carry me back to my bed."

"Oh God! I can't even imagine what your childhood was like. I didn't know anyone who lived like that."

"It was nice." Chitra paused for a moment. "But nice only for as long as I could love my father."

Maya watched the expression on Chitra's face. She was not that good at hiding her emotions, Maya thought. Her tough act was very superficial. Realizing Chitra's sadness, Maya felt she should drop the subject but said instead, "Is it really possible for anyone to stop loving their own father or mother, *An, ha?*" She hoped that Chitra would tell her that of course everyone loves his or her parents.

"*Han,* it is possible." Chitra's eyes narrowed, as if she was about to swallow a bitter dose of quinine. Maya gazed at her sympathetically. "It's possible not to love your father if only you had a father like my father."

"That must have been so sad. *Tai*, I really feel bad for you."

Not in the habit of accepting anything from anyone, even heartfelt kindness, Chitra brushed off Maya's concerns. "Please don't feel sorry for me. In fact, pretty soon you may feel sorry for my father." At Maya's questioning glance, she continued, "Because, I might outdo him. I can be as nasty as he is, maybe nastier." She laughed loudly again.

"I can't imagine you being vengeful, *Tai*. I know you are very kind. Also generous. Everyone in this town knows that."

"I may be nice to others. But I am not nice to my own father. It's hard to love someone as obnoxious as my father. One can't just love. I know that. Should I love him just because he is my father? No. It doesn't work that way. Deep down our heart only loves what is righteous, noble, and kind. Don't you think so?"

"Yes, but... he is... your father, after all."

"You can't love someone just because by some random cosmic or genetic coincidence you are born as his or her daughter. Who decided these equations of love? People? They don't know what they are talking about. What about your parents? They left you because you weren't their 'good' girl anymore. Their love for you was over, do you see it now?" Seeing Maya's troubled face, Chitra stopped.

Listening to Chitra talking of her hatred for her father, Maya remembered her cherished times with her own father. Then she remembered the recent troubled times with him, the agony on her father's face which she felt she had caused, and which never left until the day they all disappeared. She sighed.

"What's wrong?" Chitra asked.

"I feel you never could have been as mean as I have to my father, *Tai*!"

"*Chh... chh.*" Chitra's quick annoyance showed on her face. "Now, you know you never meant to hurt him. As far as I can see, your parents have hurt you more than you have hurt them. Maya, please don't think about these things anymore. Think how lucky you are that Tony loves you and wants to marry you."

Picturing Tony's excited face when he saw her after many months of separation, momentarily helped Maya to forget all the adversity she was facing. "Yes, he was very happy. And I am glad he wants to marry me."

"Listen, it is getting late," Chitra said. "Empty your trunk and box in that cupboard." She walked into the adjacent bathroom to check if the water was running without any problem.

Sitting on the bed, Maya realized that her discolored trunk and cramped cardboard box tied with old string appeared out of place. Carefully, she brought her belongings near the bed and sat on the trunk as if it was her father's lap, then observed the room as if she was in fairyland.

The soft shade of paint on the walls looked as delicious as freshly dissolved saffron in milk. A fine tapestry hung on brass rings over the windows and doors. The off-white marble with tints of sienna exhibited the opulence of the estate. Pictures of British families who were the first occupants of this estate were hung on walls. Among them was a photograph of Mr. Pandit's grandfather with a group of barristers in their courtroom apparel. Maya stood up to take a good look at them, but when Chitra came out of the bathroom, she quickly sat back down on the box.

"Are you sure this is where you want me to stay? I feel lost here. I can be comfortable in the maid's quarters if any of those are empty."

"Maya!" Chitra objected loudly.

"Really, *Tai*, we could fit my whole house in this room."

"So?"

"Nothing, I just wanted to tell you, you are very fortunate."

"Fortunate? I guess I am in a material sense." Chitra walked to the mirror above the dressing table and loosened her ponytail, shaking her hair free.

"But then, am I fortunate to have to live with a father who is so obstinate that he hates everyone, including his own self? And to have lost my mother whom I loved the most?"

"Isn't it ironic that you lost your mother to a natural cause and I lost my whole family by my own stupidity. It really hurts me deeply... I have made such a huge mistake." She hid her face behind her hands.

"Listen, you have to stop blaming yourself," Chitra said. Maya turned away from Chitra. "Maya, forgive yourself, otherwise you will go mad. And about your parents, you haven't lost them permanently. We will find them. And once you are married they will be happy. You will see." Sitting next to her, Chitra patted her shoulders.

"I am not sure." Raising her head, Maya asked, "Would *your* father be happy if you were to marry a man from a far-off land? A Christian?"

"Never mind my father." Chitra tossed Maya's question aside. Getting up, she said, "He is never happy."

Maya gasped.

"That is the difference *Tai*, my father was always happy, only... only until I brought... him..." Maya stopped but this time she couldn't hide it from Chitra and broke down for a few minutes.

Chitra let Maya cry, then, getting up, she said, "Maya, enough. You must rest now." Chitra's authoritative voice again startled Maya. At once she stood up, wiping her tears. She tucked in her *palloo* and started to open her trunk.

Chitra went to the door and turned back. "Maya, Tony thinks that you should attend the prayer at—"

"Is there a temple around that you go to, *Tai*?" Maya asked without thinking, staring blankly at the contents of her trunk.

"Temple? Maya, are you joking? I don't go to any temple. Why would I? To put up with those Brahmin priests?"

Maya looked up. Clearly, Chitra was disgusted even at the mention of temple.

"All priests are not like that, *Tai*. You should meet Harikaka and for sure you would know the difference. He—"

"No, Maya." Chitra hadn't reasoned with anyone on this issue. She regarded her conclusions about race and religion as absolutes, and wouldn't listen now to Maya's explanation either. "I don't think that way at all. They are all alike, if not worse, like my father." She laughed loudly but Maya was not amused.

"At Harikaka's temple," she went on, "even the *Mahars* and *Mangs* are welcomed. They come to do the *poojas*."

"*Hn*!" Chitra's tone brushed off Maya's suggestion. "I don't believe this," she said very firmly. "I am so sick of living with what happens in my own house, that I will never enter a temple... We, as Indians, need to do better things than sit and pray." She looked at Maya who seem disheartened. "Maya, just forget it. It will never end." Quickly she turned, saying, "I am only telling you what Tony would like you to do, that is, at least start reading the Bible, I have left it on the desk. We will do something later in the evening."

"Okay, *Tai*."

A couple of days later, having settled in at the Pandit estate, Maya went with Chitra to Seva Sadan. It was time for the clinic to open and the place was filled with people. Her eyes searched eagerly for Tony. As soon as she saw him, she went to him and stood silently before him, for a moment forgetting the people around her. Tony felt suffocated by the crowd, and Maya walked away, feeling she was a dead weight in her society.

At that moment everything bothered Tony. Now he felt he did not belong in this part of the world. This world, with its restrictions and traditions, its preconceived notions of morality and immorality, happiness and unhappiness, was too quick to judge. Too cruel, making it difficult for them to meet, and to love.

Love should be free for its expression...

He followed Maya. His boldness always made her blush. Seeing their silent interaction, Chitra rushed out to the people waiting on the verandah. Maya ran to the kitchen, Tony walking behind her. He put his arms around Maya and pulled her towards him. "Maya, I am so glad to see you again. How are things at Chitra's place?"

She drew back from him.

"It is really nice, like a dream. But knowing that I am there because my family left me makes it feel more like a nightmare."

"Don't say that, Maya. Soon things will be different. And I want to convince you of that. So stay right there." He rushed to his bedroom, and seconds later returned with a small box in his hand. "Soon you will be my wife. In the meantime, we should be engaged." His enthusiasm was contagious, which made her giggle. He held her by the hand and walked her towards the cross that hung in the kitchen. "I would like to ask you in front of the Lord."

She stepped back a few feet, feeling confused.

"Maya, please," Tony urged. She came closer, and he went down on one knee. "Maya, will you marry me?" She blushed, but did not know what to say. He repeated, "Maya, this is the way we propose in the West. So, will you marry me?"

"Tony. Harikaka?"

"Harikaka?" Seeing Maya nodding, Tony remembered. "Oh! The priest at the old temple. What about him?"

"You will have to go now and also ask Harikaka, instead of my... father."

"Yes, of course. But let me have your answer. Maya, will you marry me?"

Tears fell down her cheeks as she held out her hand to accept the ring. He kissed her finger gently as he slipped it on.

One afternoon when Chitra was out on business, Maya visited Hari. He casually asked about her stay at the Pandits' grand estate and she gave him a detailed description, adding how Chitra hated all Brahmins, going to temples and perhaps even God.

"That is because of her father," said Hari.

"Yes. And what I hear about him isn't very good," Maya said. "I have been there for a few days now but he has been in Delhi and I have not seen him, so I wouldn't know."

"Maya, you can help her. Make her understand the things that you have learnt now."

"How can I help, Harikaka? She's bright and educated but she blanks out at any mention of religion."

"When a person is blinded by anger there isn't much anyone can do. Just as the sun does not reflect in murky water, when a person is emotionally muddled he or she cannot see the truth, the Lord." Noticing her troubled look, he continued, "Well, that is enough of problems and philosophy. Now, how about the wedding plans with Tony?"

"Wedding." Her bottom lip puckered.

"What is it? Say it, *beti*. What's on your mind?"

"Before the wedding I am to be baptized so I can be accepted into the Christian religion."

"That is all right, *beti*. We seek the God, who is only one, in every faith."

"I know, Harikaka, but when they talk about these things, it scares me. As if he, he – Tony – wants to wipe out 'who' I am, or something like that. I don't know how to explain it but it scares me, Harikaka."

"Don't be afraid. You should be wed before the child is born."

"I know. But I wish to be married in this temple. If…" She paused for a moment. "If I convince him, do you think you will marry us?"

"Sure, why not? But you don't understand, Maya. Tony will never come to the temple."

"Why not? If he…" She could not utter the word "loves" in front of Hari; it would be impolite. "If – if he can, for my sake?"

"No, *beti*. It is against his religion."

"How can that be?"

"Christianity doesn't accept those who don't believe in Yeshu."

"Do you believe in Yeshu?"

"I believe in every name of God. We… I accept… but…" He stopped and continued his ritual of offering flowers to the idols.

"But what?" Maya anxiously questioned.

"But when you are a Christian, you are told not to practice any other religion. Believing in other worship is *paap*, sin, in their religion. Now do you understand?"

Maya's forehead wrinkled.

"*Beti*, don't complicate your life any more. Just do what he wants you to do."

"Do you think Tony knows all this?"

"What?"

"I mean, all the consequences of making me Christian?"

"Of course he knows. He is a missionary, isn't he?"

"How foolish I was. I thought the primary purpose of missionaries is to help the poor and sick people in India."

"Yes. They are very good at that. But their main purpose is to convert people to Christianity."

"Really?" she asked, and he nodded.

"Harikaka—" Her voice choked; she couldn't speak. She placed her head between her knees. Hari went up to her, put his flower basket on the floor, and sat beside her, stroking her hair.

"Harikaka, you think Tony betrayed me?" She looked up, her eyes begging to know the truth.

"Betrayed? I don't think so. I think you both fell in love, and why we fall in love with one person and not the other isn't our choice. One can't will to love. And one also can't will 'not' to love someone. Even when we choose to marry someone can we be sure of love in that relationship? No. That's because love isn't a choice."

He looked at her. She was looking at him as if she wanted him to continue, so somehow she would find a thread that would relieve her doubt and anxiety over falling in love with Tony. Hari continued, "Also, loving God isn't a choice. Knowingly or unknowingly we all love God, or long to love Him. But that doesn't make things easy for you. Because love for God is inherent, religion only finds a way to reach to that love. It creates a path for that love to manifest itself. But this doesn't make things easy for you because religions work as the fabric of our lives and it is hard to replace what you have been wearing since birth."

"What will happen to me then, Harikaka? What will I do?"

"Beti, I taught you enough things. I think you understood those things, and I pray that God be with you…" He rang the bells. "Now let's say the prayers. We don't want these *Devtas* to be waiting while you try to find the eternal truth, *hn*?" He recited a few mantras and prayers. At the end he sang,

> *"The Light within, The Light without,*
> *The innermost Light that exists beyond anything else,*
> *The Light of Lights – self-effulgent Light,*
> *I am Light. The self is Light. I am Shiva."*

He closed his eyes. Maya sat looking at his face, sometimes closing her eyes trying to concentrate on a prayer, but her mind wasn't still. She stood up and Hari spoke, his eyes closed. "Maya, one can also say, I am Yeshu, I am Buddha… and so on… one can see the Light of Lights in many divine forms."

"Light of Lights," she repeated in the dark sanctum, trying to realize the meaning of the words that seemed bigger than her problem, bigger than life.

Though she was blind, Mr. Pandit's aunt's hearing was still acute. A few days after Maya's arrival, she began to eavesdrop on conversations between Maya and Chitra. One morning, hearing Mr. Pandit's footsteps, she hit her head on the floor and started beating her chest, making funny noises to get his attention. Mr. Pandit finally walked in and asked, "What is the matter? Whatever you want to say, say it without this *tamasha*."

"Oh! You call this a *tamasha*? Hmm! Then you should know what your daughter is doing. Hey, God! Why did you keep me alive?"

The old woman hit her head again on the floor and curled her body into a ball. Rolling on the floor, she began to wail. Mr. Pandit never had to face her in the mornings when his wife was alive. He stomped towards her angrily, wanting to strangle her. "Stop it," he yelled, "or I am leaving!"

"Go. Go. No one cares. *Shudh Ashudh*, clean unclean, Ram, Ram!"

Mr. Pandit turned to leave but she threw herself onto the floor in front of his feet. "I will die. I will die. Kill myself," she cried. "I will fast until I die. Without a drop of water. Not even fruit! *Chhi chhi*, living in this house is a *paap*. *Shi shi shi*!" She kept clucking her tongue until she found more words to make her point. "This home is not a home. Is a hell."

Mr. Pandit walked towards the door, and she stopped wailing to listen to the sounds of his footsteps. When she heard the screen door creak, she shouted, "Chitra. Your daughter."

"Hm?" Mr. Pandit mumbled, completely uninterested, which annoyed the old woman further.

"Chitra, your daughter, has brought a woman from a lower caste in this house, even in this kitchen. *Chhi… chhi*."

"What?"

"Now you see. It's all your wife's fault. She thought she was the goddess of these low castes of people. *Shi*!" She again hit her head on the floor. "No one respects you in your home. You, my brother's son. Your wife spoiled your girl."

"My wife is dead."

"So? Hey, Ram! What have I done that I am alive?"

Ignoring her outburst, Mr. Pandit asked, "Who is this woman?"

"Why don't you ask yourself?"

"All right. I will ask Chitra."

As he started to walk away, his aunt shouted, "*Shi. Shi!*" She beat her forehead with her hands. "She is a *kumari*... with a child."

Mr. Pandit didn't look at her again. He kicked the kitchen screen door and stormed out.

In the kitchen the old lady stopped beating her head and walked to the door, and listened as Mr. Pandit kicked all the doors of the estate. She was pleased with herself. Quietly, she sat down to have tea in the house where the pregnant, unmarried woman of a lower caste was asleep.

When Mr. Pandit finally reached the door next to Chitra's room, he shouted, "Get *out!*"

Maya froze. It was he, Mr. Pandit!

He pounded on the door harder. "Get *out!*" he roared.

Maya sat on the bed, not knowing what to do. Chitra rushed out of her room and blocked the door of Maya's room with her hands, asking her father, "Why are you after this poor girl?"

"Tell her to get out of this house."

"You will have to throw me out before you throw out this poor girl."

Trembling, Maya opened the door and stood aside.

"Who brought you here?" Mr. Pandit screamed. "Penniless whore!" He stormed into the bedroom.

Chitra quickly threw herself in front of Maya, even though she knew he wouldn't touch her.

"Please, I am asking you to leave her alone. But if you harm her in any way, I won't hesitate to press charges against my own father."

Mr. Pandit stepped back.

"Out, get out!" he screamed. "I don't want her here."

"Maya, go to the bathroom and lock the door," Chitra shouted.

Maya ran to the bathroom.

"Get out, you whore!" Mr. Pandit roared, following Maya to the bathroom. "You ugly woman." He kicked the bathroom door.

"Baba, leave her alone. If you do anything at all to ruin the girl, I will make sure you will be denigrated in your circle, in a big way. Besides, she is here as my guest."

Inside the bathroom, Maya slid down the wall and broke into sobs. Mr. Pandit turned, looked at Chitra, and shouted, "You are forgetting I am the man of this house, and your father. How dare you talk to me like that?"

"It has been a long time since I felt like your daughter and that you were my father. I am ashamed of calling you that." The words flying from Chitra's mouth further burned the relations between father and daughter, which barely existed anymore.

"Enough!" Banging on the door, Mr. Pandit said, "You don't have to prove anything to me. I have had enough of you and your presence in my house." Then, pounding his fist on his chest, he screamed, "I… I own this estate and I will not tolerate anyone who doesn't obey my words and my opinions. I have worked hard. Now you are going to tell me I am nothing? Who do you think you are, you stupid girl? What makes you think I want you as my daughter? Or I want you at all? I want you out of this house. *Now!*"

"Are you asking me to leave?"

"Yes. Get out."

"All right," Chitra said calmly. "You won't have to come looking for me again. By the time you get home we will be gone."

"Don't act as if you know everything. I would like to see how you survive without me. Then you will realize how good you have had it. My aunt is right, you are a spoiled girl. You don't deserve to be a member of this family. Get out. Get out of here. I never want to see you here again." He stomped back in the room, picked up Maya's trunk and tossed it over the balcony. Chitra rushed to see it.

The trunk fell to the ground with a thud. Indoors, on the bathroom floor, the only thing Maya heard was the breaking of two dozen green glass bangles, her mother's blessing for Maya to be married. Her wedding gift!

Her mother's only wish was now broken into a hundred pieces.

Chapter Eleven

That afternoon, when Maya and Chitra arrived at the Christian
hostel, the sisters wouldn't accept Chitra, but they made room for
Maya under the staircase in a windowless room. The room had
been a storage closet before the main building was turned into a
Christian hostel for needy girls.

The hostel was in the main part of the city. Its purpose was to
bring girls from mountain tribes and train them to be nannies or
maids and convert them to Christianity. But after a couple of
weeks, most of the tribal girls would run back to their families.
However, there were impoverished girls who needed to find work
and live in a safer place. Such Christian hostels existed in many
Indian cities.

When the sisters handed Maya the keys to her room, they told
her that she should consider Daya Bhavan – the house of
compassion – as her home now, and to continue to do so even
after she was married. The Christian women in charge of the
hostel welcomed Maya as one of their own. She knew that was
because of Tony.

Sitting in her windowless room, on her banged-up trunk,
Maya looked around. The front door opened to the rear of the
building and hung loosely, leaving an opening of about six inches
from floor and ceiling. Entering through those gaps, a strip of
sunlight with the shadows of leaves moved in the room from
early morning till noon. It made up for the lack of windows,
Maya thought. Then, remembering the big room at the Pandit
estate, she wondered if Chitra would go back home. When they
had left the estate late that morning, Chitra had mentioned that
she did not have any relatives or friends in the town whom she
could confide in about her problems. But when she was told there
was no room for her at the hostel, Chitra assured Maya that she
would find many friends who would understand her situation and
open their homes to her.

After a couple of days, as Maya settled in at the Christian hostel, she was asked to attend the prayer meetings held there every evening. The prayer room was on the second floor of the building. The room was large and mostly empty, with plenty of light coming through the tightly closed frosted glass windows. Ceiling fans stirred the stuffy air around all day and all night. Except for the stir in the air from the fans it was quiet in the room. Outside, the chaos of the city seemed distant, very distant. The hostel, like all the Christian institutions in India, stood quietly even in the busiest area of the town.

At the center of the room a framed picture of Mother Mary hung on wooden poles. The bare poles had been left leaning against the wall, and seemed symbolic of the transitory state of the room. It had been left like that for many years, as if the British had left in a hurry, forgetting to take it with them.

It was like all of India – displaced. People didn't know where they belonged. No one knew what legacy of the British Empire to keep, and what to discard. For centuries now, the people of India had been forced to live with foreign things which adulterated their original culture and suppressed their self-worth.

At the Christian hostel Maya too felt completely displaced. She stared blankly into the empty room and then at the picture. Looking at the pictures of Christian saints didn't stir any emotions in her heart as it did for Tony. But the fact that she was void of emotion for Christian statues weighed on her mind. Again she tried looking at it keenly – directly into the Virgin's eyes – hoping that Mary would say something to her. But there was nothing; no sign arose in her heart that made her feel that she had known the Mother before.

To Maya, Mother Mary appeared only as a beautiful piece of art; she could not relate to her as an object of worship. She knew she should revere these figures, as the Sisters did, as Tony did, but in her heart she didn't feel any connection with them. On the other hand, she knew the closeness she had experienced with Hindu images of gods and goddesses.

While growing up, she had run to the Hindu images of gods, asking for better marks in exams or telling them to keep her grandparents alive just a little longer. But looking at a picture of

Mother Mary, she could not connect it either to her past or to her present. Mother looked too different, altogether foreign.

She looked up again, hoping to start a dialogue with the Mother, but she couldn't ask Mother Mary for anything. She couldn't ask her to understand her feelings, or forgive her mistakes. Now, even looking at the image as the "Mother" seemed eerie. Everything about Christianity started to look strange: the Mother's clothing, the names of the saints, all the foreign ways. Lifting her eyes away from the Christian symbols, she looked up at the fan that stirred the air, but as it spun, the thoughts that were settled at the bottom of her heart, soared.

God, what am I getting into? she thought, and with emptiness in her heart, she sighed.

The clock struck seven and she wished that time could go backward. She remembered earlier times when at the stroke of three she would dash out to Seva Sadan and work with Tony while they exchanged romantic looks and gestures that thrilled their hearts. Feelings of their romance and love eased her tension, and, looking around, she convinced herself that it would take some time to learn how to relate to Christian ways. With that thought, she decided to make a sincere effort. Closing her hands, she bowed her head in front of Mother Mary and chanted the verse she would say in praise of Goddess Uma, the image of kindness.

Moments later, a young girl tiptoed into the room. Sitting down next to Maya, she rubbed her face on Maya's shoulder. Affectionately, Maya put her arms around the girl, who clung to Maya even more. As Maya wrapped her arm around her, the girl's eyes danced, but only until she saw Sister Tiru entering the room. Quickly she moved away from Maya.

Sister Tiru ignored their presence.

Sister Tiru was an Indian woman in her mid-thirties, and was wearing a gray sari and a gray cape around her head. Looking at Sister Tiru and thinking about the prospects of becoming a Christian woman, Maya's face turned pale. She imagined herself in a starched and ironed gray sari. Not bad, she thought. At least I won't have to wear a frock like they show on Christian women in the cinema. Then she noticed Sister Tiru's bare forehead, without kumkum. It looked barren, like a desert with no oasis in view. She couldn't imagine herself without kumkum. Maya wondered if Sister was a widow, or maybe Christian women didn't use kumkum? But as a married woman, she knew she would always want it on her forehead.

Sister Tiru opened a notebook, and soon she was lost in her reading, as she waited to convene a prayer meeting.

Everything would be very different, Maya thought. How would she adjust to these changes? How would it feel to be Tony's wife? And to be a Christian? She looked again at Sister Tiru who showed no signs of agitation about being Christian. Perhaps she had been born in a Christian family. But then Maya resigned herself to the thought that there was no use in imagining her future. Only a few months ago, she never could have believed she would be in her present state. With that she pushed her unsettled emotions into a corner of her mind. She felt safer once these feelings were confined in a secret, dark place. These thoughts would stay closed off, shut up so tight in that dark spot that she would hopefully never have to face them, ever again. And yet she knew that the dark spot in her mind was getting darker with its bleakness and when she was alone it frightened her.

Other girls from the hostel slowly wandered into the room and, in whispered voices, began to chit-chat. Around seven thirty Sister Tiru put down her book and tapped on her desk to get their attention. Then she motioned them to join her in prayer. Getting up from her chair, Sister Tiru knelt, and Maya and the other girls rose reluctantly to their knees. Sister Tiru observed the girls out of the corner of her eye, and the girls watched her too.

No one was praying!

Shaking her head, Sister Tiru expressed her displeasure and her face wrinkled. The girls ignored it. Condemnation wasn't new to them; they knew they were unwanted, abandoned. By now they were used to receiving people's disapproval. Always. The resentment of others vanished almost instantly into the dark places of their minds, like a drop of water disappearing on a hot skillet, leaving only a residue.

Sister Tiru closed her eyes and translated a prayer. "Hail Mary, full of grace, the Lord is with thee."

Most of the girls now sat cross-legged on the floor. A Buddhist girl, Shanta, only twelve years old, touched her forehead to the ground with her hands closed in the prayer position. Sister Tiru shouted, "Shanta, forget your old ways. You can't pray that way here."

Shanta trembled and her dried-out lips quivered in fear.

"On your knees. On your knees, girls."

Sister Tiru was trying to sound pleasant, but the effort didn't last long as she yelled, "All of you. Stand erect on your knees."

Clumsily, some of the girls raised themselves up, but some remained in the same position, sitting back on their haunches. Sister Tiru had no patience for this. She pulled some of them up by their long hair until they squealed.

"Straight. Stand erect with your hands in front of you." She nudged and poked their spines with her hands and her knees. "Keep your hands in front of you. In a begging position," she sneered. "Begging should come easy for you girls."

The girls raised themselves upright on their knees.

"We are not beggars," whispered the girl who had begged for Maya's affection.

"Hmm! We are beggars in front of God. That's okay," Maya answered.

The demonstration of kneeling was over. Sister Tiru picked up a book from the desk and asked if any of the girls were interested in reading a story. One girl volunteered and read a story about a poor family who never lost their faith in Yeshu. They never failed to pray to Him and never missed the Sunday mass. Every day they asked for His help. One day, Yeshu appeared in the father's dream. He asked the man to look for berries in the forest next to their village. So the next day, the father and his children started out. After walking for a long time, they came upon a patch of berries that were heavenly, and the father knew he had never seen the fruit before. They sold the berries in a fruit market, and soon after they had the farm full of produce. Their faith in Yeshu had ended their poverty and misery.

All the stories the girls read were about having devotion for Yeshu that had resulted in the believers being given the objects of their desire. Yeshu had heard all their prayers and solved all their problems. Without fail, the hearts of these destitute girls became heavier every time they left the room.

Despite hearing the miraculous stories about Jesus, Maya secretly gathered some of her favorite images of Hindu gods, and created a temple in her room. She knew that in the coming months she wouldn't be able to go to Shiva's temple, so she designated a corner of her room for her temple. She placed a cardboard box on the floor. Covering it with a red cloth, she placed the clay statues of Lord Ganesh and Goddess Laxmi on each side. Then at the center she put the Lord Shiva's Lingam and in front of it she placed the small brass replica of Nandi – the raging bull, sitting humbly – who signified a person's ego that must be surrendered before the Lord.

On Monday morning she asked some of the girls to come to her room to do the *pooja*. A few of the older girls had ostracized Maya. They had called her a *chalu* girl, a fallen woman, who was now going to become rich by marrying a *pardeshi*, a foreigner. They never passed any opportunity to taunt her with insulting words.

That evening, the girls who came filled the tiny room, which was filled with the smell of incense. Looking at her little temple, Maya's heart grew fonder. She felt peaceful as she placed flowers and lit the oil lamp, and performed a traditional *pooja*. One by one, they all offered flowers and Maya distributed the *prasad*. Happily the girls talked about various *poojas* they had enjoyed as young girls. They shared how they had kept up with the tradition of fasting on certain days, like their mothers and grandmothers and great-grandmothers! They all felt joyous and free, recalling their old memories. No one knew exactly why, but they all whispered and made sure that no one was around, listening to them. They decided to meet every Monday evening to do the *pooja* right after the Christian prayer meeting.

The following day, hiring a rickshaw, Maya went to Seva Sadan. When they had a chance to be alone, Maya told Tony about her temple and the girls' gathering to share the *pooja*. Tony listened silently. "Tony, would you come to see my temple?" Maya asked.

He didn't answer.

"That is the first thing I am going to bring to our home," she told him. "This is what we Indians do. First, we place the gods in a new home so the *vastu* – the spirit of the home – is blessed."

Tony was mystified. What was wrong with her? She can't do that, not here, not anywhere, he kept thinking.

"You are supposed to do the Ganesha's *pooja* before you start any activity. You know that, right?" Without waiting for his answer, she continued, "But do you know why?"

She looked at him. He seemed distant. She thought if he knew more, he would realize that it all meant something. She pulled the pendent of Lord Ganesh off the necklace that hid in her cleavage. Taking it in her hands and showing him, she said, "He is prayed to for removing the obstacles in your way."

Tony took the pendant in his hand and studied it.

Excitedly, Maya continued, "I like the way Ganesha is set on the front door of every home in India, like a protector."

Tony thought, He didn't protect you or your family! But he did not say this. He knew it would hurt Maya. He liked seeing her happy again; he would like to see her like this always and forever. But he knew it couldn't go on. He dropped the pendant, thinking she had to break away from these feelings, from these false idols of God. She should know by now that she can't worship Hindu idols anymore.

With determined eyes he gazed at her. But she looked so beautiful and happy, he couldn't tell her what he had planned to tell her. Of late, many times he had wished he wasn't a missionary, so he could marry her without any further delay.

Besides Maya, there were other things that haunted him as a missionary. Every day and night he was tormented with doubts about the purpose of his mission. Before coming to India, he was convinced that Christianity was the only true religion. Then, he wanted to help people to believe in Christ. Now, he felt pressured because since he joined the Catholic mission, it had become a game of numbers: how many did he convert? And that number was never impressive either to him or to the Catholic authorities with whom he worked.

He found that most Hindus who were willing to become Christians fell into two categories. The first group were those who were physically starved and from a lower caste, and only wanted to find enough to eat. Father Paul had named them "milk-powder Christians", as the issue of discrimination against the lower castes had not been abolished even among Christian Indians. In fact, it was worse.

Then, the others were people like Mr. Vadsare, a convict who blamed Brahmins for all his crimes. He went on a pilgrimage of holy places in India and built a Hindu temple before turning Christian. Tony knew how Vadsare threatened his sons and the employees who worked in his factory and shops, telling them they must become Christians if they still wished to work for him.

To Tony's distress, he had come to realize that there weren't many who became Christian because they really loved Jesus, as he did. Thus, now, when he felt he was failing Jesus he would drown himself in feelings of guilt and self-damnation.

Noticing that Tony was lost in his thoughts, Maya sought to reassure him. "Don't worry, Tony, I will be a good Christian too," she said. "I know Yeshu will help us like he has helped all the people who believed in him. I have read all the stories."

"So you've accepted Jesus… I mean Yeshu?" Tony questioned, feeling relieved, forgetting all the things that had been troubling him just a moment ago.

"*Han, han,*" she said, trying to convince him. "He too will look beautiful next to all the other idols in my temple."

"He? Who?" Tony asked.

"Yeshu – Jesus, Tony."

Tony was crushed. In a low voice he said, "Since you believe in Yeshu, why do we need these stone idols, Maya? That is considered a sin – *paap.*"

"Oh! Tony, it is not a sin. How can worshipping be a sin? No one worships stone idols, Tony, we all worship God. Idols are only symbols, like a flag that represents a country. Don't we love and respect also the flag for what it represents?" She paused, but as he didn't respond, she continued, "When you talk to Harikaka you will understand. He will explain it to you." Her face beamed with joy. The idea of including all the gods, including Yeshu, illumined the dark spot in her mind. Finally, she felt she had this glorious plan to achieve everything: his love; their baby; their home.

And their temple, with all the images of God, together.

And she had hoped too that she could be reunited with her family.

Tony held her hand, not knowing what to say. The happy picture included everyone and everything appeared beautiful, even to him. He felt the urge to give up everything just so he could go on feeling the same happiness. Tony pressed her hand to his lips and said, "Oh! Maya, how I wish I possessed your innocence."

"Tony, is it okay to put kumkum on my forehead after the marriage?"

He held her hand tight to his chest. "I... I don't think so, Maya, but you can wear a sari."

"So it's okay to be Hindu?"

"I didn't say that," he said, letting go of her hand.

On the way back to the hostel, she wondered how a person could forget being a Hindu, even if he or she wanted to. Would Tony be able to forget that he was a Christian?

After learning about the basic teachings of Christianity, and its religious practices, for a few days, Maya was asked to attend a different class where the girls read stories from the Bible. Sister Rosa, who was from Spain, taught the class. She was in her fifties and had spent many years in convents all over India. She was chubby, full of life, and very talkative. She had come to Kulur from Goa, on the coast, where the Portuguese had settled in India. Initially, that's where she had helped many Hindus to convert to Christianity. She spoke the Marathi language mixed with Hindi and English, an odd combination that amused the girls. The meetings with her were friendly, and Maya liked the discussions that followed the readings.

One day Sister Rosa read about the Good Shepherd and His sheep. She began, "And the Lord said..." She paused and asked, "Who is the Lord?"

"Yeshu," girls chorused, and she continued.

"I assure you, anyone who sneaks over the wall of a sheepfold, rather than going through the gate, must surely be a thief and a robber! For a shepherd enters through the gate. The gatekeeper opens the gate for him, and sheep hear his voice and come to him. He calls his own sheep by name and leads them out. After he has gathered his own flock, he walks ahead of them, and they follow him because they recognize his voice. They won't follow a stranger, they will run from him because they don't recognize his voice. I assure you, I am the gate for the sheep."

At this point Maya raised her hand, but Sister Rosa had the book up against her nose and didn't notice. She continued, "All others who came before me were thieves and robbers. But the true sheep did not listen to them. Yes, I am the gate. Those who come through me will be saved wherever they go…"

This time Maya said loudly, "Sister Rosa, I have a question."

Sister Rosa peered through her glasses.

"Sister, could you please explain what Yeshu means when he says that he is the gate?"

"Only through Him are we to enter the world," Sister answered without looking up.

"But, then he is talking of his sheep; therefore He is talking of only a few, isn't he? And not the world at large?"

"Yes, *Maya*…" Sister Rosa said her name slowly, deliberately.

"How can the grace of God be limited to so few?"

Maya looked up, but Sister Rosa was busy thumbing through the pages of her book.

"Sister, am I correct in my understanding?"

Some of the younger girls giggled. Sister Rosa looked up and said, "What did you say?"

Maya repeated the question, and the sister replied, "Yes. That is why you should have the Christian faith – to save yourself."

"Save from what, Sister?"

Several girls laughed without understanding the question but knowing Sister Rosa would give an amusing answer.

"Save from the tangles of your questions, Maya."

The girls laughed again. And the smile on Sister Rosa's face did not change.

Maya persisted. "But I still don't understand. Save from what, Sister?"

The clock rang eight and Sister Rosa dismissed Maya's question by saying, "You will understand once you marry Tony, you naughty, naughty girl..." Her words were lost in the noise of girls rushing to the exit. Standing there, Maya remembered that she had not felt naughty since her brother was born and she had become the eldest of their family when she was only two years of age.

Maya stood watching all the girls leave the prayer room. This will never work, she thought. No one understood how much, and how soon, she would like to become a Christian. Only then could she become Tony's wife. Tony had not said that in so many words, but that's what she had gathered from him, again and again. When she had suggested getting married in Shiva's temple, with Harikaka, because it would be easy, since Hindus don't require conversion, he had replied, "Maya, I came to India to do the mission work, to help the poor and sick. Now, how can I betray the mission? And the Lord?"

She understood his integrity. And, truly, she respected his concern for the poor and the unfortunate people of India. She honored his work completely. For that reason she had resigned herself to the fact that she would have to change her religion.

But she had never thought that she would have to make a complete break with her own tradition. While growing up she had never given much thought to the God or the multiple images of God and religion. She only knew that people prayed in temple or at home or at a festival or when they wanted something. Other than that she enjoyed celebrating the holy festivals that went on all year long.

But now she had grown more spiritual, and she had learned to understand the ways of her mind. She had realized that her habitual ways of praying would be hard to change. But what she hadn't realized was that this would be so terribly difficult. Though she was willing to become Christian, from the bottom of her heart she could not stop being a Hindu. That was hard – not being who she had been. Being a Hindu was part of her very being, which even she hadn't known. The thought of losing that identity scared her.

She felt she would have to bury and plaster all her memories to become a Christian. And she didn't have time for all that.

Tony, Father Paul, the Sisters and even Chitra wanted her to change her religion. Quickly. But she felt she couldn't develop faith in Yeshu as her God and her savior in a matter of a month or two. She knew how Tony felt about those who became Christians for the wrong reasons, and she truly wanted to share his love for his Lord.

But the few weeks that Maya stayed at the hostel became unbearable to her. And she guessed it was equally unbearable for the Sisters and the women of the Christian hostel to have her there. She questioned all the things they believed and taught. She felt the Sisters only wanted to wipe out the Hindu ideas that the girls had grown up with and replace them with Christian thinking at once. They didn't seem to realize that changing religion meant having to change every subconscious level of thinking, and how was one supposed to do that? For that, she needed a total mind change, and perhaps only a "massive brain surgery" could accomplish such a thing.

For some girls, conversion was not a problem. They had been raised on the streets or in various institutions. They had distorted impressions about the Hindu religion. The only thing they could think about was avoiding starvation. But to other girls, conversion didn't come easily. They accepted it because it was a way of surviving. But, before coming to the Christian hostel they had enjoyed the celebrations of religious and cultural holidays at home. They had distinct and positive impressions of the Hindu gods and goddesses. They had memorized prayers and enjoyed the colorful festivals. Like Maya, they were never really happy obeying the laws of prayer meetings at the Christian hostel.

Maya told some of her friends about the old temple and Hari-kaka. She also urged them to visit him, and some of them actually dared to go with Maya. But the second time, they were caught coming in late for the prayer meeting. Their punishment was having to say the "Hail Mary" twenty-five times. Maya was excused from this, but she took it upon herself to accept the punishment since the incident had been her fault. However, before accepting it, she argued that they had been spending their time praying – the only difference was that they had been doing it at the temple. But Sister Tiru, fixing her eyes directly on Maya said, "Maya, you shouldn't say these things. You should know better, that we don't consider that prayer. It is only mumbo-jumbo."

Maya mumbled, "A prayer is a prayer. When you don't understand it becomes a mumbo-jumbo."

But still, she knew she would have to become a Christian. Even Harikaka had said so. Only, how could she forget what she knew? How could she betray her own self, where the distinct image of God existed? In absolute silence, in meditation, there are no images, Hariakaka had said; it is formless, only an awareness. Pure joy. But, otherwise when she prayed, she prayed to no formless God. There was Lord Shiva on her mind, all the time. Now it would have to be Yeshu, not Shiva. Yeshu, she told herself every day.

One night she dreamt that she was sitting on a mountain top, engrossed in the mantra to invoke Lord Shiva. As she repeated, '*Om, Namah Shivaya. Om, Namah Shivaya,*' she saw a person, and realized it was Tony, who was pushing the image of Lord Shiva aside, and she also saw Sister Tiru, who was laughing and dancing in the background.

Chapter Twelve

After leaving Maya at the Christian hostel that afternoon, Chitra soon found out that there were no hotels where she, a lone woman, could stay. And she could not stay with relatives because the idea of this princess being homeless would be so far from their minds that she did not know how she would even begin to tell them. When she stopped at some of her friends' places, she felt they were embarrassed for her to see how they lived. She knew she could live with Sarala-auntie, a friend of her mother's, but she was away on a pilgrimage.

After spending the entire day looking for a place to stay in town, Chitra asked the rickshaw driver to take her back home, but the thought of facing her father so soon after he had asked her to leave was unendurable. His taunting words resonated in her ears, "I never want to see you again, get out!" He wanted to see if she could survive without him and now she had returned, which was hard for her to accept.

So, when the rickshaw reached the gates of their estate, she changed her mind about returning home. Instead, she asked the rickshaw driver to take her to the rear entrance of the estate, where the servants' quarters were. After her mother's death the quarters had gradually become empty, except the one where Laxman had stayed on.

A few years back, two of Laxman's boys had left the Pandits' maids' quarters. But recently his married daughter had moved in to look after her father. Now her children and his son's children, all seven of them, were sitting in a semicircle, around his daughter, ready to be fed, when Chitra tiptoed past Laxman's noisy home to reach the cook's quarters.

The cook's old quarters were dusty. Perhaps she should wait until the children were fed and then go and ask Laxman's daughter to clean the room. On second thought, she felt she should clean it herself. For sure, she knew she didn't want to be

Miss Pandit, not any more. She did not want to be the daughter of a Brahmin barrister. Twenty-seven years was a long time…

In the maid's quarters, not long after she had fallen asleep, Chitra woke up to a knock at the front door. The knocking turned to pounding and she sat up. The old wooden charpoy creaked. Slowly, she became aware of her surroundings, remembering her sudden homelessness and her search for a place to stay. Again she heard the knocking, and this time it was accompanied by a man's voice. The man sounded hysterical, pleading with her to open the door. She finally realized it was Laxman. Wondering what could be wrong, she called out, "Laxman, what is the matter?"

"O-pen, open the door, *Tai-Sahiba*." He shook the padlock loudly. His voice sounded on the verge of breaking. "*Hare! Bhagawan – hare Bhagawan…*" His sobs sucked up the rest of the words. This was unlike Laxman.

She quickly unlatched the door. Laxman threw himself at her feet, holding crumpled-up rupee notes in his hands. She bent down to raise him from the floor, puzzled by his outcry. "Laxman, what is wrong? Are your children okay?"

He sat on the ground wrapping his long arms around his knees. Holding the fistful of rupees, he hit his forehead. His thin body rocked back and forth as he sobbed.

"Laxman, do you need money?"

He shook his head vehemently. "No. No, *Tai-Sahiba*. But you take this money." And he dropped it on the floor.

"Laxman?"

He didn't answer and blankly stared at the scattered notes.

"La-x-ma-n?" Chitra said more loudly.

"Go. Go somewhere else, *Tai-Sahiba*. This is not good." He took a deep breath, looking up at the sky. "Whose curse are you living, *Tai*? For the first time I am happy that your mother is not alive to see your *halat*." He moaned, holding his head in his hands.

Now she realized that *her* staying in the servants' quarters was what was troubling him. He had never been upset for himself, even though he had lived all his life in poverty, in these very quarters. For her, it was only a temporary arrangement, a matter of a few days. But still that bothered him! He could not bear her living like this at his level, even if it was temporary.

Chitra patted his shoulder. "Laxman, it's all right. I'm not alone. *Hn*? You are here with me."

He looked up and gazed directly into her eyes. "No. You don't belong here, *Tai-Sahiba*. Definitely not with us." His voice grew resentful and he repeated, "Not here. Not with us! No. We are the rag wearers." He cried shamelessly, "Penniless paupers. The worthless people." He seemed to feel no disgrace in saying these things, as if this lifetime he had no hope that he and his family might live a better life. Instead of doing something about their living conditions, he had accepted his path passively.

This outburst was intolerable to Chitra. "Laxman!" she said angrily.

But he could not stop. Ignoring her, he babbled about his perpetual miserable fate.

"We have been ignorant fools. A horde of scraps!" he moaned.

What a fool! She walked inside.

"But *Tai*," he went on, "I know this much, you are not one of us. Your kismet isn't that low."

Listening to his tragic acceptance of his poverty-ridden life, and his degradation of his own existence, she felt no one should feel that lowly about their life. Being impoverished should be infuriating. Revolting. And here he was, only crying about it as if it was a fate and couldn't be changed. She wanted him to stop broadcasting his lowly status!

Chitra had thought of these things before. She believed if she ever had to change places with people like Laxman, she would feel grossly repulsed. She would revolt and demand what rightly belonged to every human being: dignity and a fair share of wealth.

When she was about to say something to Laxman, his grandchildren ran up to him, whimpering, clinging to his neck, saying they didn't want their *ajo*, their grandfather, to be sad.

She felt burdened by everything: their emotional display, his loyalty towards her, their love for one another. She knew he cared about her, but she also knew she could not return the same care, not in the same manner. She tried to reason with him. "Laxman, situations change. People change. I am not your *Malkin Sahiba* anymore."

Her stating of the fact didn't comfort him. He rested his forehead by Chitra's feet, pleading with her to leave the empty maid's quarters.

"Laxman," she said, raising her voice, "go home. We'll see to it tomorrow."

"No. *Tai*, no. I can't sleep at the same place as you have."

His insistence on being lower than she infuriated her. This whole emotional upheaval of his, was only for the sake of her comfort. That's foolish, she thought – I should feel bad about this, not you. Idiot! But she didn't have the heart to say it.

Now all seven of his grandchildren started touching their little foreheads on the ground by her feet. Supplicating. Begging with their grandfather, not even knowing the reason for their actions, they begged for her dignity. Looking at them, Chitra felt, these people are hopelessly destroyed.

She despised this attitude.

She looked at those little heads on the floor and concluded that submission was a matter of genetics. In addition to that, she strongly believed that such attitudes were initiated and cultivated by the Brahmins. For generations, with their lofty priestcraft they had filled these poor people's heads with decadence, entrenching them deeper in their lower status. These poor souls! How would they rise in the world when they had no self-esteem, and felt less than human? Poverty had pushed them into a swamp, making them feel like a pestilence, making them inured to insult and humiliation. Now they had adopted submission as a way of life.

She had always been incensed by these ideas. Now she would have provoked him, teaching him a lesson or two, but she knew Laxman loved her. She also knew how her mother had cared for him and his family. She couldn't ignore his concerns about her.

"Listen, Laxman," she said, softening her voice, pacifying him, "I don't have a place for tonight. I will make some arrangement, say in a day or two? *Hn*?" She picked the money up from the floor and pushed it into his hand. "Don't worry about money, Laxman. I have enough. I'm fine."

"You were always like that," he said, "A winner! I remember how your mother used to comment: 'Chitra has the strength to be the queen of Zansi, how could she have been born in a Brahmin family, where women are pious and meek?' Now I know you're the Rani of the Zansi."

The Rani of Zansi, the queen who fought against the British empire, tying her baby on her back, had a kingdom; Chitra didn't even have a home! But she smiled. The memories of her mother made her feel closer to him. He seemed to feel responsible for her well being and he asked, "Barrister doesn't know this, right?"

Chitra shook her head. "He asked me to leave the home this morning, so I did."

"*Tai*, he can't be serious about it, you didn't have to."

"I had to, Laxman. He will never let me live in peace. It's about time I left anyway…"

"I am going to see Barrister. Now." He stood up.

"Laxman, it wouldn't help. Because I won't go back home as long—" She broke off, because she could not tell him how long her homelessness would last.

But Laxman was determined. He wiped his tears away and started walking towards the main house. All his grandkids sat on the floor, with proud eyes, watching their grandfather. His daughter ran into their quarters and brought his cap. Putting it on his head, he stood straight and tall. Looking at him, Chitra shook her head though she now felt better about his courage.

"Laxman, you will be insulted," she warned.

"That isn't anything new."

Watching his figure disappear into the thickets of trees, Chitra felt she should have lied about her name and her caste at the Christian girls' hostel. She should have hidden everything that identified her as Chitra Pandit.

Laxman walked up to Mr. Pandit's study. He saw through the window that Mr. Pandit was looking at some papers. Laxman knocked at the door. Mr. Pandit only cleared his throat to let him know not to disturb him. But Laxman knocked again and said, "Barrister Sahib…"

"*Hn!*"

"*Me*. Laxman, Sahib," Laxman pleaded from behind the door.

"*Hn!*"

"Sahib, please. Sahib."

"What?"

Laxman did not answer.

A moment later Mr. Pandit shouted, "If you are going to say something, then say it. I'm listening."

As Laxman walked into the room, the phone rang and he waited patiently in a corner. He saw the rich mahogany desk, the ornate carpeting on the beautiful marble floor, rich tapestry, and the pale velvet-covered Victorian settee by the wall. The contrast between this plush room and where Mr. Pandit's daughter now was, became unbearable, and his eyes filled with tears. As soon as Mr. Pandit put the phone down, he fell at Mr. Pandit's feet. "Oh! Oh, Sahib." He could not speak any further.

Uncomfortable with Laxman's action, Mr. Pandit hastily rose from his chair and stood a few feet away. "What are you doing, Laxman? You know I don't like such behavior."

"I know, I know, Sahib. Sahib, but..." He sat on his heels and with pleading eyes searched for a trace of humanity in Mr. Pandit's. Dodging this visual confrontation, Mr. Pandit stepped backward.

"If I have served you good enough, Sahib..."

"I never questioned your servitude. Have I?"

"Sahib, in the thirty-five years of my service, I have never asked for anything. But this time, Sahib... only once, I want you to do something for this poor servant."

"Laxman, stand up!"

Laxman stood up, but his eyes remained glued to the floor. He murmured, "Chitra-*Tai*, Sahib."

"What? What about Chitra?"

"She is staying at the maids' quarters," Laxman blurted.

"What?"

"Yes, Sahib." His voice choked, sounding as if it was he who was the guilty person.

Mr. Pandit turned and paced the floor.

The girl is inconsiderate, he thought. Completely unmindful. She had never been normal. Girls of her age are all married, but no... not her. Now, this? Did she really have to move out? What is she trying to prove? Is it necessary? What is the matter with her? Didn't she learn from her mother? Her mother never crossed me. She appreciated what I did for her, for them. Why is her daughter so different? She must learn my ways. Obey my laws. Respect my opinions. What is so wrong if he expected that from her? She would have money, name, power and prestige in society. All this she could have only because of me…

His forehead wrinkled, knowing he could not give her anything and she would stay at the servants' quarters.

He sighed, cleared his throat and stopped pacing, while Laxman watched him anxiously. He walked back to his chair. "If you think I should ask her to come in this house, you are mad." Folding his arms across his chest, he paused, standing erect.

"But… but, Barrister, she is your daughter. Where should a young woman go?" Laxman pleaded,

"She should have thought of that before opening her mouth. Before insulting me. If she wanted to come back she should have offered an apology."

Laxman took his cap off and stood, thumping it on his hand.

Mr. Pandit continued, "Instead she is making a scene by moving into the servants' quarters. You don't know how she insulted me this morning, in my own house. Do I need to take this kind of insult?" Mr. Pandit looked disgusted. The usual frown on his face seemed more tangled.

"But, Sahib, this one time," Laxman begged. "Only once… If you let her—" Laxman begged.

"I am glad you came to tell me this," Mr. Pandit said, cutting him short. Then, with a victorious look, he sat down in his plush chair. Leaning back and now fully enjoying the situation, he placed his hands behind his neck, resting his head on the chair's back. As far as he was concerned, the matter was over.

"Shall I tell *Tai-Sahiba* that you have asked her to come back in the house, Sahib?" Thinking Mr. Pandit had changed his mind, he was almost ready to leave the room.

"*No!*" Mr. Pandit roared.

The callousness in his voice froze Laxman on the spot.

"You tell her…" He paused for a moment, then, with an increased indifference in his voice, he continued, "You tell her that I am in need of a Brahmin woman to cook for us. And if she wants the job, only then can she stay in the quarters. The pay will be one hundred rupees a month." And feeling happy for trapping her at her own game, he laughed loudly. "I will have the most learned cook, won't I? Advocate. Hmm! A useless thing, she… she—" He stopped abruptly, then swiveling his chair towards a window he looked outside and stared into the night; he didn't notice that Laxman was holding back tears.

"Also," he added coldly, without turning to face Laxman, "if I provide the meals, three meals a day, she is to pay the rent for the maids' quarter, fifteen rupees."

"*Chhi, chhi*, Sahib. I can't tell her that. For God's—"

"Laxman, you will tell her that. Now the case is closed. And go on. Go. Go – I have work to do." Mr. Pandit looked back down at his desk, murmuring, "You're all idiots."

When Laxman returned, Chitra was chatting with his daughter. Laxman didn't stop to tell her anything. Chitra understood. With heavy steps on old feet, he walked into his home, picked up his bedroll, and spread it outside Chitra's quarters. Laxman's little grandchildren copied him.

They all slept outside her door.

Part Five

Chapter Thirteen

When Tony was asked to visit the mission's camp at Chhotanagar, unrest between Hindus and Muslims had begun in many parts of the country. While waiting for his train at the Kulur station he saw many trains running empty on the routes where the riots had already begun. He had to wait a long time before his train arrived. When his journey finally got under way the train passed many secluded temples or mosques that were burning. It stopped at a few stations, and these were guarded by soldiers. Then it skipped the other stations to make up for lost time. As the train went a little farther on, there were no signs of unrest and the atmosphere seemed normal. Later he read in the newspaper that the disturbances were mostly in the inner cities, and he worried for Maya.

He hadn't seen Maya for the past few days. He had been busy, preparing Seva Sadan for the visit from his diocese of Father John, who would arrive in Kulur upon Tony's return. Visiting Maya at the hostel involved travel and he couldn't manage to free himself from his hectic work schedule. He knew she was frustrated with the differences between the Hindu and Christian religion. But he hoped she had made amends with the women of the Christian hostel.

Right before he left, the sisters had come to visit, warning him about Maya, telling him to think before he married her. They told him that she still went to temple and followed her own Hindu rituals in her room at the Christian hostel. They couldn't tolerate that. She had been stubborn but they wished to help her, only to help him.

Tony listened to them, and spoke in her defense. She needed time, he said. They disagreed. He told them she could have easily lied to him and to them but she had been honest about her doubts of their faith.

"How can she doubt our faith?" they argued. "She works at a Christian mission, she lives at a Christian mission and she is marrying a Christian. Then why should she doubt this faith?"

Tony was speechless.

They claimed her charm and beauty had blinded him. And when he laughed at that they asked him to talk to Maya about the Christian faith, to teach her the catechism, since they weren't sure if she wanted to learn anything from them. Before leaving they warned him that she might take him away from his faith. He had assured them that was not the case. They should remember he was there as a missionary.

But Maya's turmoil and questions had raised many valid questions in his mind, questions he had chosen, all his life, not to dwell on. It had been convenient to think that Christianity was the only way. Now that comfort was gone and he wondered how could he be so naïve as to think that people could simply convert to Christianity. And yet, when it came to Maya, he had convinced himself that she would. Now things appeared to be different, difficult. Finally, he had began to think, What if she didn't become Christian – which would he choose then, his faith or his love? Which could he let go?

Neither of them was their choice, neither faith nor love.

The only choice he knew was that he had to help Maya to become Christian, and with that resolve, every time, he felt relieved.

But when she wanted to know why Jesus was the only true Son of God, and why Christianity was the only true religion, how would he answer?

He didn't know. Over and over again, he had explained to Maya that he loved his work and it came to him through Jesus. Betraying his work meant betraying all the poor people he helped. He knew he couldn't abandon the people who lived in those despicable conditions. How would he ever be able to offer them all the food, medicine and education that they and their children needed without the help of the Catholic mission? The only hope, the only way he knew, was that the Christian faith might bring about a change in their world. Also, only a few months ago when Maya had left him, serving these people had given him the only reason to continue living. Charity work made him think he was making the difference. It had been more than satisfying; it was divine. It was the work of Christ.

He believed that seeing Christ in every face of the poor had transformed him, made him happy. But what could he say when Maya had asked, "What's wrong if someone saw the face of Ram instead of Yeshu?" She had further argued that heartfelt compassion came through God, that compassion is God. Why then tack a particular face on something that's so natural to every human being?

The face of Rama? This was new.

It could be true.

In his heart of hearts Tony found himself admitting that her arguments were valid. He had always been told not to question because doubt weakened faith. And he had been able to hold it back, until now.

Now he felt that the life of faith always meant a risk of losing it. It could be as hard as an acrobat's walk on a tightrope; he had to be always steady; concentrate only on one thing, one idea. If he looked around, he could tumble. And if someone gave the rope – his faith – a little push, he could fall. It was too rigid, totally confining. It was against a man's true nature of wanting to be free. There was no freedom.

But it had given him strength.

He knew he wasn't falling, at least not out of his faith, even when he didn't have the answers to her questions.

Now Maya was telling him how Hari encouraged her to ask questions, how he told her that without inquiry God will never be known. And to aid this innate inquiry there was the methodology written by sages and known as Vedanta, which imparts the knowledge of the self. The knowledge is for entire humanity, it's universal. Thus knowing God, for anyone, wouldn't be a matter of faith. Thus, every thinking conscious being can know God, the truth, or realize it within, and not only by believing with the rational mind.

Tony had counter-argued that believing in Christ had given him purpose and leisure to live here and hereafter. Questioning or rationalizing complicates simple minds and can be dangerous. A life of faith is an easy and common way of living.

But if anyone can realize God within his heart, how is it that He is seen only through Yeshu? she had persisted.

Tony remembered how he had fumbled for an answer while telling her that she needed to understand, she needed to love Him, as Jesus.

He had resisted admitting anything to Maya or at times even to himself. The life of faith was easier when it wasn't questioned but difficult when inquired into, but then having no faith was even harder. He would feel naked, empty, stripped of love.

Tony thought he would talk to the priest about his dilemmas when traveling to the valley, as he was to bring along the priest from a town a few miles away. A scooter was arranged for him but when he arrived to pick the priest up he found that he was running a high fever. Sitting on the back on Tony's scooter, the priest kept dozing off and losing his balance, making it hard for Tony to go faster. Every few minutes Tony slowed, making sure the priest was awake. After a few times of slowing and stopping, Tony persuaded the priest to tie himself up like a backpack on Tony's back and shoulders. This enabled him to pick up speed, but he was still late reaching the valley of Chhotanagar.

As he neared the valley all the annoying questions left his mind, and he was absorbed in the beauty of the jungle. The trees were swaying with the wind, blowing exotic scents that filled the air. In the bright sunlight, vivid colored butterflies danced everywhere, kissing the flowers. Mountain sparrows, colorful parrots, pigeons and many other birds twittered from every branch. Peacocks sat with their fountains of feathers trailing on the green grass. Spreading their wings, condors circled in the blue sky, and, on the ground, squirrels zoomed, rabbits hopped, mountain goats and cows grazed. Monkeys jumped from the treetops, screaming, curiously looking down from the branches as open spaces filled with the mountain people.

Hundreds of men and women were sitting on the ground. The dark, healthy skin of the mountain folk glistened like ripples on deep river waters in bright sunlight. Many of the men were wearing scanty loincloths around their waists and held spears in their hands. The women wore jewel-toned halter-tops with long skirts falling from their waists. Ample amount of jewelry made out of ivory beads and colorful stones sparkled in the bright sunlight. They were oblivious to why they were gathered and were chatting with other women. Naked children were playing in the dirt. The tribe were called, *Suryashakti* – Power of the Sun. They were known for their hunting skills, and for making stone jewelry. They worshipped the sun and moon and stars.

When Tony arrived, the priest somehow untied himself and Tony helped him sit on the ground, under the shade a little away from the people. Then Tony went back to the scooter and carried his bag of medical supplies into a tent. Tony was surprised to find two sleepy-looking guards at the entrance of the tent. He walked past. Inside the tent, Tomas, a Christian missionary from Belgium, was sitting on a rickety chair and leaning over a table. Tomas was following with his finger over the list of names of people. He looked up at Tony in surprise and asked why was he alone, and where was the priest? Tony told him that the priest was sick and resting under the tree. He would be up in a few minutes.

Tony sat and waited, while Tomas counted the names on the lists. They totaled 345, including children. Looking up in the sky and crossing his heart, he prayed. As he closed the book, a man jumped from his seat and walked towards Tomas. Tomas opened a zippered pouch and handed the man, whose name was Bijoo, an envelope containing money he had offered to the man for getting him into this particular tribe. Bijoo ran behind the tent and counted the money. Then, pulling his trousers over his loincloth and slipping his T-shirt back on, he came back. He talked to a few men in the crowd, telling them he had received the money and he would bring them the bags of cement, knives and other tools they needed. Holding Bijoo's arms, and with their arms around each other, they formed a circle. Looking up at the sky, they prayed to the sun god. After the ritual, Bijoo left the valley on his scooter, without looking at Tomas, carefully holding his hand on the pocket with the money.

Tomas looked up at Tony. "Bijoo helps his people to sell their goods in the markets and bring other supplies from the villages," he began to explain. "He was their only connection to the other world until we, the Christians, arrived a few years ago. The mission also hooked him for their use. Later, we built camps and a church. We brought medicine and education. A couple of times a few tribal people burnt the camps to the ground, but the missionaries were persistent. We kept coming, rebuilding the camps. Only when there was famine or epidemics more people started coming to us. Slowly, now we have earned their trust. Quite a few have now become Christian and a few are living outside of the tribe." He stopped, then, looking outside the tent, he said, "Oh yes, Christianity is flourishing in the valley of Chhotanagar."

At any other time Tony would have been happy to hear that Christianity was flourishing in Chhotanagar. Now, he kept quiet and didn't show any enthusiasm about the activities of the Catholic mission.

Outside, people started to walk away. Tomas hurried outside the tent. Tony followed, not sure what to make of this robust missionary, and anxious to check on the priest. Tomas began walking briskly through the crowds of people screaming from the depths of his belly, *"Yeshu sab ka thik karega. Uski prathana tumahra dharma hai."* ("Jesus will do good things for you and praying to Him is your duty.") He walked back and forth, panting, pleading with them. *"Bolo, Yeshu ke raktse,"* ("With His blood you will be saved"), he said, coaxing them to repeat what he was saying. He was sweating heavily and people stood curiously looking at him. A few snickered at him. But Tomas didn't notice anything: he was possessed with new vigor. Finally, his dream was about to come true; people from Suryashakti had agreed to be baptized and saved!

As Tomas approached, a young man, Megh, stood up. Raising his eyebrows, he asked, *"Yeshu kaun hai?"* ("Who's this Yeshu?")

"Yeshu is your new God."

"When did the God became old or new?"

"He's new because you didn't pray to Him before."

"What's his relation with God, Sun?"

"No. That's different…"

"Do you have a different sun?" Megh asked seriously.

"No… don't ask such questions… when you… you don't know anything…" Tomas said, running back to the tent. Seeing him run, most of the women giggled as he passed them. Children ran with him, asking for sweets, pulling at his trousers.

From the tent he picked up the copper pot filled with water. And looking at the priest, who was sitting on the ground, Tomas turned to the people and told them they were saved, that soon the priest would be up.

But Tony saw immediately that all was not well with the priest. His face was red, his breath was hot and sounded heavy. Then Tony helped the priest to walk to the tent, where the priest lay down and soon seemed to lose consciousness.

Tomas placed the pot of water on the floor and shook the priest by his sleeve, asking, "What's wrong with him?"

Tony didn't answer and the priest did not respond. Tony checked his pulse. Then he checked his fever, and told Tomas that the priest wasn't going to wake up quickly.

Asking Thomas to let the priest rest a while, Tony opened the bag of medicines. Tomas brought water and sprinkled some on the priest's face. Seeing Tomas so anxious, Tony told him, "Let me take care of him, then I will help you with your patients."

"Patients?" Tomas threw his head back. "No one is sick here but me. I have planned to baptize all these pagans before it's too late, and that's why you are here to help, and not to help the sick."

Tony had not been told about the "mass conversion" because most of the time these were done in full secrecy, and those who organized these mass events didn't want the information to leak out, especially not in a city like Kulur. They didn't want the Hindu fanatics to disturb the process of baptism, which at times they did, even though baptism was entirely legal. Now, taking advantage of the tense atmosphere between Hindus and Muslims, the mass conversion was planned, as the fanatic Hindus would be fighting against the Muslims, and wouldn't worry about the conversions of a few tribal people.

"Like you, I am not near city," Tomas told Tony, "where people are different, educated, more aware of their religion. This is an open farm, thousands of souls, Tony."

Tony looked at Tomas, who was quite overcome by what he was doing. Tony could sense his joy and excitement, excitement in spreading the message. He felt guilty. What had happened to his passion? How could he start doubting the very idea, baptism, for which he had left home, crossed the ocean? How could he be so selfish?

Tony said nothing. He held the priest's wrist in his hand to check his pulse.

Tomas walked away.

He hurried back to the tent, and, picking up the lists, he went back to the people, screaming, "*Bolo, bolo... Lord Yeshu...*" Many of them began to drift off, and Tomas screamed, "Wait, wait!" Some of them stopped, looking for the gifts, but many others continued to walk away.

Tomas ran after every one of them, brought them back and made them sit, promising it would only be for a few more minutes. Then he took the Bible from his pocket. Seeing that, they stood up. They had grown tired and didn't want to listen to Tomas's stories. A group of men stood and started to walk away from him. Tomas ran to the tent, picked up a bunch of bananas and ears of corn, and pointed at the other treasures. People came near him and he let them see and feel the things but cleverly he never handed any of these items out. And again some waited in anticipation of receiving something, gazing at the baskets of gifts.

Tomas walked back to where Tony sat and glanced at the priest; Tony shook his head. Tomas dashed out again and roused the dozing guards, asking them to carry the pot of water. Then he ordered them to bring the baskets of food and boxes of trinkets.

Tony heard Tomas shouting at a mass of people, "Repeat after me. *I renounce Satan...*" Tomas waited. No one said a word. He repeated the words. Still no one said anything. Ignoring the lack of response, Tomas continued, "*I vow to be a Christian from now on. Oh! Lord Yeshu, you are the only one I will pray to.*" He looked up.

No one was repeating his words. He shouted again, "*I renounce Satan...*" A few mumbled some words after him.

Tomas paused for a moment, thinking how to end this chaos. Then he asked the people to stand in line. They didn't know what a line meant, so the guards shuffled them around and made them stand in some order. Tomas dipped his fingers in the pot and sprinkled water on the first person's head, mumbling, "I renounce Satan..." but the man stood silent, nodding. Then he gave the man a piece of chapatti bread, soaked in tamarind water instead of wine, and asked one of the guards to give the man a cross pendant tied to a black thread.

Thus the first man was baptized.

The man stood aside for a moment, looking at the pendant, but when he saw a few people coming up behind him he dropped it on the ground and hurried to the heaps of gifts.

And so it went on. Those who were baptized started filling their arms with clothes and food baskets. When those who weren't yet baptized and were waiting in line saw this, they rushed up and threw themselves on the piles of gifts. The bickering that resulted brought the process of baptism to a complete halt. The men piled up the goods in their arms. The children broke the sugarcanes and tugged at the farming tools. Tomas screamed, "Stop… stop!" as some started to run away with baskets of fruit. The monkeys came down from the trees, looking curiously at the scattered bananas. Everyone was screaming, "Give me this or that," and young women started wrapping pieces of cloths around their bodies.

Tomas blew a whistle. A moment of silence filled the space and he screamed, "Stop it! *Band karo ye sab. Hamara Bhagawan tumhe dukhase chhuta nahi karega!*" ("Our Lord cannot end your misery if you behave this way!") But the children continued to throw fruit in the air to feed birds and monkeys.

Tony came out of the tent and put his arms around Tomas. "Tomas, let it go," he said.

Tomas shook his head.

"Let it go, Tomas," Tony repeated, "It's okay."

"I can't… I can't," he cried, tears streaming through his eyes. "I will be condemned. I will fail as a Christian. I have to save these souls."

Tomas ran around picking up the scattered fruit, crying and singing a hymn loudly.

> *"I lift up my eyes to the mountain,*
> *Whence will help come to me,*
> *My help is from the Lord, God."*

Listening to his singing, the people were quieted. Then he sang even louder, possessed by new vigor, "*Whence will help come to me…"*

While singing, he noticed the fighting people and shouted, *"Tum ko narak nahi jana hai… to mat karo. Tumh bhuka nahi marana."* ("You don't want to go to hell. You don't want to die of starvation, so don't do this.")

But the people were not cowed by his threat. He tried to hold one man by his arm, trying to put his hand on the Bible to swear; but, pushing Tomas away, the man walked off.

Tomas went back to the tent. Crying, he stood before Tony who was busy sponging the priest's feet with a cold towel. Tomas whimpered, "Look at them. None of them seemed to care what I've taught them for the last so many months."

Tony stood up and made Tomas sit on a chair and gave him a glass of water.

Tomas told Tony that these people had forgotten he had helped them to build the huts. They had forgotten he had brought new tools for them to make stone jewelry. They had forgotten he had promised to sell their jewelry abroad. They had forgotten he had helped cure their sick children.

Tomas rested his head on the edge of the table. He sat quietly for a minute and then stood and told Tony that this would be his last effort. He picked up the pot of water, went outside and threw water over everyone's heads, saying again and again, "I baptize thee," and again, "In the name of the Father, and of the Son, and of the Holy Ghost."

As he threw the water, children ran into it and splashed around, laughing. Then Tomas threw pieces of chapatis into the crowd. The women and children caught the pieces of bread from the air or picked them up from the ground. He passed the cross pendants to the women, who held them in their hands. Seeing the pendants sparkle in the sun they wondered aloud if they were made of real gold. While pondering this, some used the cross as a toothpick. As he threw the last piece of bread in the crowd, he pronounced them as new Christians.

Inside the tent, holding a water-dampened towel on the priest's forehead, Tony wept as he watched Tomas baptizing the masses who did not want to know who the beloved Christ was!

Chapter Fourteen

Tony took longer coming back from the valley as the riots were brewing in and around the city of Kulur. When he reached Seva Sedan he could tell Maya had been there, attending the clinic in his absence. All the papers were neatly arranged. The medicine bottles had new name tags. Floors were washed, shining clean. Brass oil lamps were polished and burning all around the altar.

On the dining table a new tablecloth was spread and fresh flowers from the garden were neatly arranged in a chipped china vase. In the kitchen the serving dishes and spoons were placed on the counter, beside a telegram. The telegram informed them two guests, Father John from the U.S., and a deacon from Goa who was accompanying him, would be arriving a day early and then going south, where there were no riots, the next day.

Whistling a tune, Tony went for a bath and when he came out he saw the guests getting out of the rickshaw. He had never met Father John, and when he saw him standing on the street, Tony was surprised to see how big Father John looked in comparison with the small-built Indian men. His chubby cheeks and the fat around his neck made a bib of flesh around his face. He had a chiseled nose that dipped under his slightly tapered forehead. If it wasn't for his weight, with his sharp features, blond wispy hair and deep blue eyes he could have passed as a movie star. Tony ran down to the gate and shook hands with them and carried their bags to the rooms. He had never entertained guests before, and he was surprised at his excitement of having someone from home, the U.S. But, Father John seemed reserved, and spoke very little.

After supper, they went out for a walk.

They walked slowly, looking at the leisurely activities of people by the river. The young men were playing *kabbadi* in the fading light, where the dust created a film, and from the distance Tony and the Father could barely see the hulking figures of the players. Children sat on the branches of the *pepul* trees watching the game. Women resting their brass or clay pots filled with water chatted for a long while before parting from one another. And a few older men sat under the tree smoking a chillum, sharing it with one another.

Father John asked, "So, Tony, everything going well for you?"

"There are many difficulties, Father, but I would like to talk to you about a different matter." Tony turned to face Father John, trying to ascertain why the Father was visiting him. Father John had only told him that he had been asked to visit some Catholic missions around the country. But he wondered if it was more than that, whether Father John had heard about his involvement with Maya, a Hindu girl. But why should that be a cause of his concern? It was Tony's personal matter.

"Listen, Tony, who hasn't had difficulties performing the Lord's work? The Lord himself suffered, leading 'people like these' to the right path," said Father John, and he continued to talk about the greatness and the sufferings of Jesus.

Father John hadn't listened to what he wanted to say. Tony needed some answers, not regarding his work here but about bigger issues of faith and the purpose of the mission. All over the world, Catholic missions offered help by creating educational institutions and by giving medical help. And he believed that only by serving people had Jesus, the greatest missionary, instilled love for Him in His followers. And so it should be today.

But that was not how the missions were working. Tony wanted Father John to know that. He was beginning to think that their great work at times was considered little more than bribery, since in return for goods and services they expected people to become Christian. Why did our charitable, kind actions have to be bolstered in this manner? Tony had thought out all this clearly and he was waiting for his chance to say it.

Father John breathed heavily as he continued to speak without even looking at Tony. The heat was persistent and when he paused to wipe the sweat from his face, Tony quickly interjected his question about 'these people' being on the wrong path. "I don't know what is the right or wrong path anymore, or who is on it. Who am I to judge, and say, these people are on the wrong path when I am groping for right answers myself?"

Father John stopped walking. "Now, Tony, how can you

think like that?"

Tony shrugged, "Because I am no longer sure why we claim ours is the only true religion. Others can claim the same," he whispered hesitantly.

Looking directly into Tony's eyes, the Father scolded, "Have you become a Christian of weak faith?"

Tony shook his head.

"Then how can you say that?"

"How can I say that?" Tony repeated, then paused, thinking, If I accepted other religions – not followed, only accepted – as a legitimate faith, would it make me a Christian of weak faith? Did Jesus really say, don't respect other religions? he wondered, and, before he knew, he was asking aloud, "Did Jesus really say that, Father, don't respect other religions?"

The question just slipped from Tony's mouth, but when he looked at the Father he felt as if his question had shaken the Christian heavens.

It had definitely shaken Father John. A sea of anger exploded in the lines of his face and he said loudly, "What?"

Tony didn't answer.

Father John's face flushed, and his flustered expression scared Tony. Tony's fear was that he would be asked to leave India. Then he thought, No, Father John wouldn't. Then, looking at Father's still angry face, he thought, Yes, he would send him back. And hurriedly he pointed at a passing boat in a vain effort to change the topic.

Father John pushed his hand aside.

"What's the matter with you?" the big man asked, in a tone of annoyance. "Don't you see the poverty and filth here? It is a sign that there is no faith. A wrong faith has led to the existence of Satan in the form of poverty. The very presence of evil makes these people starve. If they knew better they wouldn't be suffering like this. Just count your blessings, Tony, that you can help these hopeless and poor souls towards the right path."

"I am not sure what the 'right path' is for 'these people'. Right path..." Tony repeated unconsciously. Then, trying to gather his courage, he said, "Father, please forgive me for saying these things. I would like to know how is it possible for God not to touch 'these people's' lives? Isn't some sort of faith or a philosophy necessary for a culture of this magnitude to develop? I think that in the absence of a profound philosophy, a society would have to remain barbarous, don't you think?" Tony looked at him but didn't pause for a response as he continued, "Besides, I don't know how to answer the commonly asked question, why should Jesus be the only Son of God?"

"*Tony!*" Father John stopped in his tracks.

"Father, please," Tony pleaded, standing still. "Tell me how I should think." His lips quivered. "I need to resolve these things in my head so I can go on as a missionary."

"I get it – a love for this woman has changed your commitment of a lifetime," Father John accused, staring at Tony.

So, he had heard. Tony looked away and began to walk forward again.

"Listen, Tony," the Father said changing his tone, walking slowly alongside him. "Don't waste your time interpreting 'these people's' lives. You must follow your path, which is to spread the Word and to help people take Christ into their hearts and recognize him as the one true God. That's the purpose of our mission and the life of every Christian."

Tony nodded like a child who didn't believe a word he was being told.

He knew he shouldn't jeopardize his position with the Father, so, ignoring the questions that buzzed in his mind, he said, "I agree, I agree, Father. I don't know enough to arrive at any conclusion, that's why I am looking for guidance. But I know one thing: most of the poor people that I come in contact with are good-hearted people, despite their poverty. Isn't that good?"

Taking Tony's hand in his, the Father said, "Look, the truth of whatever good they have is in front of you. It has brought them to this state of destitution. The world is moving into a new and better way of living, while they are still sitting in filth with their idols. False ideas of God, hmm!" he exclaimed, jerking his head.

Tony closed his eyes, shaking his head. He was about to say something when the sound of someone calling, "Brother Tony, Brother Tony," stopped him.

Hearing the urgency in the voice, Tony turned around and

saw two men rushing towards them, their feet throwing up dust, which sent Father John into another coughing fit. Grabbing Tony's hand, one man pulled him towards Seva Sadan. "Brother Tony, quick. Come to Seva Sadan. Brother Soma has had an accident. They have brought him to the house. Hurry, hurry, Brother Tony, he may be dead."

The other man nudged him and said, "No, he is not dead. He is only unconscious. But hurry."

Looking back in the direction of Seva Sadan, Tony saw people gathered in front of the house. "Sorry, Father," he said hurriedly, "I must run. You continue on your walk. I'll see you later."

Tony ran with the two men to the house, as Father John looked up at the sky and crossed his heart.

When Tony reached Seva Sadan some people had already carried Soma inside the dispensary. A couple of men held rags over his wounds and a smashed onion was placed under his nose to bring him back to consciousness. Soma was in worse shape than Tony had thought. He had been hit by a bus and tossed up in the air, landing in the ditch of an unpaved alley. Blood dripped from his nose, ears and mouth. His upper body was completely red.

Tony had wished many times that people wouldn't bring him the accident cases, especially ones like this, thinking he could do miracles. He had told them repeatedly that he was not a doctor, but they did not want to believe it. To them, he was just as good. Their attitude pressured Tony into helping them, and in most cases, somehow things seemed to work out well.

Tony rushed to the sink and, washing his hands, asked someone to get the doctor at once. He poured disinfectant onto huge cotton pads. The profuse bleeding from Soma's wounds scared him, and instinctively he started praying. "Oh! Lord Jesus Christ, let my plea come before you. Let Your hand help me; for I have chosen Your percept."

More people were gathering. Tony said loudly, "*Bahar jav…* go home." A man pushed some of them out, but still some stayed, moving to the side so they were not in the way.

Soma winced in pain, and Balu, his brother, patted his cheek. "*Ae'*, Soma. Wake up," he said. A couple of the men at his side also joined in, "Soma, *ae'* Soma!" and waited for his response anxiously.

Soma fidgeted but didn't open his eyes. He was dying. Tony looked at the door and said, "Go, go see if Dr. Mate is home, if not, Joshi, hurry please." Balu looked at a man and threw the keys of his scooter at him and the man dashed away.

Balu wiped the blood from Soma's mouth, and Soma again whimpered, "H-ey! R-a-m!" Christian men looked at each other, questioning but avoided looking at Tony or the deacon.

Balu cried again, "*Ae'*, Soma, open your eyes, Hey, Ram, help him." Even Balu, a converted Christian, forgot whom he was calling to for help.

Another elderly man hurried in and smashed more onions and held them under Soma's nose. Balu snatched the onion from the man's hand and cried, "Soma, *marana nahi re, marana nahi*. What will I tell your wife and children if you die?"

Again Soma moaned, "Ram... Ram... help me." This time the groan was loud and clear and Balu looked at Tony apologetically.

Soma had been baptized almost a year ago, and had attended church and mission activities like a devout Christian. But now, at his critical moment, he had forgotten his Lord, Yeshu, and was calling upon someone else.

Father John had returned and he too looked at Tony with concern on his face. But Tony was calm and worked on the bandages. He had seen this before and wasn't concerned about Soma's prayers to a Hindu god. But the deacon from Goa became upset at Soma's words. He jumped from his chair and approached Soma's bed. Soma whimpered as if he was coming out of a deep sleep. His lips moved but this time no words came, and he fell back into unconsciousness.

A loud sigh resonated in the room. The deacon patted Soma's cheeks. "*Ae'*! Soma, say *Yeshu*," he said, and then added in a kinder tone as if teaching a child, "Not Ram, say *Ye-shu, mera Bhagawan,* help me."

Tony brought a needle and asked the deacon to move aside. As he rubbed Soma's arm with alcohol, Soma again whimpered, "Ra-m, Ra-m" and rolled his head around.

The deacon looked at the Father, who looked at Tony, who

was busy propping Soma's head on a new pillow. The deacon became incensed and, pacing around Soma's bed, started mumbling, "What is this 'Ram, Ram.' *Budhu Kahinka*!" Then, as if to impress Father John, he said in English, "Don't forget, you will go to hell."

Soma again whimpered, "Ra-m."

The Christian brothers around him shook their heads. Sensing something amiss, they stepped backward, except for the deacon. Forgetting the huge pads around Soma's chest and the pain he was suffering, the deacon now thumped his fist on the side of the blood-soaked bedding. "Yeshu, Ye-shu is your Lord!" he cried out.

But Soma was slipping into the deep silence.

Tony walked back and forth from the verandah, then went down a few steps towards the gate, anxiously waiting for the doctor.

Inside, the deacon tried to put Soma's palms together in a prayer position but his hands fell limply to his sides. Then the deacon whispered at the dying man, "Soma, you don't want go to hell." And he held Soma's hands in the prayer position until Tony sat by Soma and took Soma's hands in his, checking his pulse.

Tony watched. Soma's breathing became labored, and his grunting sounds became fainter. Tony tried to find his pulse, anxiously looking at the door. The doctor arrived and the crowd moved aside to allow him to reach the bed. Immediately, the doctor asked everyone, including the deacon, to wait outside. Then he checked Soma's pulse and put his stethoscope on his chest.

It was too late.

Soma's eyes rolled in his head and he uttered his final words: "Hey Ram!"

Soma's dead body lay on the floor of the dispensary at Seva Sadan and Balu sent someone to tell Malati, Soma's wife. Shortly she came. Her eyes were swollen and her oily hair had come loose from her bun and fell across her shoulders. Kumkum, the symbol of a married woman, was smeared all over her forehead. The women in the neighborhood had wiped it away the moment the news of her husband's death was given to her. She was holding her *palloo* over her mouth to muffle her whimpers and she stopped near Balu. "See what you have done to him?" she cried.

When she looked at Soma's dead body, she hissed at Balu like a wounded snake, "Are you happy now? All those Khr-isti-en brothers of yours taught him to drive a scooter. He was slow for that sort of a thing and you put him on the motorcycle?" She stood over the body, holding the *palloo* between her chattering teeth, tears falling down on her dead husband.

Turning again to Balu, then looking at Tony, she shouted, "You, you are all mad. You killed him. You talked him into riding that scooter. Do you think he was that smart?"

No one answered or tried to console her. They all stood, mute. As she sniffled, mumbling, "You killed him... killed him..." Balu waved his hands in the air and denied the painful accusations. He walked a few feet away from her. Soma's daughter came near and looking at her dead father; she rubbed her face on her mother's shoulder, crying out loud. Patting her daughter with one hand, she thumped her forehead with the other and said, "Hey! God! What is going to happen to me now? They killed my keeper." She sobbed violently and some of the other women hastened in and started crying loudly.

A few minutes later her daughter shook her mother, then gave her a brass container of water. Wiping her tears, the mother took the pot. Seeing the closed container of water, Balu shot forward. He grabbed the pot and said, "My brother was a Christian, and he doesn't need this."

"I have to do this..." Malati cried.

The daughter hugged her mother from behind and they all struggled over the container. The three of them jerked back and forth and all of sudden the lid fell and the holy water from the Ganges started spilling onto Soma's body. Wrestling with the water pot, Soma's wife pushed it towards her husband's head, emptying it onto his face.

Tony and Father John didn't know what was happening and all the other Christian men stood around, watching. No one helped Balu either. Seeing the water running over Soma's mouth, streaking the blood, Malati let go of the container and fell crying to the floor. Her daughter sat beside her. Dropping her head between her knees, she rocked.

The men left the room. The deacon and Father John retreated to their rooms.

As the women were ready to leave, Malati told Tony and Balu that she was told that Soma's last words were, "Hey, Ram!" That proved that at heart he hadn't become a Khr-isti-en or anything like that. Now this water from the Ganges had made him holy again and she would like to keep his body here until their eldest son, Ravi, came home.

Balu and Tony stayed, waiting for Ravi to arrive. All night long, Balu told stories of Soma and Malati to Tony. He told him that Soma was very fond of his wife. Theirs had not been the traditional, arranged marriage, as they had met at the railway station where Soma worked as a ticket conductor. Because of Balu's influence, and the affluence he had gained as a result of owning a scooter renting business, Soma had turned to Christianity.

Then, after listening to Bible stories, Soma would go home and try to convert his wife by telling her how Yeshu had died for the sake of poor people and how she should take Yeshu in her heart. He didn't care for these Hindu gods anymore. Over and over again he would tell her that Hindu gods didn't exist. If they did they would have done something for the poor people in India. What kind of gods were these? Didn't they see the way people lived in India? They were unkind, so why should she pray to them?

She would say that she didn't understand any of these things. The only thing she knew was that God was not unkind. She would tell him what a Hindu priest had taught her to say: God wanted her to be Hindu and that was why she was born there. If she had been born in England or America, perhaps she would have prayed to Yeshu. She had told Soma that the gallery of Hindu gods blessed her home, and that he should leave her and their children alone and not try to convert them.

But Soma would ignore her point of view and reply, "Yeshu is the only true God. So, therefore, your god is nothing but a myth."

"Who knows the truth?" she used to ask, to which Balu had no answer.

Tony knew that Balu made fun of Soma for listening to his wife. Balu had beat his wife up until she became Christian. Then she had run away from him and since then Balu had lived a lonely life, finding a new prostitute every week.

Now Balu started to confess to Tony that at times he had interfered too much in Soma's life and now for some reason he felt guilty. Tony responded dryly, "You meant well. I know."

Tony and Balu both fell asleep in their chairs, wondering what Soma's son would do. They were awakened around six in the morning when Ravi, a boy of seventeen, arrived. A few men held him by the shoulder as he walked in the room. The white sheet covered the body from face to toe and was bloodstained. The few ice slabs that had been placed near it had already melted. The moment Ravi realized that the body lying on the floor was his father, he fell to his knees, and most of the men accompanying him started to choke. He hugged his father. Balu pulled at him and Ravi rolled his own head on the ground. He wailed out a screeching cry. Balu, sitting on the floor, held him tight in his arms, and Ravi sobbed in his uncle's embrace.

"I hardly am a man," he started mumbling, "and how can he leave like this? How can he leave us? What will happen to us?" Holding his head in his hands, he said, "Who will marry my sister, a Christian or Hindu? I don't know who will marry her," he sobbed. "God, what do you want me to do? I can't take care of them."

He freed himself from Balu's embrace and fell on the floor, letting out a louder cry. Balu held him again, saying, "I am here."

Ravi shook his head, denying his offer. "My mother and you..." he cried.

Tears filled Tony's eyes. He felt the boy was lucky to have had his father for seventeen years of his life; he himself had never known what having a father felt like. A moment later he felt guilty about thinking of his own pain in the present situation. He stood up and, putting his arms around the boy, he helped him to get up.

The clock in the hall struck seven, reminding Tony that he needed to report to the Father as per their schedule. As he went inside, he felt a strange emotion fluttering in his heart, as if he wanted immediately to get away from everyone and everything and spend his life someplace where he wouldn't have to deal with painful situations. But pushing these feelings aside, he knocked on the door.

There was no answer, so Tony quietly opened the door. There was no one in the room; the bed was made and the Father and deacon had left. On the bed was a letter addressed to Tony.

Dear Tony,

I had come this far to own up to something I am not proud of. When I was at the rectory, many of us who studied there didn't think we would make it as clergymen. However, I knew I was solid in my commitment, but taking the vows of celibacy was something different. Many days and nights I spent talking with the other men about the vows we would be taking, and many students confided in me that they were not interested in women. Others said they had lost their girlfriends and would never be able to love someone else. They had joined the Church on the rebound. For me, I felt true to my commitment to the Church and God and believed I would be the best priest they ever had. But when I talked about my commitment, some of the men challenged me in 'testing my temptations'.

I studied at the rectory in your hometown and I don't know if you remember, but I am the one who visited your sister. The fellow students at the rectory set Sharon up with me. ...Sharon was beautiful and sweet. Many a time I was afraid that I was falling in love with her but I assure you I never crossed my boundaries. Only I never knew how much my friendship also meant to her. I deceived her and I have felt terribly guilty since her suicide.

Tony stopped reading and ran out of the house, carrying the letter. He was shaking. He ran past the gate and looked in vain for Father John. He looked down at the letter and read again, *I am the one who visited your sister.* What does he mean? How could he? Again his eyes searched for Father John, across the street, beyond the river. A peon came rushing to him and Tony asked if he had seen Father John. The peon shook his head and replied that

Father John and the deacon had requested him to bring them a rickshaw by four in the morning because they wanted to catch the five o'clock train. With Soma's death, they felt it would be better if they left early. Tony listened, still looking around, his hand that held the letter trembling.

"Sahib, is anything wrong?" the peon asked, "I haven't seen you like this."

Trying not to let the whimper out of his mouth, Tony chewed his lips and looked away. He walked away, glancing at the letter, waving his hand to the peon, telling him not to worry.

He ran up the steps and dashed into his room. He sat on the bed and dug his face into a pillow and sobbed. "Oh God, after all these years! Why? My poor... sister..." he cried.

Someone knocked on his door. He looked up and, taking a deep breath, asked whoever it was to give him some time and send someone to get a priest from the church.

The letter scrunched in his hands and the words written in Father's John's beautiful script crinkled and changed their shapes.

He sat up on the bed and straightened the folds from the letter. While smoothing the folds of the letter, the deadened memories of young John's face came alive. John – John, yes, Sharon was waiting for John, her friend John. Not yet Father John, he had disappeared from the rectory right after Sharon's death. But the vague memory Tony conjured up didn't match the Father's face at all.

He heaved. After all this time, all those memories gathering in his head were as fresh as if it was yesterday. He placed his head in his hands, whimpering. Someone walked past his room and he held his breath.

He continued to read.

All these years the memory of my last visit to your home has been haunting me. I told Sharon that day that I was leaving next day and had no intentions of coming back. She should forget me and marry someone who was more worthy of her, but...

Finally, I have come here to confess to all those involved in her tragedy.

He'd got a nerve, becoming a Father. How could he cheat my family out of our happiness? All those years of sadness... Tony couldn't find any words to express his feelings of reproach.

Can I ask for your forgiveness? He read, and re-read. "Can I ask..." How could he even think of such a thing?.

No. He shook his head, no... no way. How could he forgive?

Tony's hand sank down upon the mattress, and when he looked up, the entire room whirled around him. Tears fell from his eyes as he thought of that horrible afternoon, Sharon lying on the floor, bleeding, and how he felt when he couldn't save her! Now the anger exploded in his head. He had been betrayed by this Father John, when all his life he had suffered from the feeling that he had betrayed his mother in keeping Sharon's secret. His fingers sank deep into his palm as he clenched his fist. His chest heaved in pain. It had been so long... so much suffering.

He felt alone. Left behind.

No one would understand his pain. As he fell to his knees, holding on to the edge of the bed, he asked, "Was that the only way he could 'test his temptations'? God, what kind of a man is he?" he whimpered. He sat for a few minutes, letting the tears fall from his eyes.

Then he brought the letter down on the floor and, resting his head on the edge of the bed, he read the last few lines.

As for you, you are doing the right thing. You are correcting your sin. I wish you and Maya a long and happy married life.

I know what you would like to know from me, but Tony, I don't have the answer for you. I never questioned anything, maybe because I never felt the need. Our Lord is in my heart and I can't think of anything else.

I admire your work and patience to deal with what is at hand. All night long I watched and listened to what was happening here. I hope you find the answers in love of our God.

I truly beg you for your forgiveness.

Take care. God, bless you!
Father John

The letter was crumpled and wet from his tears. Father John

wanted to be forgiven? How could he ask such a thing? Now, after all those years he hadn't come for me, and now he had come to get the guilt off his chest.

But why should Tony have to forgive him?

Father John didn't even think he was in the wrong; he claimed it was Sharon who had misunderstood him. But it wasn't only Sharon. Tony had felt, even though he was only seven, that the two of them were in love.

Sharon died for this? She was sacrificed as a test of his temptations? Tony sighed. There were many ways, many things he could have tried, but to lure my sister into an affair that killed her? He paced the tiny room, thinking, Father John too was young then, like I am now, Tony reasoned; perhaps he was driven by his desire to serve Jesus. It was an honorable wish, but Tony couldn't find forgiveness in his heart. Aren't there other ways of serving Him?

Sharon should have talked to someone. Their mother would have helped her forget about John. But then Tony shook his head – she wouldn't have helped. His mother would have blamed Sharon for seducing John. She had high regard for those involved in the work of the Church.

Now, he too was involved in the great work of Jesus.

But would he ever be able to forgive the man who killed his sister, and, for many years, his wish to leave? Father John was asking for something that was impossible. "I am a missionary, not a saint!" Tony said out loud.

But, poor Sharon! An innocent victim, a casualty of the Father's "testing of temptations".

Someone again knocked on his door. It sounded urgent this time. "In a minute," he answered.

★ ★ ★

Around nine o'clock in the morning the men started gathering for the funeral. Some were building a stretcher out of bamboo and wood sticks for Soma's body. They tied and pieced them together in a perfect ladder fashion, with extended ends to carry on their shoulders. Balu stayed away from Ravi, who was sitting in a corner of the verandah, crying. A Hindu priest arrived to perform the Hindu last rites, asking Balu if he planned to carry the body back home. If not, Soma's wife had asked him to come and do the Hindu rituals, so Soma's soul could depart in peace.

Tony stood with Balu, watching the priest. Tony felt curious about him: his ash-smudged forehead, his shaven head with the little tail in the back, and clean face. Balu whispered to Tony that he wanted the priest to do what was needed so his brother could rest in peace. Tony looked at him, but could think of nothing comforting to say.

Balu glanced at the gathered men, some Hindu and some Christian, and when the priest asked again if he wanted the Hindu rituals, he replied, "Why do you ask such a question when you know my brother wasn't a Hindu. You can go home."

Hearing that, Ravi angrily shot back, "Balukaka, let him do whatever my mother wants done."

"You stay out of this. You don't know a thing about this."

"I want to do what my mother wants us to do," Ravi said firmly.

His relatives joined in support of Ravi. "*Han han...* that's right, Soma was born Hindu."

"*Na... na* you have no choice over your birth..." said someone else and the discussion began.

One person walked up to the dead body and declared loudly, "He, he chose to be a Christian... bury him..."

"No!" Ravi shouted.

"Son, he turned Christian," a man said, patting Ravi's shoulder, "burying him would be the right thing to do."

"Bury him..." others joined in.

An older man, though, who struggled as he walked, gestured, *no, no,* with one hand and said, "Wife has the right, what she wants..."

Now they all crowded near the old man, but someone from the back mumbled, "What do women know...?" A few laughed at this.

There were still more comments.

"His life became a hell after he changed..."

"His whole family suffered..."

"He didn't know what he was getting into when he became a Christian…"

"He is dead…" someone reminded them.

A man said, "Christian or Hindu, he was a good man…"

"He betrayed every god," one commented.

"He is doomed for a hell… if you cremate him… remember he was a Christian… for his…"

Ravi started shaking, squeezing his elbows against his stomach. The older man held him and started chanting, "*Hare Ram, Hare Ram*," and coaxed him to chant. "*Hare Ram… Hare Ram*," he whispered which helped to quiet Ravi. A few Hindu men joined in and chorused, "*Hare Ram… Hare Ram*…"

"Stop it. This isn't your temple," a Christian friend screamed.

"*Hare Ram… Hare Ram*…" the men sang loudly. Ravi started sobbing hysterically.

"Bury him…" Balu announced.

"No, that's not what his son wants."

"You are all fools," said an old relative. "This way he will become a ghost…"

"*Han… han*… Ghost… *Bhut*… do what is right or I am leaving this place…"

"I am too… cremate him if you like… if you want to see him haunting you as a ghost…"

The words "bury, cremate, ghost – *bhut*" flew from their mouths and hung in the air. The men suspended their thoughts as the fear of unknown gripped their hearts.

No one agreed or knew what was right or wrong in the situation. Tony didn't know either. Soma was Christian but he died saying something else. So?

He waited for a Christian priest to arrive.

But who would be right? Was it even a matter of right or wrong? Did the person really turn into a ghost and come back because the body they inhabited had not been destroyed properly?

Malati's relatives ignored Balu, and asked Ravi to help from the right side of the stretcher. They told Balu they were taking the body home for his wife to decide.

They tied the body on a stretcher. The priest threw flowers and powders with offerings of rice for his last safe journey to his home. Balu ran to the stretcher. Pushing the priest aside, he brushed off all the flowers and held the garland in his hand.

"He is my brother," he cried. "Oh, Soma... you can't do this to him." But they picked up the stretcher and chorused, *"Hare Ram, jai jai Ram."*

Balu took the cross that hung around his neck and dropped it on the sheet. Ravi tried to remove it from the sheet but the Hindu priest patted Ravi's shoulders and placed the cross along with the flower garlands and asked Balu to hold the front end of the stretcher. The Hindu men chorused again, *"Hare Ram, jai jai, Ram..."* Balu and other Christians sang, *"Jai Yeshu, jai..."*

Tony stood, wondering whether to join the funeral procession of a man whose lifeless body was now claimed by others who believed their actions would help him either to reach heaven, turn him into a ghost or reincarnate to another life...

Part Six

Chapter Fifteen

What would it be, girl or boy, and where would it sleep? Of course it would sleep in their room at Seva Sadan, but which corner? Maya was sitting in her windowless room, planning the future. Near a window would be nice, babies like to stare at the color green – she had heard her mother say that when her younger siblings were born. She had helped her mother with her deliveries and now she thought that would come in useful. It would have been nice, though, if her mother had been there to help her. Mothers are better as grandmothers, her grandmother used to say. But, not wanting to dwell on the past, she put her mind to the list of shopping items and left the hostel.

After buying some wool and pieces of cloth and threads, and picturing the tiny bonnet and bib, and booties, she daydreamed about making many color combinations for her baby's clothes. She thought of cute bows and dainty trims or a little contrast lace. But while shopping, she missed having her mother with her, and the more she missed her, the more she became determined to give her baby a grand welcoming. She shopped until the shops began to close, somewhat earlier than their usual times because of the riots.

When she returned to the hostel, she noticed a trail of scattered petals, kumkum, and ashes of incense stretching from her door to the hallway. Who could have done that? she wondered. A kitten? The one that always licked the milk bowl by her temple? Shaking her head, she tried to turn the key in the rusty lock, but it hung open. Had she left without locking it? She flicked a light switch on and was stunned at the condition of her room.

A box she had used for the temple had been trampled. The clay statues of deities had fallen and were in pieces on the floor. And the Lord Shiva's Lingam, made out of stone which couldn't be easily broken, were missing.

For the last few days her little temple had given her the

assurance that things would be normal again. The hope of adding Yeshu to her temple had helped her pass one day at a time. Now all that had been shattered. Who had done this cruel thing? she wondered, putting the bag of shopping away. Could it be Sister Tiru? Or the older girls, who hated her? It couldn't be Sister Rosa.

She silently picked up the pieces of the statues: a hand – the blessing hand of Lord Rama. A face – the kind face of Goddess Laxmi. Though broken, all those forms still gave her some strength. She put all the broken pieces in a bowl, then touched her forehead in front of the broken altar, but no prayer came to her mind. She was angry and vengeful. "I will find out who did this and why," she said out loud. That evening she didn't attend the prayer meeting and went to sleep without talking to anyone.

Next day, she walked out of her room and out of the building, without signing herself out, which was what she was required to do.

Once out of the hostel she really didn't know where to go. Knowing Tony would be busy or wouldn't be around, she hailed a rickshaw, thought of going to Chitra's but gave the driver the address of Father Paul's church.

On the way she noticed people were rallying against the Kashmir war. For the first time, relying upon the Muslim majority of the region and encouraged by a public leader, Pakistan had made a surprise attack on the area and was taking over the territory that was officially under the Indian government. This had become a cause for jubilation for the Muslims and anger for the Hindus all across India.

At midnight, in a town square of a city, the Muslims had slaughtered a cow that belonged to a Hindu. The Hindus worshipped the cow as the embodiment of earth, the giver of life. It was sacred. The act of butchering a cow infuriated the Hindus and, as a consequence, the anger over the Muslims' actions were growing in every part of the country.

Peace rallies crowded the streets with photos of Gandhi, but the sentiment was far from uniform. Other groups screamed bloody murder for Muslims or for Hindus. Police jeeps zoomed around the streets, and the patrols on every street corner were increased. Every temple and mosque was guarded around the clock, while devotees went in and out quickly. People rushed to bazaars to buy household supplies, yet the bazaars appeared nearly empty as the main entrances were closed, so that in the event of a riot the businesses could shut down at once. The atmosphere was tense, and since these scenes had been going on now for several weeks, Maya realized it was only a matter of time until the simmering conflict burst into flames.

Maya worried for her family. She knew how her father hated the fighting between Hindus and Muslims. Her father had many Muslim friends with whom he had happily shared and exchanged social and cultural events. But now, judging from the way people were behaving, and asking herself if her parents would have ever accepted Tony, she wondered if religious tolerance was only an idea, a philosophy to read about, but not something that could ever last long in practice.

Her rickshaw passed a Muslim neighborhood, then, slowing down, it approached and stopped at the Christian school and church premises.

The two-story yellow school building was as since the children had been allowed to go home early because of the fear of impending riots. The other side of the school was the church building, and the two buildings were connected by a breezeway. The gatekeeper told Maya that she would find Father Paul in his office. Inside the school compound everything was peaceful, untouched by the country's uproar, like a little Buddha in the midst of chaos.

The peon who sat idly outside Father Paul's office asked Maya to sit on the bench outside of his office while he went looking for Father Paul. Maya sat there, wondering what she should tell the Father. Should she talk about her destroyed temple? And Sister Tiru's behavior towards all the girls? Or class discussions that didn't answer her questions? Or why conversion was necessary for her to marry Tony? Why the mission…

Then she wished she wasn't there to complain about the Christian hostel or the purpose of the mission. Asking these questions was useless. Closing her eyes, she rested her head on the wall.

She opened her eyes when she heard Father Paul saying, "Maya? What brings you here in the middle of this unpredictable afternoon? Come. Come. You look tired. I'm glad you finally came by yourself to visit me." He instructed the peon to bring two cups of tea.

Maya followed him into his office. He had seated himself at his desk and gestured for her to sit across from him. "So," he said, "I can tell, you are here to talk about something. Tell me, what's on your mind?"

"Nothing really. I shouldn't be bothering you."

"Maya, give me a chance, I can tell something is on your mind. I would like to help."

"It is just that I am confused. And I am angry."

"Why are you confused? And at whom are you angry, Maya?"

She gazed at him, unsure of how to tell him what was on her mind.

"Maya, I assure you, our conversation will stay in this room."

"The sisters... I am angry at the sisters at the hostel," she blurted out, then waited. Father Paul didn't respond and she continued, "They... they... I don't know who... but someone demolished my temple in my room."

"Really?" he said, sounding confused.

"Would you approve of that, Father?" she asked, looking at him intently.

"It really is a difficult situation, Maya." He leaned back in his chair.

"Can you understand my problem, Father?" she asked, eager to receive some help.

"I do. However, Maya, you cannot live in their house and break their rules."

"Rules? What rules? And how can there be such rules in India?" Maya questioned, leaning forward.

Father Paul raised his eyebrows but did not answer.

"Really, the sisters never told me not to do *pooja* in my room. Besides, I did attend every prayer meeting."

"That's good."

"Yes, Father, I really did and I am trying to learn the Bible. I know Tony wants me to. The sisters don't believe that I am trying to be a Christian, but believe me, I am trying. Only, until now, I did not know what it meant to be Christian. But now I know, and since I know that I am not supposed to accept any other religion as a true religion, I can't become a Christian. How can they expect me to think that my mother and father, my grandparents, my uncles... the whole society here is based on false principles? I can't, I can't take this, not anymore."

"No – you shouldn't," he said, not knowing what to say. "But give yourself some time."

"But you know I don't have time." She looked down, ashamed of having to be in her situation. She didn't want her baby to be born without his father's name. "You know no one will be more in a need of baptism than me. But, on the other hand, what is the sense of going ahead with the baptism if you don't accept the very principle it wants you to believe? I cannot take Christ in my heart as the only God and Savior. I have tried to believe, I know the verse by heart, 'I am the way, the truth, and the life. No one can come to the Father except through me.'" She almost sounded as if she was mimicking the sisters. She looked at Father Paul but he was staring out of the window.

When he turned, she continued, "When I have understood that God is one, and as the one consciousness He is worshipped in many different forms, then how can I believe that I will see God only through Yeshu? The more they tell me to forget my understanding of God, the more it becomes clear to me that it isn't that easy." Her voice rose, then cracked. She paused and took a deep breath. This was useless, she thought. How did she expect Father Paul to understand her ways of thinking?

Father Paul took the pitcher that was behind his desk and poured water into a glass. Maya wiped her face with a handkerchief. Slowly she sipped the water, avoiding looking at the Father, who she knew was looking at her.

She wished Tony was around and she was visiting him instead. This was hard. She and the Father hardly knew each other.

"Maya, are you feeling okay? Do you need to rest?" Father Paul asked.

She shook her head. "What... what can I do, Father? Tell me!" There was severity in her voice. She looked at the Father, and he nodded. Maya said, "Tell me. I am desperate."

She rested her forehead on her hand. Father Paul arose from his chair and paced around his tiny office. She had an urge to get up and leave. She felt she had hurt enough people, and Father had been so kind that she didn't want to cause friction between them. She looked up, her baby moved around in her belly and she sighed. She had to get to the bottom of her problem. She also knew that the baby would maybe be born before its time. She wanted the baby to have his father!

For a few minutes it was quiet in the room. The peon tapped on the door and brought the tea tray in. Wiping her face, Maya stared outside blankly.

Passing a cup of tea to her, Father Paul said, "Maya, listen to me carefully. I consider this conversation as a confession. God is kind. He will forgive you."

"I don't understand, Father."

"I am saying that baptism is next Sunday. Just go on with it. You have confessed to me."

"Confessed? What does that mean, Father?"

"Say, you have admitted your weakness and pleaded for God's forgiveness. Now you can be free to move on."

"If you confess, God forgives," she repeated, trying to understand what was being said. So the Christians believe that God forgives even if one didn't believe in the Christian faith. That was not what she had understood. "Father, are you telling me God forgives even if I don't believe in the Christian faith?"

Father Paul rubbed his fingers against the wooden arms of his chair. But he said nothing.

After waiting a few moments for his answer, she said, "You are kind, Father. I hate to be in this position. But how can I forgive myself just by admitting or confessing? How could I live with myself? It won't relieve me of the pain that would come from being unfaithful to Tony and his faith. Confessing to you won't change the fact that I cannot be a true Christian."

"Maya, be kind to yourself. Now I know how you feel about it and we will work at it. We will pray for you."

"God knows I need all the prayers I can get. But Father, I would like to know if there is any way you could accept me as I am."

"Of course we like you, Maya."

"I meant as a Hindu? Will you accept me as a Hindu. I can't forget that I am a Hindu."

Again it was quiet in the room. She stared at the floor then looked at her wristwatch as Father Paul cleared his throat. "I like your honesty, Maya. I have seen people becoming Christians for the wrong reasons, and without any qualms. It's good you know what it means to be a Christian." He paused, then, taking a deep breath, he said, "But, for all practical purposes, you can't afford to stay Hindu. Can you?"

He looked at her and she nodded, "Not if Tony wouldn't marry me without being a Christian."

"Tony is a nice young man, but he can't accept being married to a Hindu girl. He is a missionary, Maya. He has chosen missionary work by his conviction. He has to follow the path of conversion. By no means is he a ruthless missionary but he is a missionary. He has to comply with the faith of the mission. If you don't convert, you will make his position very difficult, Maya."

"I know, Father."

"Then, why not go with baptism as planned next Sunday?" he asked.

She nodded, then tried to smile. For a few moments they sat, engrossed in their thoughts, sipping tea. Slowly looking up, she asked, "Father, can I ask you one thing?"

"Sure. What is it?"

"Do you really think Jesus is the only Son of God?"

"No – I mean, why do you ask me such a question?"

"I am sorry, Father. I really would like to know what you think. I'm sorry if I asked you the wrong question."

"The question is not about it being wrong, but doubting everything doesn't make our life easier either." Father Paul placed his hands behind his neck and looked up at the ceiling. He appeared about to say something more when the peon knocked on the door.

Without waiting for permission, the peon hurriedly came into the office and said, "*Tai*, the rickshaw-wala is afraid of the riots. He is saying…" He hesitated, then continued. "In your condition he does not want you to be caught in the middle of the riots. If you are ready, he will take you back. Otherwise he is leaving."

Father Paul stood up hastily. "I think he is right. You better get going. You never know what will happen tonight."

Maya walked slowly to the door. Father Paul hurried out the door and called the peon back to ask him to accompany Maya to the hostel.

As she got in the rickshaw, Father Paul said, "Good luck then, Maya. I will see you on Sunday."

"Let's hope things calm down," she said, and waved goodbye.

When they reached the main road, it was after six o'clock. The streets were deserted and the bazaars abandoned. The police patrol was tight. A policeman stopped Maya's rickshaw and asked the driver where they were going and why they were in this part of the town. The peon jumped out of the rickshaw and told the policeman he was only going to drop Maya 'at her place. The policeman noticed her pregnant condition and, tapping his baton on the handle of the rickshaw, told them to hurry home.

They turned into a back alley, and they hadn't gone far when they heard the commotion of a mob running past them. The mob knocked a policeman down to the ground. Everyone in the mob carried something in their arms and threw it when they came closer to the mosque and to Muslim shops. Flames burst out, whipping the air. The peon again jumped out from the rickshaw and helped the driver to push it, with Maya inside, to the opposite street. Another mob emerged from this alley and ran past them to join the people on the main street. At a corner of the street, the rickshaw driver, the peon and Maya stood, stranded but unhurt, watching the people running about wanting to kill one another. An army truck drove up in the street ahead of Maya and her companions. Guards emerged with batons drawn and began running in the direction of the mob.

Wearily, the peon and rickshaw driver pushed the rickshaw, looking for a safe way out. They passed a few alleys quietly before coming to a group of people who had covered their faces and heads with cloths. This group demanded that they hand the rickshaw over to them. The rickshaw driver was ready to run but the peon pulled his cross out and, kissing it, told the people that they were Christian, and needed to get this woman to the hospital. The mob was not interested in hurting Christians. Hurriedly, the mob leader told them that if they went the back routes, they would see the Christian house along the river where the woman might get medical help.

Maya was relieved to hear that they meant Seva Sadan.

Chapter Sixteen

When Maya's rickshaw pulled up at Seva Sadan, Tony was at the dispensary making his notes about the few patients he had seen. He heard Maya's voice and hurried outside.

"Maya, what are you doing here?" Seeing her, he smiled. "Is everything all right?" His eyes widened. The creases on his forehead showed his worries but the smile peeking from his lips gave away how happy he was by her sudden appearance.

This type of reaction on his part always amused her. It told her he cared for her, very much. Truly, she thought, love can break many barriers. With that thought, at once, she was at ease and it released her from the anxiety she had endured for the last few days. "Guess what happened?" she said, sounding as adventurous as when she had come during the rainstorm.

"I couldn't." Looking at her now really big bulging belly, he said worriedly, "I hope you weren't caught in the middle of the riots."

"You guessed it right. That's exactly what happened. I had gone to see Father Paul…"

"That's great, you went to see Father Paul – but after all that time, why today?"

"That's a long story. But when we got out of that area the mob we came across wanted this rickshaw driver's rickshaw, but…" Excitedly, she told him how she had ended up there.

"Thank God you're all right," said Tony. He took a deep breath. "And you're laughing. Soon you're going to be a mother, sweetheart."

She blushed, then laughed again, and seeing her so jubilant, he too relaxed. He went out to pay the rickshaw driver. The driver and peon left.

When he came in, she was in the kitchen, looking for something to eat. He reached out and held her in his arms, and she wrapped her arms around him. Kissing her, he whispered, "I missed you."

"I missed you... more..." They kissed again, whispering, "Miss you, miss you," again and again.

"I am so glad you had to come here, Maya," he said, while setting the table in the adjoining room. "I've been missing you so much I had dreams of kidnapping you."

"Kidnapping from whom?" she asked. "The sisters? They would be happy to see me go." After the words slipped out of her mouth, she waited in the kitchen with some apprehension.

But he was still enjoying the dream of kidnapping her, and she was relieved to see the smile on his face when he came back into the kitchen and said, "But I couldn't decide whether to kidnap you on a rickshaw or on a bicycle." They both laughed.

After dinner they sat in the verandah. Here the night was untouched by the riots and the river was calm. The breeze fondled the trees, lingering leisurely on the long fronds of the coconut trees. The rustling of the leaves and the rhythmic sound of water ripples were soothing under the star-studded skies. A lonely night bird was cooing while searching for his mate.

As she felt Tony's love, Maya's mind was refreshed, restoring her sense of being wanted. She didn't think it right to mention her problems at the hostel, or the process of conversion that she would now be going through in a matter of a few days. She also didn't want to talk about the wedding, which would be in church. She had no idea what it would entail. The sisters would have told her, but...

He wrapped his arms around her and showed her some stars in the sky. She showed him the Saptarshi, the Big Dipper, and told him that on the first night of the wedding the husband shows the star of Arundhati to his new bride. She pointed at the fourth star, Vashistha, and said the star of Arundhati is right around or over the fourth star of the Dipper. The bride and groom see it together because the marriage between the sage Vashistha and Arundhati is considered the holiest. It began with the beginning of the creation and would last till the end of it, so they were given their place in these celestial forms.

"That's a beautiful story," he said. "When I sat alone late at night on the verandah, these star-studded skies made me miss you even more. I always tried to remember the Hindi songs you used to translate for me. Can you sing one for me?"

"Now?"

"Why not?"

"It's been a while since I've enjoyed romantic feelings from the songs, but I will try." She laughed, reminding him of her old light-heartedness. She cleared her throat and whispered the tune and then translated it:

"There may not be a moon or star left around,
But I will remain yours, forever and ever.
If for any reason I have to be separated from you,
Don't think I don't love you,
Wherever I may be, but I will remain yours, forever and ever."

"Wow! I like that. But why are love songs mainly about separation and longing? That's over for us. Teach me how to say, I will remain yours, forever and ever. Like those stars in love."

For a few minutes she taught him the Hindi song and they laughed as he tried to speak the unfamiliar words.

"Learning a new language is fun, especially the way you teach. It wasn't fun when I was trying to learn it in the U.S. But everything seems fun now, because..." Suddenly his voice became louder, "Because, now everyone knows *I love you*, Maya."

She giggled.

"Love has no boundaries. It's free." Excitedly, he continued, "But people think love is binding. Even in India when someone falls in love I hear this expression, *Bandh gaya*. To them, love is bondage. Doesn't the word 'bondage' have a negative connotation? I feel we are bonded, but it has freed me from my loneliness, and given me strength and inner freedom." He laughed, then asked, "Does that make sense?"

She chuckled, "Yes..."

"I feel free because I am happy or I am happy so I feel free, I don't know. I have never been so happy in my life before, Maya. Holding your hands, I would like to tell the world..." He held her hand up in the air, saying, "I love Maya! I love Maya!" His voice grew louder and echoed in the surroundings.

"Shush, Tony." She pressed his hand, bringing it down.

Lowering his voice, he said, "Don't stop me, Maya, I want you to know how happy I am." His shy face gleamed with new lines of passion.

"I know, I know. I too am happy, but…" she said, "I hope we respect each other's wishes and are honest with each other so that we can be happy forever."

"We will, Maya, I have no doubts. Your wish is my command."

Their hands intertwined, and they moved back, resting their backs on the wall. Then he kissed her hand. He held her in his arms, and she leaned against his shoulder, putting her hand on her belly.

"I have a feeling it is a boy," she said.

"Really? Can I touch?"

"Of course." She held his hand on her moving belly. The baby jerked inside and Tony laughed. Maya tried to laugh also but she felt a throbbing pain. "Tony, have you thought of a name for our baby?"

"Sure. Many different ones."

"*Hn?*" Now facing him, she asked eagerly, "What are the names? Aren't you going to tell me?"

He looked at her mischievously but did not respond.

"Tell me. Tell me, *ne*, Tony."

Enjoying her zeal, Tony said coolly, "I thought I would surprise you."

"You can't do that." Her eyes sparkled like dazzling black pearls in the dim lamplight. Lost in their magic, he smiled as she continued, "Besides, here, we name the baby on the twelfth day after the baby's birth, and I can't wait that long."

"Good! But what do people call the baby for twelve days?"

"*Chendu, Fendu,* all the names of love." She laughed. "But tell me, tell me now, what would you like to name him? Or her? Then I will tell you what are my picks…"

Tony fell silent, thinking about all the baptisms he had attended at church and the parents who had fussed with their babies. How would he feel if his baby were not baptized? He shuddered. My baby won't be baptized: that… that was unheard of. But Maya too was never baptized. And he had concluded that one day she would be baptized and they would be a Christian family. He also remembered his childhood years when he didn't believe in God, and how angry he was at everyone. And how in his teenage years he felt life had no meaning and how he was always sad.

But all that had changed as he had taken a liking to Father Carlos and then to Christian teachings. It had given him hope that he would meet his sister Sharon in heaven. Without that hope, perhaps, he never would have become a missionary. He wondered what kind of life his child would lead when eventually they settled back in the U.S.

In his own mental debate between his love and faith he still feared his life becoming a life without faith, and now he doubly feared for his child.

The baby should be baptized, if nothing else.

Now he knew, no matter what he had thought, he couldn't give up his faith. And most important he wanted the same for his child. He or she couldn't be raised without a faith, his faith.

Seeing his sudden repose, Maya too became serious, holding his face in her hands and turning it towards hers. "Tony, we will name the baby whatever name you want."

"It's not whatever I want, Maya, we need to think of lots of other things for the baby also," he said, and looked away. He was hesitant to share what was on his mind.

"You know," she said, looking intently at Tony, who still looked distant, "I went to see Father Paul today, there..." She wanted to be very careful in how she told him about her decision.

"Yes, but you didn't tell me what you talked about," he said, without looking at her.

"Talked about you," she chided, again not wanting to open up the topic of her baptism. She didn't want to let slip that it would only be for his sake and she still had doubts about the whole thing.

"I'm glad that you found someone to talk to against me." He tried to smile.

"I didn't talk *against* you," she said, tucking the curls from behind her ears into the hairpins. "I talked not against you... but talked about Christian faith..." Noticing the changed expression on his face, she stopped.

"What? About the faith? What did you say to him?" He spoke rather tersely, and she moved away from him a bit.

"You didn't tell him about the sisters?"

She didn't answer.

"Did you talk against them, Maya?"

"Mainly I talked to him against the faith, the Christian faith. I wanted to tell him that if I can't believe that Jesus is the only Son of God—"

"You didn't, Maya! He's a Catholic priest, you didn't tell him that! You telling me all about your thoughts is one thing, but..." His voice was sharp.

"I had to, Tony." She too became a little bolder than usual. "I can't go on pretending what the sisters and others want me to pretend."

"They don't want you pretend anything. They only want you to have faith in Jesus." He stood and walked a few steps away from her.

"And do you have a formula to create that faith?"

"Maya..."

Seeing the sudden change, even in the way he looked at her or called her name, she felt he was looking like her father, at once distant, forgetting his love for her.

Just moments ago he had sung the songs of love as the highest virtue, and now look what had happened, merely because she had spoken against his faith. Or at least, he thought she had. Why can't he be true to his feelings? It angered her. Holding her lip in her teeth, she took a deep breath. "You are all the same. At the hostel the sisters want me to forget that I am a Hindu. You want me to instantly have faith in Jesus and Father Paul wants me to think that since I have confessed I will be forgiven by God. It's all confusing and nothing is clear." She said all this in one breath, her voice wavering at the end.

Ignoring her faltering voice, he replied, "Nothing is clear because you don't want to admit that you don't want to become a Christian. You would rather me go to a temple to get married and live like a Hindu."

"Tony, I never said that and you know it."

"You didn't say it but you implied it, many times."

"So, what's wrong with that? What's wrong if I want you to go to temple? At least I am not asking you to change. Am I?"

"I am asking you to change because you are pregnant and—"

"And you think that because I am pregnant it is only my fault?"

"Not again, Maya, I never said that."

"You don't have to say it. My mother was right when she told me not to protect you, that men only know one thing."

"And now you believe her? I know only one thing? Hmm!" He paused, his voice raised. "I am taking full responsibility for what happened between us. You are the one who left me and your parents deserted you, what kind of people—"

"Tony!" she cried, hiding her face between her hands.

He knew he shouldn't have said that but he didn't know what had come over him and what was making him say these things. Why was he hurting her when all he wanted was to envelop her in his arms and tell her, "Let's get married." Instead, with thoughts of the baby's future, something else was being said. Why? What was bothering him?

He walked away from her, and she ran inside.

He looked across the river. He was angry with himself for saying the things he had just said to her. Standing by the very edge of the verandah, he thought how much he had thought of telling her he was thinking of quitting the mission because the missionaries or the church didn't raise a helping hand unless they knew they could spread their faith. And, of course he hadn't told her about Soma's family; and how he felt that dividing families by converting a man of the house couldn't be an act of kindness. Also, it pained him to think about how the Church encouraged acts of "mass conversion" for those who didn't know a thing about his beloved Lord, Jesus Christ. And yet, he had just realized that he couldn't be without his faith. Then, how did he expect Maya to leave her faith? He knew that was unfair.

His faith was second nature to him. But now he also loved Maya, and though he wanted to give her everything, he couldn't let go when she talked against his faith. It hurt him too much, even though in the past he also had raised many doubts about the activities of the Church. But he felt that his own doubts were a different matter. He had some concerns, but it wasn't as if his faith was under full-scale attack. When she asked, "Do you have a formula to create that faith?" he felt as if she was attacking everything he believed. Everything he had worked for had collapsed before him.

But was she responsible for that? *No.*

He knew his doubts had begun since he had come to India – no, maybe way before he came, he had to admit. The only difference was that she had him face the truth and it wasn't pleasing. Now she was upset and he needed to tell her that he couldn't live without her, he loved her too much. But he didn't love Jesus any less either.

Tears fell from his eyes.

He didn't want to be separated from Him. He would be lost, purposeless. How could he walk away from his mission and live life without purpose? Maya would become the purpose of his life. But would that be enough?

He looked in the direction she had fled. Right by the entrance door on the wall was the photograph of Christ holding a dark-skinned child on his lap. Christ seemed to be staring directly at him. Tony stood up and kneeled before the Lord. "Lord, I love you, I love her," he cried. "Help me, God. Tell me I don't have to choose between you and her."

He stood silent. "I am the light of the world" – the words from the Bible echoed in his ears. "If you follow me, you won't be stumbling through the darkness, because..." he stood up, his feet shaking, "you will have the light that to leads to life."

His face was drawn. He looked at the picture of Jesus again, then resting his head next to the framed picture, he said, "Am I losing Your path and going into the eternal darkness, Lord?" But he feared to look into the eyes of the Lord. He knew the answer, 'If ye forsake Him, He will forsake ye.' Or, 'He that is not with me, is against me.' Could that be true? Could Jesus have abandoned people like that? Tony didn't want to believe that Jesus could have said such a thing. Jesus forgave even those who put him on the cross. He was full of love. He invoked love in people's hearts. Tony had felt His Love, pure love!

He lifted his eyes, and looked at the eyes of the Lord, which were filled with compassion. He still could feel His love. Unconditional love! It loosened the knot in his mind. It freed his heart from the fear of drifting away from Jesus. He felt free to love Him even if it meant not following everything that had been said in His name. Lifting away his eyes from His, he looked outside.

The stars were blinking in the dark skies. Long fronds of co-conut leaves moved with the breeze, and for a moment fireflies flashed specks of light in the dark empty space.

Maya had locked the bedroom door and for a long time he sat staring at the stars and an empty, torn spider's web that was hanging at the edge of the roof.

In other parts of Kulur the night grew darker and the rioters louder. Most people, who weren't active in the riots, sat in their homes, frightened, anxiously listening behind closed doors to the noise outside. At times, everything was quiet. Then, suddenly, there would be the sound of breaking glass and the smell of firebombs. The noise of lathis beating on the ground would become louder and louder only until it crashed against the people. Putting their hands on the ears of their children, people heard shouting and the running of many heavy feet everywhere, sometimes coming closer, terrifying them, and at other times rushing away from their homes, easing their fears.

All through the night, in the back rooms of their homes, peaceful men and women even debated about the existence of God. While pretending to be asleep, children heard the stories from their elders and their prayers to destroy others' way of worshipping God, and under their blankets the children played wars between gods, developing a hatred for the other religion.

Hindus and Muslims who didn't live in their own segregated neighborhoods had quickly vacated their homes. The well-to-do people hired Gurkhas, mountain men from Nepal, as security guards for their homes.

That should have included the Pandit estate. But there were no Gurkhas there. Laxman's daughter was waiting for Laxman to drive Mr. Pandit home from his out of town trip. She paced the patio outside the quarters, feeling worried for them.

Soon, they drove in, and before going into the house, Mr. Pandit asked Laxman to keep an eye on things. So, before going to his quarters, Laxman decided to go out. He took a rag from the trunk of the car to use as headgear to disguise himself if necessary and shoved it in his pocket. Slowly he walked out through the estate gate.

He hid around the corner to see if he could find anyone who would give him information about tonight's activities. If he saw Muslim men, he would greet them with Muslim greetings – "*Shalom alekum!*" But he did not come across many people. As he walked farther, into the low-income neighborhoods, he knocked on the few doors of those he knew, but no one opened their doors. After spending an hour or so without finding a clue about whether riots were brewing, he walked back to the estate. He knew that the Pandit estate was rather secluded and that usually people were afraid of Mr. Pandit, so he thought they might stay away.

After Laxman had had his dinner, his daughter gave him a note that had been given to her by his neighbor, whom he called Firoz-uncle, a Muslim friend of the family. Laxman's family, being in the business of butchers, had always lived in the Muslim neighborhoods, and Firoz-uncle and Laxman's families had been friends for generations.

Laxman felt uneasy and feared for the safety of Firoz-uncle and his family. With some concern, Laxman held the note close to his eyes and read:

Laxman,

The Pandit estate is in the plan. For Allah's sake, move out of the house. God be with your master.

Uncle

Laxman immediately burnt the paper over the oil lamp. He asked his daughter to gather her children and sleep at the back quarter. He said he would lock the door from outside so no one would suspect that anyone was inside. And if they heard sounds of danger they could run out through the back door and hide beyond the old well.

Before going out to see if he could find Firoz-uncle, he went to warn Mr. Pandit. But Mr. Pandit did not take the Muslim threat seriously, telling Laxman that his old butcher buddies were butchering his courage. And he was not afraid of those beef-eating Muslim rascals.

Ignoring Mr. Pandit's remarks, Laxman gathered a group of people, including Mr. Pandit's old employees and waited for the rioters to invade. Every hour Laxman walked the grounds but found no one loitering around the estate. They all sat behind the walls of the courtyard where Mr. Pandit's Grand Impala was parked.

By the river, Rahim, the gang leader, vowed to torture and kill Mr. Pandit for insulting Muslims, particularly Rahim's father. But the rest of the rioters were mainly gathered to burglarize the place, and they waited with their bags. Around two o'clock, when Laxman and others had fallen asleep, Rahim's gang quietly entered from the back entrance. Using signals, they divided themselves into four groups and dispersed around the property. From all sides they came in, pounding on the doors, and the sounds of banging and the breaking of glass windows shook the ground. Behind the bushes, Laxman awoke and sat up.

The Muslim men who were coming towards the courtyard paused behind the car. As a couple of the men raised their rods, the leader of that group shouted, "No, we will drive that out."

"And how are you going to hide this bus?" one questioned, looking at the size of the Impala.

"Who would drive it? And what about petrol? *Na, baba, na.* This would sure get us in trouble."

"You are all cowardly," the leader replied, trying to open the driver's side door.

Right then Laxman and his friends struck at them with clubs. The sudden attack startled the Muslim men, who raised their rods and lathis and started to fight back.

From the other sides of the thicket, Hindu men who had heard the sounds of pounding and breaking hastily ran inside the property. As they came closer they slowed their pace as fear lurked in their hearts. They weren't trained to fight. But they came slowly towards the verandah and as soon as they faced their adversaries in the verandahs and in the courtyards of the estate, they found extra courage and chorused, *"Jai Bajarang Bali ki Jai."*

In the dark night the clubs, cricket bats and iron rods were raised, *thhut... thhut... thhut* echoed the sounds as if it was just a drill, until the wounded started to collapse. The men, old and young, Hindu and Muslim, even those who had been and maybe still were neighbors, who had helped one another out in crises, were now trying to mortally injure members of the other race and religion which had survived through many centuries of wars. The cries of the wounded and the profanities of angry men filled the air. They cursed each other with the holy names of their gods.

Laxman fought with his clubs. He tried to pull at their scarves, wanting to expose their faces. He wanted to make sure he wasn't killing Firoz-uncle or his sons by mistake. In doing that he took a number of blows on his hands, and his fingers started to bleed. His grip on the baton he was holding was beginning to loosen but he wouldn't let go of it. His arms became shaky and then his wrist broke. As the rods hit him in his head, everything seemed vague. The baton fell from his hand. The other men hit him mercilessly on his chest and his hips till he fell to the ground and lay there motionless.

Outnumbered by Muslims, one by one many Hindus fell to the ground and some ran into the thickets, fearing for their lives.

The group of Muslims entered the main part of the house and charged onto the verandah. The polished brass swing trembled and they yanked it from its hook and tossed it in the yard. They shouted loudly, *"Allah ho Akbar."*

Some fought over the brass statues of welcoming ladies, till one of them said the statues were of Hindu women, so they spat on those and tossed them out also. In the dining hall they crashed the etched glass panels and stole all the silver and gold articles – flower vases, photo frames, and tea sets. They tore the curtains and ripped the oil paintings.

They quickly moved to the bedrooms where they took clothes, linens, shoes and jewelry. They took everything they could and damaged what they could not.

Behind the closed doors of his bedroom, Mr. Pandit listened to the sounds of the rioters. Sitting on his bed, he trembled with fear, saliva dripping on his nightshirt. Trying to stop his hands from trembling, he crumpled up the bed sheets with his hands. He looked around for a weapon, but he couldn't get up. He was frozen stiff.

He had never trembled before anyone and he tried to hold himself upright without shaking. There was nothing to fear, he reminded himself that he was a very powerful man. The power of his words had made people tremble.

Now, his words had brought him to his destruction, perhaps his end.

After a few moments, when he didn't hear anyone coming to his bedroom, he relaxed and stopped trembling. He stood for a moment, thinking, Let them take whatever they want. He knew they wouldn't dare enter his room. But just in case they did break in, he tried to think of something that could soothe the rioters. He would offer free legal counsel to their entire Muslim community. He would fight to have more Muslims in the state government. Anything, he thought, anything, to bribe those bastards and to save himself. Later, he knew he would see these penniless trash in court.

His plan to make false offers of help made him feel better and he wiped the sweat off his face. Going under the sheet, trying to lie still, he stared at the ceiling.

But no name of God came to his lips.

In a few minutes he heard someone outside calling Rahim's name. He went stiff again, and at once he knew that none of his survival tricks would work. He scrunched up under the sheet, thinking how to jump from the window and whether he would survive the fall. His heart started to skip beats as he heard banging on the closed doors.

"Open the door. *Ae kutte*! Your end is very near."

Mr. Pandit cowered in terror. He recognized that voice. It was Rahim.

Rahim was laughing loudly, and he continued, "I have been dead since you insulted my father. My father is with Allah. But you? You will go to devil, your *dost*, buddy!" he roared.

The pushing on the door increased. Mr. Pandit felt the thrust on his chest. The hinges creaked. As the heavy wood started to crack his jaw was locked; he felt he was gagging. He could neither move nor respond verbally as he saw the wooden door caving in.

He knew his end was near.

Bang, bang – the men were slamming on the door with their shoulders. With crowbars they were ripping through the frame. The door was about to collapse any moment. The next moment, as the door came off its hinges and made a loud crash as it landed on the marble floor. Mr. Pandit urinated in his pajamas.

With his last spark of energy, he ran to the window.

Roaring, Rahim caught him by the arm and whisked him back and forth like a rag. Mr. Pandit's mouth foamed and he resisted by turning his body away from his assailant. Rahim held his arms and pushed him to the wall. He shoved a club under his chin, stretching it upward while Mr. Pandit gasped for breath. His face turned deathly white. The other rioters switched the lights on and a gang of them rushed in. Mr. Pandit closed his eyes.

People started ransacking his room and for few moments Rahim just watched, still threatening Mr. Pandit. Then Rahim tied his hands and left him cowering against the wall. Keeping an eye on Mr. Pandit, he joined in the mass theft. After bagging a few trophies, he returned to Mr. Pandit and slapped his face. Mr. Pandit raised his tied-up hands and Rahim hit him on the shoulders. As Rahim's arm went up, Mr. Pandit ducked. "*Dekho*, I – I..." he begged, trying to murmur something that would save his life.

Rahim roared, "Shut up. I don't want to talk to you, *sala, nalayak*." He cursed and hit Mr. Pandit again as the other rioters pushed forward to give a blow or two. They hit him while holding their looted possessions in their other hand. When Rahim saw Mrs. Pandit's photograph hanging on the wall, he stopped beating Mr. Pandit and held his hands up for the others to stop beating him too.

"You lucky bastard, you were married to a kind woman. Because of her favors to my family, I will spare you from them." The others stepped away.

Rahim took another rope from his pocket. "You gutter-mouth

pig!" He spat on the floor, then tied Mr. Pandit's feet. When he noticed Mr. Pandit's wet clothes, he fell into a fit of laughing.

"This will give something for my Hindu friends to laugh at." He took a bottle of ink out of his pocket as Mr. Pandit pushed his face to the floor. Grabbing the few strands of hair from the back of Mr. Pandit's almost bald head, Rahim spread the ink on Mr. Pandit's face, painting it black. Some ink went in his mouth. He shook his head vehemently, struggling to spit it out. He started to choke and cough. The coughing became faint and the shaking slowed as Rahim slapped his face. Soon he fell unconscious.

Then Rahim stood, and the rioters dragged Mr. Pandit, cheering for Rahim. Stepping out of the room, Rahim pushed them away.

"Move! This pleasure is mine," he said. Then he threw Mr. Pandit, like a sack, over his shoulder and dashed outside. In a moment he had disappeared into the woods.

★ ★ ★

Around four in the morning at the Pandit estate, the police drove in and blew their horn, giving all the looters a warning, but it was more of a chance for them to run away. Before the jeep had come to a halt, the straggling looters disappeared. Some simply ran out through the front doors but the police made no effort to catch them. Instead, they just walked around, making announcements that the rioters should surrender peacefully.

No one came forward.

Chitra was residing with a friend of her mother's, who lived not very far from the Pandit estate. Someone had alerted her and she walked in right behind the police. It was the first time she had been to the estate since the day she had walked out. A policeman walked up to her and asked if she would identify the men who were unconscious. She recognized a few: their old gardener and his son. Then she noticed Babu and some other men she didn't know, their old maid's husband and Laxman's sons and their friends. There were many more men; known or unknown, they all seemed to have united as Hindus. Now, they all were wounded. Most of them didn't even flinch when touched. It was as if they were dead.

She asked for Laxman, and then for her father, and was told that Laxman had been taken into his quarters and they didn't think Mr. Pandit was at home. She sighed, "Thank God! But do you know where he's gone?" The policeman shook his head. "The only person who can tell about him is Laxman", she told the policeman.

"But his daughter is saying that Barrister was at home," an assistant to the police whispered. Chitra turned, and the policeman said, "*Tai*, don't go inside."

"Why?"

"Don't go, it's not a pretty sight."

"Not a pretty sight? I need to find my father. And go get the doctors, as many as you can find."

The officer replied that the ambulance and the doctor were on the way and she hurried forward.

Walking over the debris, Chitra went inside. She stood by the entrance of the living room. The fabrics on the settees and chairs were slashed and tables were smashed. The windows were broken, curtains were torn or missing, and curtain rods were hanging in the air. All the paintings were thrown on the floor. Broken pieces of glass and china vases and statues crunched under her feet as she cautiously walked into the room. Where could he be hiding? He couldn't have remained downstairs, she thought. She went to her father's office. All the paperwork was strewn around. The rugs were rolled up, ready to move. All the drawers of the desks and cabinets hung out, emptied of their contents. Mr. Pandit's leather chair had long gashes in it, and she wondered with alarm what would have happened if he had been sitting in the chair. She noticed with relief that there was no trace of blood on the wall or on his chair. She looked for the telephone. It was missing. Her heart pounding fast, she ran out of his office.

As she walked through the hall she had an urge to call him, *Baba... baba.* She hadn't called him that for many years and she knew she couldn't, even now. She ran to his bedroom, certain that he was too smart for these people to find him and hurt him.

The door of his room had fallen on the floor, and the policeman asked her to wait outside. Her heart sank with fear and she stood in place for a few moments. Her eyebrows curled and she held her quivering lips between her teeth. A surge of anger rushed through her – how could they? He isn't an ordinary man, my father. She shook her head, shaking off the thoughts, denying the overwhelming concern for her father.

But her inner voice said he had had it coming to him. Since he had always treated people like dirt, this was bound to happen sooner or later. People aren't that naïve anymore, she thought, they seek revenge. But who could tell him... he was a man who dwelled on his own pride.

She was sure though that he had somehow missed the attack on himself. And thank God her mother wasn't around to witness this. Of course it wouldn't have happened like this had she been alive... the whole town loved her. It's only him... but where could he have gone? Could he be hiding around the neighborhood, or had he reached the police station before the hooligans had entered? She stared out into the thickets; it was still dark, he couldn't have gone that far. He may have gone at the most to the huts of some fishermen, but they had collapsed, broken in from all sides. She sighed.

Chitra was standing, thinking, when a police chief came out of Mr. Pandit's bedroom. Seeing her standing in the balcony, a little away from the door, he said, "Chitratai, don't go inside."

"Why? I am a lawyer," she said, and crept in anyway.

There were a few splashes of blood on the wall. The black ink stains on the marble floor had streaks of red floating in them. The door that opened to the balcony was wide open, and she dashed to it to find any evidence of his escape.

"He's too smart; this can't be his blood," she said to an investigating police officer. "These people must have fought among themselves while looting."

After making sure he wasn't hiding inside the building they walked around the property, and around the thickets. But there was no trace of Mr. Pandit. Coming back, Chitra sat on the steps of the verandah, thinking, He was told about the danger, even an invasion, but he wouldn't listen. He never had listened to anyone, so why would he now? And now he was missing. She wondered, would he be alive? And where would they take him? But she still didn't believe that he could have been taken away. She told the police that she felt for sure he had made an arrangement before these people had crashed in, and fled before the troubles.

A few of the Hindu men who had run away from the Muslim mob peered out from the trees and shouted that they had come to help Laxman and weren't part of the looting mob.

"Come out in the open," a police officer shouted, "you will be safe."

As they approached cautiously, the policeman asked, "What do you have to tell us?"

At first no one spoke, but when the policeman shouted, "Are you going to give some information or do you want to be locked up?" for a moment they were all silent, but all at once they started to tell their story, excitedly.

"One at a time," Chitra said loudly. "But before you give detailed reports on who saw who, I want to know if any one of you have seen my father? Does anyone know if he was inside or had gone away before they broke into his room?"

They all stood quiet. Then there was some whispering amongst them, and one man took a policeman aside and told him that Rahim had carried Mr. Pandit on his shoulder and gone out by the rear entrance. But they didn't know in which direction he had gone. When the officer told that to Chitra, she said loudly, "No," shaking her head. "That can't be him," she said in a firm tone. "They were all thieves, they have looted the house. What are they going to do with him?"

They all murmured something and she ignored it. She did not believe that anyone could dare to carry her father like that. "You are wrong," she said, confirming her opinion. Then to test their answer, she asked, "What do you mean, they carried him away?" Chitra gestured, making a dragging motion. "Like that – or literally carrying him on the shoulder?"

No one said anything.

Then someone said, "*Tai*, Rahim had only come to get the Barrister."

"What?"

"Yes, *Tai*, Rahim…"

"Any one of you know Rahim?" the police officer asked.

They shook their heads. One man whispered, "He's very dangerous if anyone crosses his path."

While they were guessing at where Rahim may have gone, Laxman's grandson came running, telling them that his grandfather was conscious and had asked to see Chitra. She rushed to his quarters, thinking, Thank God, he's conscious. Chitra went in and sat next to him, looking at his bloody hands and chest. Tears filled her eyes. She put her hand on his cheek, and Laxman slowly said, "Sorry, *Tai*... I... couldn't help your father..."

She stroked his head, and said, "Don't worry, Laxman, you know he can take care of himself."

He shook his head and said: "Rahim took Barrister to his father's grave." This was near where Rahim lived! At once Chitra stood, and walking out she gave the information to the police chief.

Someone had informed them that Rahim wanted Mr. Pandit to apologize to his father.

Right away the chief police officer with a couple of other officers rushed to the jeep.

"Wait, I will go with you," Chitra said.

"No, *Tai*, women don't go to such places, you will be better off here. We will send for you as soon as we know something about the Barrister."

As two police jeeps approached the inner part of the town, they passed through streets full of wrecked shops, toppled vehicles, charred homes and buildings. Destroyed mosques and temples were only part of the wreckage. On disgusting bloody paths, butchered animals and the dismembered parts of bodies were spread out all over the city. Whimpers and shrieks from broken hearts and people with broken limbs made the place sound like a city of ghosts filled with pain.

In a few minutes they had passed the Muslim neighborhood and came upon a burial ground, where Rahim's father was buried. The burial ground was small and disheveled. Many tombs were covered with red cloths. At the entrance, the inspector turned on the searchlights from the roof of the first jeep. A few yards away, some men started to run off into a swamp filled with tall grass. The jeeps couldn't go any further as there was no room between the tombs. Leaving his jeep, the police officer ran to the spot where a man, tied into a bundle, had been dumped.

A couple of policemen pursued the men running into the swamp. The chief officer instructed, "Make sure you catch Rahim. He's probably one of them."

The chief officer untied the sheets and saw that the man lying inside was Mr. Pandit. He was gagged, his face was swollen, the bleeding had stopped but the bed sheet and his clothes were stained. His hands and feet were bound. He was unconscious. The officer couldn't find his pulse.

They removed the gag and freed his feet and hands. The officer put his ear to Mr. Pandit's chest and said, "Take him to the hospital, he's alive."

They put Mr. Pandit in one jeep and the other vehicle was sent to get Chitra.

As Mr. Pandit was being carried into the private hospital, Chitra rushed in. Looking at his swollen, ink-painted face, she swallowed a lump. The wounds on his forehead were deep. His right shoulder was torn and broken. Dried blood was sticking to his scalp. His cracked lips had turned black and blue, and dried-out foam caked his mouth, from which blood and saliva drooled.

Tears fell from Chitra's eyes onto her father's chest. How could they do this to him? She looked away from his face. She had never thought his haughtiness would eventually bring him to such a sorry condition. Her eyes brimmed with tears and she was startled as they fell onto her cheeks. To her surprise she wanted to cry loudly. She wanted to tell him that she loved him and she was sorry she hadn't been there when he needed her.

She pressed his limp body closer to hers, wiping the blood from his face with a handkerchief. Her tears fell on his face. He whimpered. He barely could open his one eye. When he saw Chitra, crying, he moved his left hand. She held it in hers and he gently squeezed it. Tears fell from his eyes. She wiped his tears, thinking, "Love isn't a choice."

Chapter Seventeen

Early next morning when Tony woke, he saw that the door of Maya's room was slightly open. He whispered, "Maya..." There was no answer. He stood, thinking he should wait, that she was just tired. For a few minutes he paced in the front room, thinking about how to make up with Maya. It would be difficult. But he would be patient, he reassured himself, and they would manage their differences amicably. If she understood how he felt, then... and as the clock struck eight times he stopped pacing and walked back to her bedroom. He knocked on the door but when she didn't answer he peeped inside the room.

Maya wasn't there.

He ran out of the room towards the verandah, calling "Maya... Maya..." There was no answer, and the hollowness of the empty space gripped his heart. Again he ran into all the rooms. He went from the kitchen to the backyard and then to the dispensary. He stood in front of the window, his eyes searching beyond the street by the riverbank.

Maya wasn't there, nor was she inside the building.

His heart pounding fast, he again called loudly, "Maya... Maya." He ran outside. On the verandah the peon was fast asleep.

Tony shook him and the peon sat up. Tony asked if he had seen Maya. Rubbing his eyes, the peon thought for a few moments and then said, "Not since we went out."

"Didn't you hear the gate? It always makes such a loud noise."

He shook his head. "I am sorry, sir, but I was fast asleep. But maybe she's just gone to the corner to buy milk or something."

Tony shook his head. He knew she didn't like to go out alone as the people around the neighborhood knew what had happened and made nasty remarks. Besides, nothing would be open this early or even later, because of the riots.

He ran across the street to the riverbank. "Maya... Maya," he called loudly, but his words echoed back to him. He asked the few fishermen as their boat pulled in near the bank if they had seen Maya, a pregnant woman, or whether one of them had taken her across the river in his boat. No, no, one by one they all shook their heads.

He ran from there and held his head in his hands, blaming himself. "Oh God, what have I done? Where did she go? How could I be so cruel? Oh God, help me."

As he walked he came near the Hindu temple, and ran inside. The man sleeping by the entrance said, "Sahib, take your shoes off."

Tony took his sandals off and threw them outside the temple. There was no one inside. There was no one by the altar. He went down deep into the dark sanctum. It was empty.

Help me, God, help me to find her before I burst into pieces, his heart cried. He went back to the house, hoping she may have returned. He asked the peon, who shook his head. He fell on the steps of the verandah and cried to himself, Where did you go, Maya?

The sun was rising on the horizon and the river had acquired sparkling gold tones. Birds circled in the sky and the temple bell began to chime, but none of this eased Tony's heart. He sat thinking, questioning, where would she have gone? Everything was closed, and the buses and trains were not running. She couldn't have returned to the hostel. She couldn't have gone too far from Kulur, and he would find her, even if he had to walk down all the alleys talking to every person in town. Thinking that she couldn't have gone farther, he felt better.

At ten o'clock the temperature had already risen to 45° centigrade. The empty, black tar roads exhaled petroleum vapors and the leaves on the trees drooped. Even the roadside pigs and three-legged dogs weren't roaming about the alleys. Buffaloes slept in the water and there weren't any signs of life on the riverbank except for the frogs raising their heads, catching insects.

As the sun rose higher in the sky and Maya still hadn't returned, Tony took his bicycle and started pedaling towards Hari's temple. The streets in the outskirts of the town were tree-lined, and this made the scorching heat more bearable.

The temple was too far for her to have walked, but he hadn't found the rickshaw driver who had said he would be sleeping in his rickshaw, so he thought maybe she had coaxed him to take her to Hari.

After riding the bicycle from the outskirts of the city he finally reached the temple. He had no doubts that this was the one Maya had been telling him about. He rode down the path, lined with the large *pepul* trees. The temple was smaller than he had thought and there was no one around, as he expected.

Standing by the entrance, he wanted to call Maya's name, but the tranquility of the place held him back. This time he took his shoes off and went in. There was no one inside the temple, not even Hari. He went back to the entrance and noticed there wasn't a single pair of shoes there. Maya would never enter the temple with her shoes. He stood by the entrance and looked around. She wasn't there.

God, where could she have gone, on such a day? How could he let her go? He stared at the ground, which had cracked open in the heat. How could she survive this heat in her condition? He would never forgive himself if something happened to her and the baby. He glided down the steps and walked to the right side of the temple where he thought he heard someone talking.

As he walked a little further the sound became a little clearer. He heard a deep voice and as he stepped closer, he felt drawn to it. Around the *pepul* tree was a raised plinth made out of clay where a few men were sitting cross-legged on the floor. Among them were a couple of white men. Before them an old man was sitting on a mat and talking. Right away Tony knew that was Hari.

Tony walked up to them and stood at one side. No one moved or even looked at him. Hari glanced at him and Tony sat on the edge of the plinth. He looked around for Maya but didn't see her. Again, Hari looked in his direction, gave him a nod and continued his talk.

"Religion is not found in any doctrines, in dogmas, nor in intellectual argumentation; it's not about one person or a deity." Hari spoke first in Marathi and then slowly explained it in English, word by word. "It's about being and becoming; it's realization. The highest goal of religion, *any* religion, is to attain what we call in India, Yoga. It means union, Union with God.

"And that union with God is attained only through our internal nature. This conquering of the inner man through understanding releases the subtle workings that are within the human mind. Knowing the wonderful secrets of our spirits is the real nature of *any* religion: Union with God.

"Once we understand that and once we practice that, then only love and love alone will prevail. You will realize God, the Truth of the sameness and omnipresence of the Soul of the Universe as God within yourself. The Soul is not bound by the conditions of matter. In its very essence, it is free, unbound, holy, pure and perfect.

"Meditation is the nearest approach to reaching the soul, to the spiritual life – the mind that is resolved. It's the one moment in our life when we are not at all material – the soul thinking of itself, free from all matter. This marvelous touch of the soul can change your life entirely."

Hari again glanced at Tony who, in spite of his state of mind, was now listening.

"And once you have realized this, you can worship everything as God. Every form is His temple. Such is the God that Vedanta preaches, and such is His worship without any boundaries, or limitations... *Om*! Peace, peace."

Closing his eyes, he whispered a prayer.

After the prayer, Hari stood up, and Tony went to him. Hari asked enthusiastically if he had good news.

Tony shook his head.

"But Maya's all right, isn't she?" asked Hari.

"I don't know..." Tony was on the brink of breaking down and Hari asked him to come into his hut, which was right behind the tree.

Hari spread a mat on the floor for Tony but Tony stood impatiently at the door and asked, "Have you seen Maya?"

"No, why? What's wrong? And why would she come in the middle of these riots? Isn't she at the hostel?"

"Yes, but last evening she was caught in the middle of the riots and ended up at Seva Sadan." He stopped, his lips trembling.

"Then?"

"We... we... fought..."

"So, you two had a fight." Hari laughed.

"Harikaka..." Tony paused, then looked at him. "Maya calls

243

you *kaka*, can I call you the same?"

"*Han, han.*"

"Harikaka, it wasn't a simple fight. I said some harsh words to her." He told him what had happened.

After listening, Hari said, "Listen, she may have gotten upset with your words. But she will come back."

"No, I know how she had left me once and was determined not to come back. She... she... may not return. Somehow she comes here to—" His voice was breaking, and Hari patted his shoulders.

"Don't worry, I will ask around. And if I find her, I will bring her to you."

"Thank you, thank you, Harikaka," said Tony. He dashed to his bicycle without looking at him again.

The streets were still empty, but near the city limits the army patrols were noticeable. Tony pedaled his bicycle with heavy feet. He hadn't eaten all morning long. But his thoughts weren't on his body; he kept thinking about what had gone wrong the previous night. Why had he been careless about her feelings? He had wanted to work things out but by then she had gone to sleep. And he also went to sleep thinking she was tired and they would talk tomorrow. He had no idea how he was going to reconcile with her; it was difficult for him when she spoke against his faith.

But he wanted to tell her he wouldn't insist anymore about his faith. "The highest goal of religion, *any* religion, is to attain Union with God, and that Union is recognizing one is not just the body-mind-sense complex, but the one is the very Existence, the absolute Truth, the Bliss." He had just heard those words from Hari and though he hadn't understood them completely, instinctively something felt right. He tried to remember more of Hari's words. "Once we seek the Union with God, then only love, and love alone, will prevail." Yes, God's presence is in loving, not in following any doctrine. This, this wanting to be loved and wanting to love someone is so inherent to human nature that it's hard to scrape off or escape. This, the love, is the core part of our existence, which is as inherent as the fragrance of a rose, the sweetness of sugar; it's the breath of living. Love!

He felt, last night, the love he perceived from Jesus, also

accepted his love for Maya. He was certain that if Jesus loved him, he loved Maya as well.

Yes, yes, and he wasn't going to let go of Maya either. They loved each other so much that it had helped him to grow spiritually and now their love would supersede all the other differences. They would be united forever, like the song she had sung last night. He tried to remember the words. "There may not be a moon or stars left around. But I will remain yours, forever and ever."

He began to whistle the tune, but a few minutes later worries about Maya clouded his mind. Without any transport she couldn't have gone far. Going back to the hostel was impossible for her. No city buses or trains were running. Then where did she disappear to? She didn't have any friends around here, not anymore.

Again Sharon's suicide came to his mind. Oh God, she's pregnant! So young, just like Sharon. But she wouldn't try something like that. No, she had survived the worst event, her parents leaving her. But then he was her hope, and now he too had hurt her.

He pedaled faster.

When he reached Seva Sadan, the peon had left. Maya hadn't returned. He went inside and walked to the bench by the altar and sat. Looking into the searching eyes of Jesus, he said a prayer, "May the Almighty God have mercy on me, and forgive me, and forgive my sins and bring me to everlasting life, amen."

After a few moments he cried out, "I need to know, Lord, where Maya is! Please give me some indication." He sat there for a long time, saying, "Oh Lord, please help me, forgive me…"

He stood and paced the floor, then stood by the window. Then he paced the verandah. Then he went into the kitchen and to the rear yard and then paced the floor. When he thought he had heard the gate opening, he ran outside and stood by it. Then he walked to the street and stood in the middle, in the blazing sun, hoping to see someone who may have seen Maya. But he didn't come across anyone.

Again and again he rode his bicycle throughout the neighborhood. If he met anyone, he asked, had they seen Maya? No one had seen her and most of the streets and alleys were deserted.

Sometime in the afternoon he sat by the shrine, and this gave him a few moments of peace. He closed his eyes and Maya came to his mind. Holding her image in his mind, he kept pleading for her to return.

The image of Jesus emerged in his mind. He remained focused on the image. Slowly, every muscle in his body relaxed. Every joint loosened. His breathing became slow and rhythmic. The image of Jesus remained. It gave him a sense of inner sanctity. The longer he meditated upon that image the greater sense of peace he felt.

Slowly the image of Christ began to fade. But Tony didn't move. The words of Hari resonated in his mind. "You will realize God, the Truth of the sameness and omnipresence of the Soul of the Universe, as God within yourself. The Soul is not bound by the conditions of matter. In its very essence, it is free, unbound, holy, pure and perfect."

The image of Jesus reappeared in his mind and he experienced total silence. Soon, all the images faded. All the words dulled. All the senses freed his mind and it centered on the pure being. No longer did his mind reflect on any thoughts. The sorrow of losing Sharon, of not having a father, the guilt that he had betrayed his mother – they all faded. He transcended his longing for Maya, her love and his faith. He felt absolute peace. He stayed in that state for a long time.

When he was waking up from his meditation, he felt an indescribable sense of inner wholeness. It wasn't an ecstasy. It was peace, a peace that didn't depend on anyone or anything: not Maya, or any external image or thoughts of God.

He didn't know how long he had stayed in the meditation. His eyes closed, he moved his arm a little; he was alive. He heard his heart ticking in rhythm, and he remained in the same position, not wanting to come out of his deep meditation. Slowly, thoughts started to gather in his mind: yes, Maya would be back.

A few minutes later there was a knock on the door and he slowly stood up and opened it.

Maya was standing before him.

He showed no reaction; it was as if she had just gone around the corner and he had known she would be back.

Seeing him so unemotional, she turned around, ready to leave. She had come back only to tell him that she was leaving. And now he was acting as if he didn't even know her, she thought. She was about to step down when he came out of his deep thoughts.

"Maya…" he called and quickly walked out the door. "Thank God you are all right," he said, putting his hand on her shoulder.

She stood still. His grip tightened on her shoulders and she snapped at him, "Let me go, Tony, I can see you weren't expecting me to come back at all."

Tears started forming at the corners of his eyes, and while trying to recover his voice, he said, "What are you saying? I have been looking all over for you."

She said nothing, but raised her eyebrows a little.

Again he went to embrace her but Maya glanced at a couple of women by the gate watching them. He refrained. "Maya, where have you been?" he asked.

She stared at the floor, but he couldn't stay away from her. He held her hand and pulled her in. She looked back at the women and nodded goodbye.

As soon as they were inside the house he tried to embrace her. Pushing his hands aside she stepped away.

"Maya, please, I am very sorry. Tell me you won't leave like this." He put her hand to his lips. She pulled it away.

"Where were you? I have been looking for you all over. This morning I even went to see Hari."

"You didn't," she said, and he was crushed by the distrustful tone in her voice.

"Yes, I did and he was right. He told me for sure you would be back. But where were you?"

She sat on the bench and he sat beside her. He turned the table fan towards her face. Her hair blew around her face and he kept gazing at her. She looked more determined than ever. Her hands holding the edge of the seat, she looked ready to get up at any moment.

Where had she been and what was she planning to do next? He went into the kitchen and brought out two glasses of water. She held the glass in her hand, while he swallowed his in one gulp, not moving his eyes from her face. She was rubbing her fingers on the glass. He stood peering down at her.

"As soon as the riots are over, I will be able to go. Till then…"

"Where would you go – and till then what?"

"Till then…" she paused, avoiding looking at him.

"I will stay with Harikaka," she said. "Auntie would take me."

"Which auntie? What are you talking about?"

"Mrs. Mate, the doctor's wife."

"How did she come into all this?"

"When I left Seva Sadan at early dawn, I was having pains in my abdomen. I hadn't slept," Maya said. "Dr. Mate was taking his walk by the river and he saw me there, and thought I was crying so he woke his wife up. Auntie knows me."

"And?"

She didn't know how to tell him that she was again leaving him, this time for good.

"Auntie took me to their house, heard what I had to say, which was very little but then she let me cry on her shoulders. She fed me and asked me to get some sleep, giving a strict warning to her husband not let anyone know that I was there, because all the neighborhood children would come bothering me."

"God, that's all there was to it? You weren't really leaving me?"

"You sound as if you wanted me to leave, I am go – going away." She sniffled. "I am going to Nasik," she said slowly. "There is an ashram for unfortunate women like me."

He wrapped his arms around her shoulders. "You can't leave me, you can't." Pushing his hands aside, she stood and moved away. "I am leaving," she said.

"But why, Maya? Why?"

"Chitra was right. People only love those who are good. One wrong thing has wiped out my goodness. My father didn't think I could have made a mistake. He dropped me as if I was a leper. When you thought I didn't wish to be baptized, you too sounded, all of a sudden, like my father. You feared I might not convert. I wouldn't be the nice girl that you expected, so you too wanted to disown me."

"I never would disown you, what did I say that makes you think I would disown you?"

"It's not what you said, it's what you didn't say."

"What did you want me to say, Maya? I don't understand you at all… sometimes."

She was still angry. Tony shook his head. "One moment you are happy, the next you are gone."

"Now I am telling you that I am leaving and not coming back. So you won't have to worry about me."

"Would you please tell me what you expected me to say?"

"Now it's too late. You couldn't love me as I am. You can't marry me as I am."

"That's not true," Tony said emphatically, "I am marrying you as you are, pregnant with my baby and all. I wouldn't want it any other way."

"I am not talking about the baby. I am talking about me *not* being a Christian. You don't even know that next Sunday I was going to be baptized—"

"But… I don't want…"

"Let me finish," she said. "I had decided that I would go along with the plan of baptism, not because I wanted to or because I am in this desperate situation or because it made much sense to me, but only because I love you. I care for you… so you wouldn't have to give up the mission…"

"Giving up the mission is one thing but giving up the faith would be another."

"I know that. I never asked you to change your faith but all night long I kept remembering how you thought I was attacking your faith, your God, and I felt my baby is better off not knowing his father than not knowing the truth about God."

"Maya, you are not being fair."

"Wasn't that important to you – serving Him, having love for God? You too lived not knowing your father, so it would be the same for your child…" Her voice had an unusual edge. "I never knew anything about God, or hadn't thought about it, but…"

"*Maya, what's happened to you?*" he questioned rather loudly. "Growing up wasn't easy for me and I wouldn't let that happen to my child under any circumstances."

"I am sorry, Tony, everyone has been telling me all kinds of things but now I know what I want. I want to depend only on myself, take care of my baby and me. I can't worry what the world says. And what the religions talk about."

"Maya, can we set our differences aside?" he asked. She didn't answer but stared at his sincere, kind face. "I am sorry about what I said last night. I know our love will find the strength to resolve everything. I loved you, Maya, as you were – a Hindu – so I wish to marry you as a Hindu."

"I don't believe this. Not at all." She turned her face away from him, saying, "Not anymore."

"I understand you are angry but believe me, Maya, I love you. And nothing else matters, not anymore."

She looked at him and repeated, "Not anymore?"

"Yes," he said, "Nothing else matters anymore except one thing."

"Except what? I should be baptized..." She gave a hollow laugh.

"*No*," he said loudly. "You don't have to be baptized. I know you have become bitter about it all, but hear me out. One thing I want you to know. Though I always will remain Christian, I don't believe in conversion anymore." He paused, waiting for her response. She didn't say anything and he repeated, "Since I don't believe in conversion, it won't be hard for us."

"You don't believe in conversion? Since when?"

"No, I don't." He raised his voice. "You can take it however you want but I have been thinking about it now for quite a while. I just couldn't come out and admit it to you." He walked away and stood by the shrine, facing her.

"You couldn't tell me? Why? Didn't you think it might have helped me or relieved the tension between us?"

"How am I supposed to say anything, Maya, when the very belief on which the mission is built has failed? At least in my mind... and that... that's been... hard." He paused, giving a sigh. "I have understood, finally I have found the answers, and resolved my dilemmas." He turned to the shrine. Looking at it, he remembered the verse from the Bible, "Nothing can separate us from this love. Death can't, and life can't. The angels can't, and the demons can't. Our fears for today and worries about tomorrow, and even the powers of hell can't keep God's love away. Whether we are high above in the sky or in the deepest ocean, nothing in all creation will ever be able to separate us from the love of God that is revealed in Christ Jesus our Lord."

For a few minutes neither of them said a word.

"Tony, I am sorry…" she said softly, "I know how much this mission, Yeshu, meant to you…"

"Don't worry. This doesn't mean I don't love Jesus, it only means that if God can work through the hands of Jesus it is possible He can also work through other hands. This is the verbal proof about how I feel about you. Also, now, I am more at peace. I have no fear. You do not fear when you love all, accept all."

He walked to the front window and stood gazing outside, where the river was calm. Looking at the subtle ripples and in them the reflections of moving clouds, he said, "The only thing I want is for us to be together… I don't want to lose you, Maya… as I have lost everyone in my life…" Unable to speak, he rubbed his finger on the windowpane.

Maya went to him and put her hand on his shoulder. Without turning around, he put his hand on hers. "Don't leave me, Maya, please. I love you and I want to spend the rest of my life with you and our baby. How can I prove it to you that I accept you as a Hindu?" She pressed on his shoulder. He stood silent for a moment. "Maya," he said. He turned and put his arms on her shoulders. She stepped backward and he pulled her closer, "Listen, I would even name our baby Shiva or Krishna, a name of a Hindu god that you like."

She looked at him – what was he saying?

"Would that help you?" he asked, searching in her eyes. She looked away and stood silent. He let her go and turned, facing the window.

It was hard for her to believe what he had just said. But he had said that before the shrine, before Yeshu. It had to be very hard for him to have come this far. She didn't want him to say these things just to please her, to win her back. But she knew he meant it. She looked at the picture of Yeshu. His face full of love and His watchful eyes reminding her of the same kindness she had felt in the eyes of Rama. There was hardly a difference in feelings to be perceived from the messengers or incarnates, or the images of various gods. She was happy he had understood, and she was happy that she too felt love for Jesus in her heart.

He was still standing with his back to her. She again put her hand on his shoulder, pressing it. He turned around and held her in his embrace. As he held her tight in his arms, she whispered, "And if we have twins we could name one Chris and one Krishna, or one Mary... and one... Meera?"

While tears were still in their eyes, they both laughed.